A sudden sense of foreboding slid within Joan's veins, but she forced herself to ask, "What must I do?"

"You must go to him this night, and surrender your innocence," Annle answered. "Then the curse cannot touch him, because his essence will be bound to yours. And if he is a man of honor, he will wed you to save your virtue."

For a moment, she could hardly breathe. *I cannot.*

How could she even imagine such a thing? She knew nothing of seduction, and the price was far too great. Her mind spun with the implications.

Yet, earlier, he had started to speak of a betrothal once more. She had cut him off, believing it was impossible. But what if she was mistaken? What if she could find a way to break the curse and seize a life with Ronan? Was that not worth the risk?

Author Note

Forbidden Night with the Prince is the third book in the Warriors of the Night series.

In this story, Joan de Laurent is deeply superstitious about marriage, since every man she has been betrothed to has died. But when she meets Irish prince Ronan Ó Callaghan, she longs for an end to the deaths and a new beginning. Ronan is intrigued by the beautiful noblewoman who only wears white and refuses to wed. But will an unexpected attraction, a potion from a wisewoman, and one forbidden night be enough to break the curse?

Book one in this series is *Forbidden Night with the Warrior*, the story of Warrick de Laurent and Rosamund de Courcy. Book two is *Forbidden Night with the Highlander*, the romance between Rhys de Laurent and Liana MacKinnon. You might also enjoy the story of Aileen and Connor MacEgan in *The Warrior's Touch*, part of the MacEgan Brothers series.

If you'd like me to email you when I have a new book out, please visit my website at michellewillingham.com to sign up for my newsletter. As a bonus, you'll receive a free story, just for subscribing!

MICHELLE WILLINGHAM

Forbidden Night with the Prince

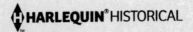

Recycling programs
for this product may
not exist in your area.

ISBN-13: 978-1-335-52284-9

Forbidden Night with the Prince

Printed in U.S.A.

HARLEQUIN®
www.Harlequin.com

RITA® Award finalist **Michelle Willingham** has written over twenty historical romances, novellas and short stories. Currently she lives in southeastern Virginia with her husband and children. When she's not writing, Michelle enjoys reading, baking and avoiding exercise at all costs. Visit her website at michellewillingham.com.

Books by Michelle Willingham

Harlequin Historical

Warriors of the Night

Forbidden Night with the Warrior
Forbidden Night with the Highlander
Forbidden Night with the Prince

Warriors of Ireland
(linked to *The MacEgan Brothers*)

Warrior of Ice
Warrior of Fire

Forbidden Vikings

To Sin with a Viking
To Tempt a Viking

The MacEgan Brothers

Her Warrior Slave (prequel)
Her Warrior King
Her Irish Warrior
The Warrior's Touch
Taming Her Irish Warrior
Surrender to an Irish Warrior
Warriors in Winter

Visit the Author Profile page
at Harlequin.com for more titles.

To Beth Broderick, a great friend who always has time to talk while our dogs play together. I appreciate all that you've done for me, and thank you so much for your friendship. Irish and Cocoa have a real-life canine romance, and thank goodness they're both fixed or we'd be overrun with puppies.

Chapter One

1175

Joan de Laurent was cursed.

Most folk believed she was foolish in such thoughts, but in her heart, she knew it was true. She had already been betrothed twice, and both men had died before they had wedded her. One had perished in battle while the second had fallen ill with the pox.

For some reason, God did not want her to be married. She was convinced of this, and moreover, any man who dared to seek her as his bride would draw his last breath before the wedding Mass was over. The people of Montbrooke believed it, too. Men crossed themselves whenever she walked by. The women avoided her, particularly those who were pregnant. Some of the children ran away from her, and had she not been the daughter of an earl, they might have accused her of witchcraft.

Joan had done everything in her power to prove them wrong. Every gown she owned was white, a symbol of her innocence. She wore an iron cross around her neck to keep away the fairies. Her dark hair remained veiled at all times, and she went to Mass every day.

But she could feel their stares burning into the back of her head. She heard the whispers and knew that their hearts had turned against her out of fear. No men wanted her, despite her father's attempts to arrange a third betrothal. Why would they, when it meant a death sentence?

Joan had resigned herself to a life of prayer, one where she would never marry or conceive a child of her own. And that was the problem. She loved babies with all her heart. After her brother's wife, Lianna, had given birth to a daughter, Joan had been overwhelmed by love for this beautiful girl. It was her secret that she desperately wanted to be a mother. The need burned within her in a fervent desire. She had been lonely for so long, shunned by everyone. She longed to fill the emptiness by cradling a beloved child against her breast, to rest her lips upon a soft head and feel that soul-deep love.

You are too old, her mind chided. Four-and-twenty was an age when most women had several children, whereas Joan was still a virgin. There was little hope of her ever marrying or bearing a child.

But her father had no intention of letting her serve the Church. Instead, he'd sought a betrothal with an older nobleman from Ireland. Her intended husband already had heirs, and Murdoch did not need children from her.

It should have been the perfect arrangement—and yet, she was afraid of this marriage. She didn't want to see another man die, though the sensible side of her brain knew her fears were foolish. But no matter how many times she told herself it was only a coincidence that her previous bridegrooms had died, she couldn't quite dispel the belief.

After weeks of travelling, they arrived in Ireland. Her father, Edward de Laurent, had sent her brothers, Warrick and Rhys, to accompany her and to witness the vows. Warrick had lands in Killalough, and he'd brought dozens of soldiers with him to protect his wife and children at his estate. Rhys had brought half a dozen of his own men to guard them on this journey.

It was raining, and Joan held a woollen cloak over her head as the cart rolled through the mud. She did not see a castle anywhere—only thatched huts upon a hillside. Deep inside, panic gripped her lungs. Her hands were ice cold, and she fought to calm the rush of nerves.

Everything will be all right, her head tried to reason. *I don't want to marry an old man*, her heart wailed. *He may be kind. His children could become yours.*

But deep inside, she believed Murdoch Ó Connor would die if he married her. It felt as if she were bringing a curse upon an innocent man, one he didn't deserve. How could she even think that this marriage would come to pass?

Her brother, Warrick, reached out and took her hand. He said nothing but squeezed her fingers. Yet, his silent reassurance did nothing to ease her terror.

Joan stiffened her spine and let the hood fall back to her shoulders, regardless of the rain. She hardly cared about how it would soak through her veil and braided hair. The frigid weather matched her uncertain mood.

Rhys glanced back at them and said to Warrick, 'I don't know if this will be a good alliance for Joan. Murdoch may be a chieftain, but...' He shook his head, eyeing the decaying homes.

Joan didn't know what to think of this place. It appeared as if nothing had been done to maintain the ringfort. The thatch was rotting on the rooftops, along with the wooden timbers. Why, then, had the chieftain allowed it to fall into disrepair?

A few bystanders stared at them, but none smiled in welcome. Instead, it seemed as if the people were confused by their arrival. Several murmured in whispers, staring at them.

'Do you think they knew about this betrothal?' Joan murmured.

Rhys only shook his head. 'I cannot say. But I want you to remain with Warrick while I find out.'

'I could send one of my men to speak with them,' Warrick offered. He had brought an Irishman from Killalough to act as an interpreter.

'It does not matter,' Joan whispered. The burden of this betrothal weighed heavily upon her, and she was certain it would not end well.

She tried to calm the storm of her nerves when the cart drew to a stop at the gates. Rhys called out to the guards, announcing their presence, but the two men appeared uneasy for some reason. There was a strange quiet throughout the ringfort, an air of ill fortune that bothered her. The Ó Connor guards allowed them inside, but Joan turned to Warrick. 'Something is wrong.'

He nodded, keeping his hand tight upon hers. 'I agree.'

Her brother helped her down from the cart, and one of the Irishmen came to greet them. The man could not speak the Norman language, but from his gesturing, Joan guessed that he wanted them to follow.

There was a sombre mood as they entered the largest dwelling, and Joan took a step back in shock when she saw the body laid out upon a table. Her fingers dug into Warrick's arm, and she closed her eyes, feeling a wild surge of hysteria.

Her intended husband was dead, just as she'd feared. But instead of being relieved at her new freedom, Joan wanted to weep. For it felt as if she were to blame somehow.

Three betrothals. Three deaths.

She could only believe that the curse was real, and she could never marry anyone. A crushing weight seemed to close over her chest, numbing her to all else.

A younger woman approached, her eyes red from crying. She spoke only Irish, but Warrick's translator conveyed what had happened. Her father, Murdoch Ó Connor, had died only this morning. There would be no betrothal, though the woman did offer her hospitality if Joan and her brothers wanted to stay with them this night.

'We thank you,' Rhys said gently, 'but we will return to my brother's house.' He offered his condolences with the help of the translator and guided them back outside.

Joan gripped her brother's hand, trying to keep back her own tears. Warrick drew her away, rubbing the small of her back. She struggled to keep her feelings shielded, but it felt as if God were laughing at her.

She would never have the husband and family she wanted. She would never bear a child of her own. Raw frustration coursed through her, and she let go of her brother's hand. It wasn't fair. Why should she be different from other women? Why could she not find a man to love?

Her brothers brought her back inside the cart, and only a few miles later did Rhys speak. 'I am sorry, Joan. But perhaps it's for the best. I don't care what our father intended—Murdoch was far too old for you.'

'I should have known better,' she blurted out. 'Every man I am betrothed to dies.' Warrick reached out for her hand again, but she jerked it away. 'You know it's true.'

'You have been unlucky when it comes to a betrothal, I know, but—'

'Unlucky?' She glared at him. Her voice grew higher in pitch. 'Those men are *dead*, Warrick. It's far worse than ill luck. It's a curse.'

'I don't believe in curses,' Rhys argued.

I have no choice but to believe in it, Joan thought. In the past seven years, she'd had three failed betrothals and every man had perished. There was no other possible explanation.

'We will return to Killalough and decide what we should do now,' Warrick said. 'Do you want to go home to England?'

'I don't know,' Joan whispered. She stared out at the rolling green hills of Ireland, feeling so lost and uncertain. If her brothers brought her home again, she would have to explain to her father that yet another man had died. And, though it was through no fault of her own, she did not want to face Edward's annoyance.

'You could stay with Rosamund for a time,' Warrick suggested. His wife was a close friend of Joan's, and for a moment she considered it. If nothing else, Rosamund might help her find a way to fill up her days.

'Or we may wish to consult with the king of the MacEgan tribe at Laochre. He may be able to arrange a new betrothal, if you wish,' Rhys suggested.

That was the last thing she wanted. Joan was weary of being a pawn, offered up to strangers in the hopes of making a strong marriage alliance.

It was time to put aside dreams that would never be. Better to live her life as she chose and to make her own decisions.

Ronan Ó Callaghan was a prince exiled from his kingdom. In a matter of hours, his birthright had been stripped away. His stepbrother Odhran had overthrown the king and slaughtered innocents, seizing the throne for himself.

And you did nothing but run, his conscience taunted. *Coward.*

Never would he forget the resigned look upon his father's face when they had taken him hostage. Brodur had met Ronan's gaze with the sadness of one who had expected failure. And that look had cut deeper than any sword.

Guilt suffocated him, though he knew Odhran would have killed him if he'd stayed. Someone had to seek out help and bring back their allies to retake the fortress. What good would it do his people if he was dead? They needed outside forces to help.

And yet…he had to face the reality that this was a betrayal that had come from within. Although Odhran and his mother Eilis had lived at Clonagh for only the past five years, they had slipped behind his father's defences. Brodur had trusted them, only to be betrayed by his wife and stepson.

Some of his kinsmen had chosen Odhran's side and turned their backs on their king. There was no way to know who had remained loyal and who was a traitor.

Fury burned within Ronan, along with the need for vengeance. He had escaped with the clothes on his back, a sword, and a single horse. And now, after riding for two days, he had reached the Laochre stronghold of the MacEgan king.

King Patrick ruled over the southern province, and the MacEgan tribe was numbered among their allies. Ronan intended to humble himself and ask the king for aid in taking back his lands at Clonagh—no matter the cost.

The square towers of Laochre were a blend of wood and stone, for King Patrick had rebuilt the castle in the Norman style. The MacEgan lands stretched for miles, from the hilltop of Amadán, all the way to the coast. Even the island of Ennisleigh fell under their dominion. If anyone could help him, it was this tribe.

Ronan rode towards the gates, ignoring his own exhaustion. He hadn't slept in days and had only stopped for the horse's sake, not his own. No doubt he appeared like little more than a beggar, for his armour was stained with blood. But he would meet with the king and appeal for help.

The soldiers allowed him to enter, and Ronan gave his horse into the care of a stable lad. His vision blurred, and he fought back the weariness that struck hard. He hadn't eaten in so long, the smell of food hit him like a physical blow. It was only the years of training and discipline that made it possible to hide the exhaustion and hunger.

He started to walk up the stairs when he glimpsed a woman on the other side of the inner bailey. She stood out from the others like a beam of sunlight. There was no doubt she was of noble birth from the snowy-white gown she wore in the Norman style. She was veiled, and a lock of dark hair rested upon one shoulder. Though she had a subdued beauty, her smile caught his attention and held it.

Who was she? Possibly a relative to Queen Isabel, but he could not be certain.

Out of the corner of his eye, Ronan saw a young girl, possibly three years of age, running towards the woman in white. *That* was the reason for her smile. The girl hurled herself into the woman's arms, and the woman laughed as she picked her up, kissing her cheek. He guessed it was her mother.

But then the young girl pointed directly at him and whispered to the woman. The woman studied him, her smile fading. Then she shushed the girl and took her hand, leading the child away.

A grim ache tightened within him. Though he knew it was only a child's curiosity, it felt like an accusation—as if he were a monster come to life. A cold chill slid over his spine as he thought of the children who had fought at Clonagh, trying to save their fathers.

And the one whose death was his fault.

You were not meant to be their prince, the dark voice of his conscience whispered. *Ardan was destined to be the king, not you.*

His gut tightened, and he forced away the shadowed guilt. There was nothing he could do now except try to mend the mistakes he'd made. He was here for only one purpose—to seek help for Clonagh. The last thing he needed was the distraction of a woman.

When he reached the top of the stairs, Sir Anselm approached to greet him. The Norman knight had been a loyal vassal for several years now, and he had visited Clonagh on several occasions on behalf of the MacEgans.

'My lord, this is a surprise.' The knight raised his knee as a gesture of respect.

But although Ronan was a *flaith* and a king's son,

the traditional greeting only reminded him that he was Lord of Nothing right now. He had been unable to stop the attack on Clonagh, and many would blame him for it.

Ronan followed the knight inside the *donjon*, his mood darkening. It was difficult to remain patient, for he recognised their urgent situation. He needed soldiers to help him retake the fortress, well-trained men who could seize power from his stepbrother without harming his people.

Sir Anselm led him inside, and Ronan strode through the Great Chamber. Dozens of men and women were gathered at one end of the *donjon* where the king's brother, Trahern MacEgan, was telling stories. King Patrick and Queen Isabel were seated at the dais along with their young son and two other men—Normans from the look of their armour.

Sir Anselm led him towards the steps, and the king's attention centred upon him. Ronan realised that he should not have entered their keep in such a state, covered in enemy blood. The queen's expression faltered with sympathy, and she summoned a servant to her side, leaning in to whisper a command.

'I was not expecting your visit, Ronan,' King Patrick said solemnly. 'Come and dine with us.' He motioned for him to sit at the end of their table. A servant brought food, and it took Ronan a great effort not to devour the bread and stew. He'd eaten next to nothing over the past few days, and he finished the food within minutes. The servant brought him more, and he managed to eat more slowly during the second helping.

King Patrick introduced the two men as Rhys and Warrick de Laurent, and he switched into the Norman tongue so the men would understand. Ronan was glad that his father had forced him to learn many languages, though he'd resented the education at the time of his fostering. Even now, he wasn't certain why the king was drawing these men into the conversation, but they appeared to be warriors. Ronan welcomed help from any source, whether Norman or Irish.

The king began by saying, 'I did hear that Clonagh was attacked a few nights ago, and that your father, King Brodur, is a hostage. Our neighbouring tribe at Gall Tír informed us of this.'

Ronan nodded and continued speaking in the Norman language. 'A few nights ago, my stepbrother Odhran gathered his forces and took my father prisoner.' He began relating the story, keeping all emotion from his voice when he spoke of those who had died. A part of him still felt that he should have stayed, despite the danger. But he knew that the MacEgan allies were their best hope.

Once again, his attention shifted when he saw the woman in white entering the Great Chamber. She balanced the little girl on her hip, lowering her to sit among the other children who were listening to the bard. The child squirmed and then got up to wander around the gathering space. The woman trailed the young girl, keeping a close watch over her.

For some reason, the two Normans tensed when

they saw his distraction, and Ronan forced his gaze back to them. 'I have come to ask for soldiers,' he finished. 'I cannot let my people suffer beneath Odhran's rule. But they were too afraid to fight back against their own kinsmen. And I need to restore my father to his throne.'

The king exchanged a glance with the other two Normans. It seemed as if he was asking their opinion, and Warrick de Laurent spoke at last. 'How many men do you need?'

'Two dozen,' Ronan answered. 'Three would be better, but if they are strong fighters, it will be enough.'

'And once you take back Clonagh, what means do you have to keep it?'

He paused. 'Once I restore my father to his throne and drive out Odhran, we should be able to maintain order with the remaining men.'

A flicker of doubt crossed King Patrick's face. 'What happened to Queen Eilis during the attack?'

The mention of his father's wife renewed his anger. For Eilis had betrayed him as surely as her son. 'She supported her son's rebellion and did nothing to aid my father.'

At that, King Patrick sobered. 'I know what it is to face treachery from within your own castle walls. But you cannot exile your father's wife. That is Brodur's decision to make.'

He had not considered those implications. His father might not set his queen aside, and if so, Ronan would be unable to displace the woman, even if he did take back Clonagh. 'What do you suggest?'

The king exchanged a look with the de Laurent warriors. 'You should claim the throne for yourself and take a wife. One with an army of her own who can defend Clonagh from any further threats. Keep the men there for at least a year, and then you will know who is truly loyal.'

Ronan tensed at that, for he had no desire to wed anyone, especially after all the mistakes he'd made. 'I will not hide behind a woman's skirts. Or in this case, her soldiers.' His negligence had cost others their lives, and it was better if he remained unmarried.

'Rhys and Warrick came to Ireland for their sister's betrothal,' the king began, 'but her intended husband died. You may want to consider a Norman alliance with them. They hold lands at Killalough, and they are looking for a new marriage for their sister.' Patrick reached towards his wife's hand, and the queen smiled warmly at him. Then he ruffled the hair of his son. 'Meet her and decide for yourself.'

No. He would never bind a woman to him for the sake of her soldiers. Better to hire mercenaries who would leave once he had no further need of them. He had forsworn all women since his brother's death. And that would not change.

Before he could refuse the offer, Rhys de Laurent interrupted. 'Although I am willing to consider a new betrothal for our sister, I should warn you that Joan is…somewhat opposed to marriage.'

Good. It was far easier to refuse a marriage with

a reluctant bride. The man's warning eased Ronan's tension, for he didn't intend to consider it either. 'Forgive me, but I am more concerned about the safety of my people. It has been two days, and I need to bring men to overthrow the usurper as soon as possible. Any discussion of marriage must wait until I have freed them.'

The two Normans exchanged a look. Then the younger brother shrugged. 'We may be able to help you. But I will leave that decision to our sister. If you can convince her to grant you the soldiers, then you may have the men.'

It was clear that her brothers had a greater interest in arranging a betrothal for their sister than in offering help to a stranger. Ronan was beginning to feel like a pawn, commanded by invisible hands.

He hid his annoyance and met Warrick's gaze squarely. 'Is she here?' He had to be careful not to anger these men by outwardly refusing her. Instead, it might be better to convince the Norman lady that they were not suited.

'Joan is sitting with my daughter,' Rhys answered. 'Just there, in the white gown.'

A strange sense of premonition filled him, for the woman in white had intrigued him from the moment he'd seen her at Laochre. Her dark hair framed an innocent face with clear blue eyes. She was beautiful, but there was a sadness surrounding her.

'I will meet with her later, if I could have a moment to wash?' He directed his question towards the queen. 'I might make a better impression when I'm not covered in blood.' Though he had no intention of courtship, the delay would give him time to decide how to handle the situation.

'I will send you a bath and someone to tend you,' Isabel answered. A serene smile slid over her face, and if he didn't know better, he'd imagine she was plotting something.

As he followed the servants away from the Great Chamber, he had the sense that his life was being rearranged.

'You've gone mad.' Joan stared at her brothers, making no effort to hide her anger. 'Do you honestly believe I will agree to another betrothal after what just happened? I won't do it.'

'Go and speak with him,' Rhys suggested. 'I am giving *you* the opportunity to choose your next betrothal. He may be…different from the other men you meant to marry, but he *is* an Irish prince.'

'Think of what you are saying,' she insisted. 'Every man I've been promised to has died. Do you think I want to bring a death sentence upon someone else?'

'You are letting your fears command your life,' her brother said quietly. 'I will send him to you, and you can make that decision for yourself. His name is Ronan Ó Callaghan.'

Joan knew exactly which man her brother was referring to. The moment the prince had ridden into the inner bailey wearing bloodstained armour, he had caught her notice. There was an untamed savage quality to him, as if he cared naught about anything or anyone. And yet, when she'd noticed him staring, her skin had prickled with sensation. His green eyes burned with a fierce intensity that stole her breath. His blond hair was cut short, and there was a rough bristle upon his cheeks.

She had been playing with her young niece, Sorcha, and the little girl had also noticed the man. Joan had been about to bring her inside when Sorcha had pointed at him and said, 'He's the man you're going to marry.'

Joan had shushed her niece, knowing that it was only the fancy of a small child. At times, Sorcha seemed to have traces of the Sight, where she predicted things before they happened. But not this time. Joan believed it was best if she never accepted another betrothal—not until she learned how to break the curse.

Her brother, Warrick, drew closer. He was quiet and not as overbearing as Rhys. He studied her a moment and then said, 'Ronan Ó Callaghan needs our help, Joan. His stepbrother attacked their tribe and took the king as a hostage before he stole the throne for himself. He asked if we would send men to aid his cause.'

'You may help the prince if you wish, but that doesn't mean I'll marry him.' She saw no harm in them strengthening ties with Irish nobility, but it didn't mean she would stand back and allow her brothers to manipulate her life.

'No one is forcing you to do anything you don't want to do,' Warrick reassured her. He reached out and squeezed her hand. 'I'm only suggesting that you give it a chance. Meet with him and see what you think.'

And what good would that do? She simply couldn't imagine trying a fourth time for a husband. No matter what she might desire, Fate had forced her to be alone. It had become her life, this gnawing loneliness that stretched out before her. Furthermore, she couldn't imagine that this man would even cast a second look at her. She was four-and-twenty, far too old for a husband.

'If you want to help him, then do so. I am not stopping you,' she answered quietly. 'But I will not be betrothed again.' For a time, her brothers fell silent, no longer arguing. This was her life, was it not? And despite her desire for a child, she would suppress those dreams if it meant avoiding the curse.

A moment later, Queen Isabel joined them within the solar, and she held the hand of her young son Liam. She wore a gown the colour of rubies with a silver torque at her throat and another thin band around her forehead. 'Will you come with me, Lady Joan?'

The urge to refuse came to her lips. But they were guests here, and she could not disregard the rules of hospitality. Warrick was trying to forge a strong alliance with the MacEgans for the sake of his holdings in Killalough. It would not do to offend the queen.

'Of course,' she murmured, following Queen Isabel into the hallway. Joan knew full well that the queen might try to talk her into a marriage with Ronan. But she had no intention of becoming the victim of matchmaking. Instead, she feigned ignorance and changed the subject. 'Your son is such a dear boy. He looks about the same age as Sorcha.'

Isabel's face brightened. 'Liam is a good lad, though he does get into mischief.' She lifted him to her hip and dropped a kiss upon his head.

The boy squirmed in her arms and demanded, 'I want to walk.'

The queen let him down and motioned for a servant to come forward. 'Take Liam to his nurse. It's late and time for bed.' She leaned down to kiss his cheek. 'I'll come and say goodnight soon.'

He kissed his mother and hugged her before following the servant down the hall. The familiar longing filled Joan's heart, though she braved a smile. 'You must be very proud of him.'

'I am. I hope to have many children, God willing.' But there was a slight sadness in her voice that suggested she might have lost a child before.

Another maid followed them down the hall towards one of the chambers. The queen turned the corner and then stopped in front of the door. 'I know your brothers told you of Ronan Ó Callaghan's troubles. He is an ally of ours and a friend.'

And here it was—the queen's attempt at matchmaking. Joan steeled herself and forced a smile. 'Warrick did tell me, yes. But he also spoke of trying to arrange another marriage for me.' She took a slight step back. 'If you are asking me to speak with the prince for that reason, I must refuse. I do not wish to be married.'

The queen laughed softly. 'Your brother's ambitions for your marriage stretch high, if that is what he believes. No, Lady Joan. You are Norman, like I am, and you know our customs well. I have given Ronan our hospitality, and we will grant him men to aid in his cause.'

Her reassurance eased Joan's tensions somewhat. But she asked, 'Then why have you brought me to his chamber?'

'After the battle, Ronan asked for a hot bath. I would have asked one of my ladies to serve him, but I thought you might wish to do so. You could meet the prince and decide if your brothers should fight with him.'

It was the custom of noblewomen to help bathe their guests, and Joan understood that the queen was granting her the opportunity to learn more about Ronan Ó Callaghan for her brothers' sake. 'So long as you are not trying to set up a betrothal.'

The queen shook her head. 'His family was trying to arrange a marriage to another king's daughter from Tornall, from what I have heard.'

It felt as if a weight had lifted from her shoulders, and Joan could breathe again. 'I am very glad to hear this.'

Queen Isabel smiled at her. 'Go now, and see what you can learn for your brothers' sake. You need not fear that we are arranging a marriage.'

Joan inclined her head and entered the chamber. Ronan was not inside, but the queen assured her that he would arrive shortly. The servants had already filled the tub with hot water, and Joan busied herself by arranging the soap and all that she would need.

Knowing that this man was merely a guest and nothing more eased all the tension from her mood. She had tended many visitors in her father's castle over the years, and this man would be no different.

After a time, the door opened and Ronan stood at the threshold. He was a tall man, and she guessed that the top of her head came to his chin. His chainmail armour was covered in blood and would need to be cleaned. Beneath the shadows of his green eyes, she saw weariness and strain. His blond hair was matted, and she wondered what it would feel like to touch his unshaved cheeks. She could not deny that he was attractive, and she forced a calm smile on her face.

From the wry expression, it seemed that he, too, believed others were trying to make a match between them. He spoke in Irish at first, and she shook her head, for she did not understand his words. Then he drew closer and spoke in the Norman language, 'Did your brothers arrange this?'

She shook her head. 'The queen did.' With a light shrug, she said, 'But I am here to tend your bath, nothing more.'

He stared at her for a moment, as if he wasn't certain whether to believe her. She met his gaze frankly, for what did she have to hide?

At last, he asked, 'Will you help me with my armour?'

'Of course.' She aided him in removing his outer tunic, followed by the heavy hauberk. The weight of the chainmail was staggering, but she laid it carefully on the floor, along with the tunic. 'I can arrange for a servant to clean it for you tonight, if you like.' The sight of the dried blood was sobering, for she realised the extent of the fighting he had endured.

'Thank you. I am Ronan Ó Callaghan,' he said.

'I am Joan de Laurent. You met my meddling brothers, Rhys and Warrick, not long ago.' She smiled at the prince, not wanting him to be ill at ease around her—especially when she had no intention of following her brothers' wishes. 'Pay them no heed.'

He nodded and stripped off his remaining armour until he stood only in his trews. Joan kept her gaze upon the floor and took the rest of the heavy chainmail, averting her gaze as he stepped into the tub of water. When she was certain he was covered, she turned around.

A strange flush suffused her cheeks at the sight of him. His broad shoulders were exposed in the narrow tub, and he was heavily muscled. Water droplets slid over his bare skin, and she felt a strange ache within her body. So very odd.

'Is the water warm enough?' she asked.

'It is.' He reached for a cake of soap, but she took it first and dipped her hands in the water, lathering it. The Irish prince was silent while she moved behind him and washed his back. He flinched slightly when she scrubbed away the dirt with a linen rag. It was a task she had done for many of her family's guests, a common courtesy.

Yet, somehow, with this man, it seemed different.

She was conscious of his bare skin and the touch of her hands over the firm male flesh. With her hands, she scooped water over the soap and rinsed it away, following the path with her hands.

'Were you wounded in the battle?' She didn't want to inadvertently hurt him by touching a sensitive place.

But he only shook his head. 'Nothing serious. Only a few bruises.'

Joan tried to behave as if he were an ordinary visitor, but the truth was, she *did* find him attractive. He was nothing like other visitors she had tended in the past. Not only was he handsome, but his body appeared hewn from stone with its hardened muscle.

Her cheeks burned with the flush of interest. If he had been her first betrothal, she would have been quite pleased about him claiming her innocence. She liked what she saw, and the very thought of a man like this touching her made her feel breathless. Suddenly, she was beginning to understand the teasing remarks she had overheard by other women in the past. Washing this man made her own skin tighten with anticipation, and she became more aware of him.

'You must be weary after this journey,' she said. 'It looks as if you rode here straight from the battlefield.'

'I did,' he admitted. 'It took two days to reach Laochre.'

Her heart softened at the realisation that Ronan had sacrificed everything to reach the MacEgans quickly. It was evident that he'd gone without sleep and food until now, hoping to help his people. He was a man of honour, and she admired his inner strength.

Ronan was so quiet, it seemed that his thoughts were troubling him. She helped him lean back, and she filled a pitcher with warmed water, pouring it over his hair. It was a strangely intimate task, and the air grew heated as she lathered soap into his hair. He closed his eyes and relaxed against the tub. Joan found herself staring at his muscled arms and the way the water slid over the hardened planes.

She could almost imagine herself kissing this man, feeling his arms around her. A sudden aching caught her between her legs, stirrings of an unfamiliar desire. She didn't understand these feelings, but her breasts tightened beneath her gown.

To distract herself, she rinsed the soap from his hair. Ronan opened his eyes and caught her gaze.

'You have a soothing touch, my lady.'

All words fled her brain, and she managed only a nod. His green eyes stared into hers, and she found herself fascinated by his mouth. She forced her attention back to the soap in her hands. 'I—I was sorry to hear that your father is now a captive.'

Ronan's expression turned grim. 'He is. But not for long, I hope.'

She knew he needed an army to help him fight, and she understood that this was not a king's son who remained behind stone walls while his men fought to defend the Kingdom. This man would venture into battle with no fear, only aggression. His bloodstained armour proved it beyond all doubt.

Ronan sat up, resting his arms on the wooden tub. It was time to wash his chest, but her heartbeat quickened at the thought. She wanted to touch him, to slide her fingers over his bare skin and explore his body. Beneath her palms, she felt the rise of his pectoral muscles and his swift heartbeat. His broad chest filled the tub, and she suddenly imagined him standing up, fully naked.

What was the matter with her? She sloshed water against his skin to rinse it, and hurriedly pulled back to fetch the drying cloth.

'Do you know why they sent you to attend my bath?' he asked in a gruff tone.

Joan fumbled for a reason. 'B-because you are a king's son and an honoured guest.' She took the cloth and spun, holding it out and averting her eyes. She heard the splash of water as he stood. He took the cloth from her, drying himself while she turned her back.

When she risked a glance, she saw that he had tied the cloth around his hips. His abdomen was ridged, and a slight line of hair directed her gaze lower. Her breath caught as she imagined the rest of him, but she dragged her attention back to his face.

'Queen Isabel said you are promised to another,' she reminded him. 'The King of Tornall's daughter, I believe.'

His expression twisted. 'No, she is mistaken. There is no formal betrothal between us, despite what my father wanted.'

Though she revealed no reaction, inwardly she

wondered if the queen had brought them together on purpose. It was indeed likely.

Ronan crossed his arms and stared at her. She couldn't quite guess his thoughts, but his gaze passed over her slowly as if he were memorising her features.

She fumbled for something to say but could not come up with a single word. He was staring at her as if he found her beautiful. And a piece of her spirit warmed to it.

'Is something wrong?' He took a step closer and reached out to touch her nape. The warm wetness of his hand was a distraction she hadn't anticipated.

'What are you doing?'

He pulled at her veil, revealing her long dark hair. 'I want to see you. It seems reasonable enough, given how much you have seen of me.'

She gaped at that. 'No, that is unnecessary.' She reached out for her veil, but he continued to stare, holding the length of linen under one arm. Joan let out a sigh and stared back. His green eyes held interest, which she didn't want at all. 'Give me my veil, my lord.'

But he held it and ignored her command. 'You are fair of face. It surprises me that you are not yet married.'

Because they all died, she wanted to answer. *It was quite a hindrance.*

Still, her vanity warmed to his words. She wished she could stop herself from reacting so strongly to this man. And so, she squared her shoulders and changed the conversation in a new direction. 'I bid you good fortune in winning back your castle and rescuing your father.'

'I need your brothers' help,' he admitted. 'But they will not give up soldiers…not unless you can convince them to fight for my people's sake.' His voice was deep and husky, and her wayward thoughts turned down the wrong path.

Now what did he mean by that? He was a stranger to her, and she had no reason to intervene on his behalf. But she could not deny that he attracted her.

'I am not opposed to helping your cause,' she said slowly, 'but how do you suppose I should convince my brothers? Do you intend to pay them for their soldiers?' Warrick and Rhys would never endanger their men on behalf of a stranger—even if he was an Irish prince. 'They will want something in return.'

'I can offer them an alliance and protection for Killalough, once my father is king again. But I leave that answer in your hands,' he said. 'You will know what your brothers want in return better than me. And if you do manage to convince them on my behalf, I would grant you your own wish.'

Joan nearly choked at the offer. It wasn't as if she could ask this man for a baby. *That* was a conversation she could never imagine. Even so, she felt the flustered heat rising once more. Wild thoughts entered her mind, of lying naked upon her bed. Would Ronan enter her chamber and touch her intimately? Would he claim her body night after night, in the hopes that his seed would take root?

She closed her eyes and forced the sensual vision

away. Despite the curse, she could not imagine falling into such sin. Not to mention, her brothers would eviscerate him for touching her.

'N-no, I don't need anything from you.' She clenched her hands at her sides, trying to calm the restlessness within. But it was difficult with him wearing only the drying cloth and standing so near.

'I think you do. But you don't want to tell me what it is,' Ronan predicted. His voice was low and deep, almost tempting. She started to turn away, but he caught her hand. 'Why is that?'

Because it would be a terrible mistake. Even if she enjoyed his body in the way her brothers' wives had said she would.

No, she had no choice but to remain untouched for the rest of her life. It did not matter that she wanted a baby of her own. She had to content herself with her nieces and nephews. Why, then, was the thought so bleak?

'Well?' he prompted. His thumb stroked the centre of her palm, and her body yearned for more. She imagined him caressing her in other places, and it sent a flare of need between her legs.

Stop this, she warned herself and straightened. 'I don't have to tell you what I want. Only that it has nothing to do with you.'

'You don't like me.' From the way he said it, it seemed almost like a challenge. And he was wrong—she liked what she saw very much. He unnerved her in a way no man ever had.

But she kept her tone calm and said, 'I like you

well enough. But that doesn't mean we need to make a bargain between us. I will speak to my brothers, but the choice is theirs as to whether our men will fight for you.'

He studied her a moment and told her, 'Your brothers wanted me to barter marriage in exchange for their army.'

She wanted to curse at their meddling. 'No,' she said firmly. 'That will never happen.'

The prince was silent for a moment, and the only sound in the chamber was the dripping of water. 'Good. Then we are in agreement.'

His blunt statement should have reassured her, but she had not expected his refusal. Instead, she waited for him to elaborate. 'I cannot be wedded right now,' he continued. 'My first concern must be for my people.'

Joan understood that. He had been forced into a desperate position, one where lives were at stake. And she offered her own sympathy. 'You are right to fear for them, and I hope you can save them. I will do what I can to convince Warrick and Rhys. But they don't want to accept that marriage is the last thing I want.'

'Especially to a man like me.' There was a mocking note in the midst of his deprecating remark.

Joan softened her voice. 'If I ever intended to marry, I would consider you—or at least, a man like you. But as I said before, I cannot wed anyone.'

Ronan released her hand, his gaze penetrating. She was acutely aware of him and the heat of his skin. It took an effort not to rest her hands upon his hewn chest, sliding her fingers over the ridge of thick muscle.

'Your brother told me that your intended husband died,' he said. 'I am sorry for it.'

It happens too often, she wanted to say but didn't. Instead, she answered, 'I had never seen him before. I didn't know anything about Murdoch.'

'What will you do now?'

She shrugged. 'I may enter a convent. Or perhaps I will return to my father's house and look after him, now that he is a widower.' She glanced down at him, still distracted that he wore only a drying cloth. 'I should go and let you get dressed.'

'Not yet.' His demeanour shifted, and he took on a commanding tone. In that moment, he was a prince in every sense of the word. 'I need an army to help take back my kingdom. The MacEgans will help, and possibly your brothers' men. But once they leave, my father's stepson will only drive our supporters out again.'

Her brow furrowed, for she didn't quite understand what he wanted from her.

Then he continued, 'I need men who will dwell among us until I know who is loyal.'

'Why not ask the King of Tornall?' Joan suggested. 'Surely he would send men to help you.'

'As I said before, I have no formal alliance with them—only an understanding. But if I ask him to send soldiers...'

'He would want you to marry his daughter,' she finished.

'Yes. And I have met Siobhan. She is not as reasonable as you are.'

At that, she almost smiled. *Reasonable* was not a word most men used when describing her. 'You think I'm reasonable because I don't want to marry?'

'Yes.' He took a step closer. 'And you may know how I can convince your brothers' men to stay longer.'

Her gaze shifted towards his bare skin, distracting her again. 'They would stay for a time if you paid them. But how long do you think they are needed?'

'Half a year, at least. Perhaps longer.'

She was beginning to understand why her brothers were suggesting a betrothal. Such a length of time would be difficult, not to mention costly.

But Ronan raised his green eyes to hers and asked, 'Do you think you can help me persuade your brothers?' His voice was deeply resonant, like an invisible caress. Her wayward imagination conjured up the vision of his hands around her waist, pulling her near. She felt herself yielding, wanting something she could not name.

'I—I don't know. I could try.' And with that, she fled, no longer trusting herself around this man.

Chapter Two

Ronan could not deny that Joan de Laurent had caught his attention. He had been unprepared for the rush of arousal that struck hard when she'd caressed his skin. His shaft had grown erect beneath the water, and her gentle touch had made him imagine her hands elsewhere.

He gritted his teeth, forcing back the image. He had not touched a woman in months now, and he refused to loosen the tight hold upon his desires. The last time he had seduced a woman, it had ended in tragedy. He could not allow himself to weaken again, though his body was rigid with need.

Joan wasn't the usual sort of woman he normally desired. She carried herself like a holy woman, wearing white and an iron cross upon a chain. If anything, her earlier remark about becoming a bride of the Church seemed likely. She was a virgin and not the sort of woman he normally pursued.

And yet, she had washed him like a woman who desired a man—as if she, too, had her own hidden needs. He hadn't missed the furious blush in her cheeks, as if she would die before telling him of her desires. There was something she wanted, but her refusal to admit the truth only intrigued him more.

There was no doubt that her brothers had intended to offer Joan's hand in marriage, hoping she would ascend to an Irish throne. To them, it was an alliance that would elevate Joan's rank and bring honour to her.

But they knew nothing of the sins Ronan had committed. He never wanted to be King of Clonagh, especially after his brother's death. If he could have given his life for Ardan's, he would have done so a thousand times over. For the burden of guilt never left him. Not a day went by that he did not blame himself.

Joan de Laurent wanted to be left alone, and that was the wisest course for both of them.

This morn, he dressed himself in the clothing Queen Isabel had left for him and departed his chamber. It was later than he'd realised, and most of the castle had already broken their fast. Though his body had needed the rest after not sleeping for days, he couldn't quite suppress the feeling of guilt at lying abed for so long.

Ronan didn't bother with a full meal but took bread and cheese from a servant as he passed through the Great Chamber. The night of sleep had cleared his head, and now he had to make plans for his attack.

He strode through Laochre, feeling the tug of envy. The castle was massive in size, with Norman soldiers and Irishmen training side by side. There was a sense of order, with each person having a place to fill. It was exactly what he'd hoped for Clonagh. His father and brother would have wanted the same.

The darkness of grief shadowed him, bringing with it a rise of anger. His brother had been kind, responsible, and beloved by all their people. Whereas Ronan had cared naught about what anyone thought and lived his life as he chose. He deserved to lose everything—but his brother hadn't.

It wasn't right or fair. *He* should have died, not Ardan or his young son, Declan. But his failure had caused both their deaths, and Ronan would never forgive himself for it.

He watched the men training, and soon, Warrick and Rhys de Laurent joined him, one on each side. For a time, Ronan said nothing at all, though he knew their silent question. But Joan de Laurent was an innocent—a good woman who didn't deserve a sinner like him.

Warrick studied him for a moment, his gaze piercing. At last he said, 'She told you no, didn't she?'

I didn't ask her, Ronan thought. But he raised an eyebrow and avoided a direct answer. 'Why should she agree to wed a man she doesn't know?'

'For the same reason she agreed to wed three other men she'd never seen,' Rhys added. 'Because our father arranged an alliance.'

Ronan eyed the man. 'Among my people, we don't marry a woman without knowing her first. I only met Joan last night, and we've spoken for less than an hour.'

'Our sister won't let you know her. She has already decided never to marry.' Rhys stared back at the soldiers. 'But that isn't what's right for her. She needs a husband and a family of her own.'

'And you've already decided this, have you?' Though he didn't understand Joan's reluctance to wed, he was not about to force the issue.

'Our father would be pleased with the idea of Joan wedding an Irish prince.'

Ronan had no doubt of that. But neither he nor Joan had any interest in marriage. And yet, he wondered if she could convince her brothers to come to an arrangement. He stalled an answer, asking, 'If she did agree to wed, how many men can you offer me?'

'Two dozen Normans and fifty Irishmen,' Warrick answered. 'My wife inherited property at Killalough, and we can add our forces. Add the MacEgan soldiers, and it will be enough to retake Clonagh with minimal bloodshed.'

He believed Warrick. That would make nearly seventy-five highly trained men and possibly two dozen more from Laochre.

'If our sister agrees to wed you,' Rhys continued, 'I will send my two dozen Norman soldiers to remain at Clonagh until you've driven out the traitors. If Joan is pleased with the marriage, I will send more.'

Ronan said nothing, but his instincts warned him that Joan's brothers would accept nothing less than a union between them. He decided not to reveal his reluctance, stalling for more time.

'You have three days to convince her,' Warrick

said. 'If she has agreed to wed you by the end of those three days, then we will send the men.' He paused a moment. 'But if you hurt our sister at all, in thought or in deed, I will burn you alive.'

Which was exactly what a brother was supposed to say. Ronan didn't react at all, and then Rhys added, 'Or burning might be too fast. Flaying could be better.' There was a knowing smile on his face, and he cracked his knuckles.

'Before you decide to kill me, you should wait until there's a reason for it,' Ronan answered.

'True.' Warrick clapped him on the back. 'I must return to my wife at Killalough, and Rhys is coming with me. We will assemble our men and leave Joan in the care of Queen Isabel.' He regarded Ronan with a steady gaze. 'Three days.'

Joan sat against the inner bailey wall with Sorcha, watching over the child as she made flower chains out of dandelions. For a moment, she allowed herself to imagine that this was *her* little girl and not her brother's. The young child sat down in Joan's lap, and a surge of yearning filled her. This was what she wanted—to have a child of her own. It was a physical hole inside her, and she knew her time was running out. She should have been married five years ago, and now, she might be too old to bear a child.

The thought of returning to her father's house to live among people who were afraid of her was disheartening. And yet, what else could she do? She didn't dare wed again.

Her brothers wanted her to marry whether she wished it or not. Unbidden came the thought of Ronan Ó Callaghan. Joan could not deny that she was intrigued by this man. There was a strength about him, not only physical, but he seemed like one who was strong-willed and stubborn. If anyone could stand up to her brothers' overprotective ways, it was Ronan. All he wanted in return was men to help him protect his people.

And suddenly, as if in answer to her thoughts, she saw him watching over them in the distance. Sorcha stood and hurried towards him.

'Sorcha, wait.' Joan tried to bring the child back, but it was too late. The girl was reaching her hand up to Ronan, while the daisy chain tipped from her dark hair. Joan wanted to groan, for heaven only knew what Sorcha was telling the Irish prince.

Ronan appeared wary of the child, as if he knew not what to do with her. Sorcha put her hand in his. 'You come,' she said. Without waiting for him to agree, she led him towards Joan.

When the pair of them were a short distance away, Ronan looked as if he were searching for a way to extricate himself. 'I should go,' he started to say, but Sorcha tightened her grip on his hand.

'No. You have to see Lady Joan. She's waiting.'

Waiting for what? Joan wondered. She couldn't quite imagine what the little girl wanted, but the determination on Sorcha's face rivalled the strongest warriors. Ronan had no choice at all, except to obey the child's wishes. She tried to hold back her amusement at his discomfort but could not quite manage it.

'And who have you brought, Sorcha?' Joan asked. 'Do you think he needs a flower chain?' She could not resist teasing him, for the prince appeared uneasy being led about by a three-year-old.

The child shook her head. 'No. The flowers are mine. You hold his hand.' She brought the prince closer and then reached for Joan's hand, joining them together. 'There.'

She was startled by the warmth of his callused palm and the way his fingers covered hers. Joan was about to pull away, but Ronan closed his grip. He wore a dark leather tunic and leather arm bracers. His trews covered his powerful thighs, and a sword hung at his waist. Though he was a prince, he was also undeniably a warrior.

Sorcha began walking away, as if her task was now complete. Joan asked, 'Where are you going?'

'I'm hungry, and Father is waiting for me.' She pulled the drooping flower chain back on to her hair and then hurried up the stairs to her father. Rhys scooped her into his arms and held her against his hip.

Joan wasn't certain what to say except, 'My niece is not subtle, is she?'

'She is very bold for one so young.' He released her hand and then asked, 'Why did your brother bring her to Ireland?'

Joan walked alongside him as they passed by the soldiers. 'Rhys and Warrick came to witness my wedding, and Sorcha was rather demanding about wanting to attend. Truthfully, I think Rhys brought her along because Sorcha can be challenging. His wife, Lianna, just gave birth to another baby, and he thought it would give her time to rest with their son.'

Joan wished she could have stayed in Scotland to cradle the newborn, for there was nothing more wonderful than the feeling of an infant nestled against her heart.

'Do you have many nieces or nephews?'

'Two nieces and two nephews,' she answered. 'Sorcha is the eldest. Mary and Stephen are twin babies, born to Warrick and his wife, Rosamund. Edward is Sorcha's little brother, who was only born a month ago.'

Ronan eyed her and ventured, 'You want children of your own, do you not?'

Joan nodded without thinking. Then she stopped herself and said, 'I do, but I suppose it is not meant to be.' She could not imagine a fourth man dying before their marriage. The idea made her shudder.

'Why do you say that?'

She didn't know how to answer him, for he would never understand her reluctance. Instead, she kept her answer simple. 'After three failed betrothals, I do not believe I will ever marry.'

He waited for her to elaborate, and when she did not, he stopped walking. 'Why not?'

Because they all die. Her face reddened, and she shrugged. 'You will say I am foolish if I tell you the reason.'

'You are foolish,' he repeated with a faint smile. 'Now tell me the reason.'

An unexpected laugh broke free before she could stop herself. Perhaps she *should* tell him the truth, and then he might leave her alone.

Joan thought a moment and said, 'If you were betrothed to a woman, and she died before you could wed, it would be a misfortune. If it happened a second time, you would feel uneasy. But after it happened a third time?' She shook her head. 'I am cursed never to marry. If I am betrothed a fourth time, that man will surely perish.' She raised her chin to face him, waiting to hear his protests.

Yet he didn't smile or scoff at her fears. Instead, he seemed to consider her confession, and he asked, 'Was that why you refused to marry any man?'

She nodded. 'I do not want to bring death, simply because I am cursed.' Again, Joan waited for him to mock her beliefs, but he only remained pensive for a time.

At last he said, 'Many of my men have their own beliefs regarding life and death, especially in battle. One wears a red ribbon around his left ankle, and he claims that it saved his life. Another has not cleaned his armour in over a year.' He wrinkled his face. 'God above, but it reeks.' Then he relaxed and added, 'You are not alone in your way of thinking.'

'My brothers don't believe me. They think it's only a coincidence. And though they may be right, I cannot help but feel responsible for the deaths of each one.'

Ronan began walking alongside her once again.

'Would you have married any of those men, if they had not died?'

A tightness caught within her chest. When she was seventeen, she had been thrilled about her first betrothal. Her girlish dreams had blossomed as she had imagined a husband and a family of her own. But then those dreams had been shattered, time and again.

At last, she nodded. 'The first two were good men, from what I could tell. The last one was…older, but I could have managed.' Though the idea of bedding Murdoch Ó Connor was not particularly a welcome one. Joan couldn't quite visualise lying with such a man.

Although she could easily indulge in the unholy thoughts she'd had about Ronan. His muscled body, sleek from water, had tempted her in ways she didn't even understand. She had felt an echo of sensation when she had run her fingers over his bare skin.

He caught her stare and she blinked, wishing her blush had not betrayed her interest. Better to gain control over her senses and put an end to these unspoken desires.

Ronan stopped walking near the barbican gate. In the distance, the coast was visible, and the sun shone upon the water. 'Do you want to walk a little further?'

She thought about it for a time, wondering if she dared to be alone with him. He seemed like a man of honour, and she doubted if he would harm her. Unfortunately, she couldn't say the same for his own well-being, given what had happened to the men in her past.

With a shrug, she said lightly, 'If you think it's safe to be in my presence. You still might die.'

Ronan's mouth curved in a smile. 'I'll take my chances.'

As they continued through the gate and into the open meadow, Ronan studied Joan's appearance. She was indeed an attractive woman, though the white gown made her face appear too pale. She veiled her dark hair, but he had seen for himself how the wild locks tangled around her shoulders with a hint of curl. Any man would be pleased with her beauty.

She would have been a perfect second wife for his brother, Ardan. Ronan could easily imagine the pair of them—his quiet, kind-hearted brother and this woman. Joan was virtuous and gentle, someone who deserved a good man for a husband—not a hardened warrior like himself. The shadowed thread of regret wound around his conscience before he forced it back.

'When will you return to Clonagh to take back your lands?' she asked quietly.

'Within a few days. I need to scout out their defences.' His mood darkened at the thought of his people living under the threat of Odhran. His stepbrother's rebellion had struck hard with a ruthless strength, and it gnawed at Ronan's conscience. Odhran had used hired mercenaries to slaughter their guards and take hostages. King Brodur had been seized, and Ronan had cut down four men, trying to save his father from captivity.

But when his enemies had attempted to surround him, he'd had no choice but to run.

Shame darkened his mood, though he knew patience was necessary for the success of this conquest. He needed men to accompany him and information about his enemy's weaknesses before he could invade.

Joan remained silent during their walk, staring out at the water. They continued through the grasses, passing by grazing sheep. He walked alongside her, and he could smell the faint scent of flowers emanating from her skin.

With each moment he spent at her side, he felt the silent chiding of Fate. He'd been a man who had lived in the moment and sought pleasure wherever he could find it. Now, he wasn't suited to being anyone's husband, and he had nothing to offer. She was right to turn down the betrothal.

'I think you should put aside your reluctance and wed the King of Tornall's daughter,' Joan suggested. 'You could ally yourself with her father's men and defend your people. She is Irish, like you, and it would unite your kingdoms.'

It was a sensible suggestion, and one he had considered. But there was a greater threat to his clan if he accepted help from that tribe. 'If I do that, then King Tierney might try to claim Clonagh for his own. He will exert his own political power because I would owe him a debt.'

Joan gave a slight nod of acknowledgement. 'Perhaps.' She walked to the edge of the clearing, and looked out over the sea. A short distance away was the island of Ennisleigh, a fortress the men used to scout invaders attacking by sea. There was a ruined keep that stood there, one they had not bothered to rebuild. It gave the appearance of no threat at all, but Joan knew that there were many soldiers guarding the outpost day and night. It was a deliberate means of protecting Laochre from seaborne invaders.

'The island is beautiful,' she said softly. 'I do love the sea. Is Clonagh far away from here?'

'It is. The fortress lies two days north,' he admitted. 'We have forests but no coast.'

They stood for a while, watching over the waves. Strands of her dark hair escaped from her veil, and Joan tried to force them back. The winds grew stronger, and at last, she laughed, removing the veil entirely. The dark curls framed her face, and her cheeks were rosy from the chill. Only a few months ago, he would have stolen a kiss and tried to tempt her. She made him want to push back the boundaries between them and find out whether there was a woman of passion beneath her innocent exterior.

When she saw him staring, her smile faded. 'Is something wrong?'

Only an urge that he shouldn't have. He brushed back the strands of hair from her face, cupping her face. He studied those deep blue eyes that mirrored the sea, and admired the curve of her cheek. Unlike a young maiden who would shy away or giggle, she met his gaze openly.

She was untouched, a woman of innocence. Her white gown reminded him of that, and he knew she would never consent to a marriage. But Joan de Laurent intrigued him. He wanted to taste those full lips, to see what sort of secrets she was keeping from the world. And more than that, he wanted to understand why this woman had captured his attention.

Her hand moved to cover his, as if she wanted to pull away. And yet, she didn't. The touch of her fingers upon his was spellbinding, and he locked his gaze with hers.

'What is it?' she whispered.

He let his hand drift downward to her shoulder before he held her waist in both hands. For a moment, he kept her captive, simply watching. For a woman who did not want to marry, she made no effort to escape him. Instead, she waited for him to answer her question.

'Even if there were no curse, we could not wed. We are not suited.' He knew it down to his bones. Joan de Laurent was a good woman, the sort who deserved a decent man. Not one who had caused a tragedy for his family.

'I agree that we are very different,' she said quietly. 'You are an Irish prince, and I am the daughter of a Norman earl. We have nothing at all in common.'

His hands moved up her spine, and he felt like a bastard, wanting to push back the boundaries between them. But she was a forbidden craving he wanted to taste.

'It's more than that, Joan. Trust me when I say you would never want a man like me.' He drew his hands down again in a soft caress, resting them upon her hips.

She closed her eyes as if his touch had burned through her. From the colour in her cheeks, he knew the effect he was having on her, but he wasn't ready to let her go—not yet.

'W-why would you say such a thing?' she stammered. 'Have you done something terrible?'

He had. Something so terrible, he dared tell no one at all. And if he didn't gather his self-control, he was about to trespass upon this innocent woman's virtue.

'It doesn't matter, does it? Since we will never wed.' He released her from his grasp, expecting her to pull away from him. But she kept her hands upon his chest, above his beating heart. He wore no armour, but the simple heat of her palms burned through the leather tunic, arousing him deeply. He remembered how it had felt when her slick hands had soaped his wet skin, and desire had taken hold of his senses.

'I don't think you're as bad as you say you are,' she murmured.

It was almost a challenge, and one he was prepared to face. He reached back to her waist and pulled her closer.

'You're right, *a stór*. I'm far worse.'

And with that, he lowered his mouth to hers and claimed a kiss.

The heat of his mouth was scalding, a demand— not a request. Joan tasted his longing, and when he held her closer, her hips pressed to his. She could feel the hard ridge of his arousal, and to her shock, she responded to him, growing weak with need. Never in her life had she been kissed like this, though her first two betrothed husbands had kissed her. Her breasts tightened, and she could not catch a single breath as Ronan claimed her.

His tongue slid within her mouth in a silent temptation, and she could do nothing except surrender. What startled her the most was her own racing heart. She wanted this man, yearned for his touch. He attracted her in all the wrong ways until she hardly cared at all. His hands threaded through her hair, tangling the strands as he kissed her hard. She opened to him, yielding to the onslaught until she could scarcely catch her breath.

You cannot have him, her mind warned. He was forbidden to her, and she should not give in to these longings. Else he would die.

But she was kissing him back, meeting him with the answer of her own veiled desires. For so many years, she had been promised to strangers with her father's seal upon the betrothal—just before those men had lost their lives. The sweet stolen kisses had stopped when she'd lost each one. And she'd never realised how much she needed a man's touch until now. It was as if someone had ripped apart her inhibitions, exposing her deepest desires. She faltered at the thought of Ronan claiming her body, giving her a child.

But the thought of seeing his sightless eyes staring back at her brought a tremor of heartache.

No, she could not take the risk of his death. Not even for one forbidden night.

Joan pulled back from him with reluctance, knowing that she could not surrender to her desires. At least, not unless the curse could be broken—if that was even possible.

'I won't apologise,' he said gruffly. 'I wanted to kiss you.'

'I don't need an apology,' she murmured. Her heart was racing, her skin tightening with unspoken need. Between her legs, she ached, and it was a struggle to calm herself. 'But we both know it was a mistake.' They would never marry, and she could not risk falling into temptation.

His eyes locked upon hers as if he didn't believe her. 'You kissed me back.' There was a pointed question in his statement, but she had no idea how to answer it.

Instead, she blurted out, 'It would have been bad manners not to.'

At that, he threw back his head and laughed. His green eyes warmed with humour, and he rested his hand on the small of her back. 'So it would.' And though she knew it had been unwise, she did not regret kissing him.

Ronan guided her back towards the castle, and for a time, she held her silence. She knew better than to imagine that this man wanted her for anything other than her brothers' soldiers. He wanted to take back his fortress, nothing more.

The prince slowed his pace and studied her. 'You

surprised me, Lady Joan. And it makes me consider another possibility. Would you consider a betrothal with me, even if we did not marry? Your brothers would grant me the men I need, and I would grant you whatever you desire.'

'I—I don't know.' She had never considered the possibility, but the very thought of wedding a man like Ronan made her blush. One kiss had turned her knees to water, and her heartbeat was still racing.

'Surely there is a way we could help each other.'

She steeled herself and stopped walking. Did she dare to tell him the truth of what she wanted most? Likely not, for she hardly knew this man. It shamed her to admit that she wanted a child so badly, she was willing to consider bearing one out of wedlock.

He had suggested a betrothal without an actual marriage. It made her wonder if that was a way around the curse. Ronan seemed to be a kind man, and there was no doubt she felt an attraction to him.

Would it be so wrong to surrender her virtue to this prince and take him into her bed? Or was the risk too great? In the eyes of the church, a formal betrothal was nearly the same as a marriage. She would not be the first woman to lie with her intended husband before the vows were spoken.

Her brothers might kill him, even if the curse did not. But she could not deny that Ronan had awakened sensual longings within her.

Her face felt as if it were on fire, but she decided to tell him the truth. 'You asked me what I wanted.'

'Yes. Name it, and if it is in my power to give, this

I will do.' He turned to regard her. His green eyes gazed upon her with interest, and she felt her blush rising again.

'The truth is, I want a child of my own.'

For a long moment, he stared at her in disbelief. She could not read the emotions on his face, but it seemed as if she had struck a nerve. It made her wish she hadn't spoken at all. Perhaps he didn't desire her after all, despite the kiss they had shared. Perhaps he found her lacking, a woman to be pitied. Her stomach twisted with humiliation, but at last he spoke.

'A child is something I cannot give you. Not ever.'

The finality in his voice startled her, for although she had expected a refusal, she had not anticipated the cold anger in his voice. She didn't ask him why, for it was clear that he did not want to speak of it.

So be it. There would be no betrothal between them, and they would go their separate ways. It should have been a relief—and yet, she felt a sense of regret. Ronan Ó Callaghan was the first man she had been attracted to in years. His kiss had taken her breath away, leaving her wanting more. But it was not meant to be.

As they returned to the castle, the weight of silence descended over them.

Joan had originally planned to return to Killalough with her brothers, but Queen Isabel had begged her to stay for the Samhain festivities. She would rather have retreated to their fortress, but Warrick and Rhys had told her to stay, to appease the queen and to keep good relations with the MacEgan tribe. They would send an escort for her within a few days.

She had no doubt that they were trying to arrange a match with Ronan. Although she had already told them it was not a possibility, her brothers were ignoring her.

The autumn air was crisp, and Joan strode through the inner bailey, carrying a basket of turnips. Several of the children followed, begging her to save the largest turnip for them to carve. Tonight, they would place lights within the turnips and carry the lanterns to keep away the evil spirits.

She found that it *was* entertaining to carve the turnips into faces. After distributing the turnips among the children, she chose one for herself and went to sit upon the stone steps leading to the battlements. With a small dagger, she began cutting into the vegetable, attempting to form eyes within the reddish-white mass.

Footsteps drew nearer, and a shadow crossed over her. When she glanced up, she saw Ronan standing there. He was holding a large turnip of his own. Joan wasn't quite certain why he had come to speak with her. It seemed that he'd been avoiding her since he'd kissed her. Now, he was behaving as if nothing were amiss.

Without asking, he sat down beside her and compared their turnips. 'Mine is bigger.'

She almost laughed, for it sounded like exactly something her brothers might say in teasing. There was a hint of wickedness in his eyes, and she realised he was trying to mend the awkwardness between them. Her mood softened, and it did seem that he wanted to become friends once again.

And so, she met his teasing with her own response. 'Size doesn't matter, my lord.'

A sinful smile curved over his mouth, making her flush. 'I've heard otherwise.'

'Most people say it's what you do with your size that matters,' she parried. His grin widened at the entendre, and she added, 'I have two brothers. Your jest is not a new one.' She carved a notch in the turnip, but her blade slipped and nicked the vegetable.

'Is that meant to be a face?' he asked. He took out his own dagger and began notching his turnip. Which was, in fact, bigger than hers.

'It is.' She wasn't particularly artistic, but it did have the necessary parts. 'Those are the eyes, and that's the nose.'

'You cut his nose off.'

'No, he was wounded in battle. It's still there.' To emphasise her point, she cut a line across the surface. 'That's a terrible scar. He was trying to save his lady from the enemy and suffered for her sake.'

'And she was taken away and was lost forever,' he finished. 'He died of a broken heart.'

'That wasn't the ending I had planned.' She carved another notch into the turnip, attempting to make the face smile. 'I was thinking that she would see beneath his scars to the man he truly was. And then he would bring her home with him to love for always.'

'That isn't what happens in real life, Lady Joan.'

Joan set down her knife to look at him. With a

shrug, she said, 'It's my story, and I can end it however I like.' She wasn't entirely surprised that he had disregarded the love story. Her brothers would have done the same.

'Wouldn't it be more interesting my way?' he suggested. 'Unpredictable is better.' He continued to carve at the vegetable, flicking bits of the turnip to the ground.

'I prefer a happier ending. One that ends in love.'

'Love doesn't always end happily.'

The dark tone of his voice suggested that he had experienced even more loss than she'd imagined. Had he loved a woman who had died during the attack on Clonagh? Or worst of all, had it involved a child? His vehement statement that he would never sire children made her wonder what had happened. A sudden ache caught her, for she had not thought of this. 'I am sorry if you lost someone you loved. Did it happen during the attack?'

He let out a slow breath. 'No. It was a few months before.'

She didn't know what else to say, except to touch his shoulder with sympathy. The sudden flash of interest in his eyes caught her unawares, for she had not expected it. She pulled back her hand as if it had caught on fire, feeling embarrassed.

To distract herself, Joan tilted her head to get a better look at the turnip he was carving. At first, it seemed only like a series of lines. Then he turned it towards her, and she was startled to see the gnarled face of a grandfather etched within the vegetable.

It was truly remarkable that he had captured such a powerful image with only a few strokes of the blade.

'Oh, my,' she murmured. 'This is wonderful. You cannot possibly risk burning this carving with a candle.'

He shrugged. 'It's only a turnip, Lady Joan.'

Did he truly not grasp the talent he had? Why would he deny his skills? She reached out for the turnip and then asked, 'Have you ever made other carvings? Out of wood, perhaps?'

'It's nothing of importance.' With that, he stood. 'Add my turnip in with the others. The children can light them and carry them tonight. I will go and help with the bonfires.'

Joan kept the turnip but had no intention of giving it over to be burned. Instead, she put it with her own, marvelling at the detail he'd captured. Ronan had a depth of talent she would never have guessed. The simplicity of his carving touched her heart.

'I am keeping it,' she told him. He eyed her for a moment, and then shrugged as if it were nothing. But it revealed another side to this man, one that intrigued her.

In the distance, many of the MacEgans were gathering wood and loading it into wagons to be brought to the hills for the Samhain fires. Before Ronan left her side, there was a sudden outcry near the gates.

Joan rose to her feet and saw a man and a woman arriving on horseback. The man had blond hair, lighter than Ronan's, and beside him rode a dark-haired woman of such beauty, Joan felt like an old crone. A young girl rode behind them on a smaller horse. The girl's brown hair was braided neatly, and the woman kept glancing behind her to ensure that the child was well.

'Who are they?' she asked Ronan.

'Connor MacEgan is the king's younger brother. It looks as if he's taken a wife.'

Joan moved closer, with Ronan following behind. Connor helped the woman down from her horse, but when Joan drew closer, she saw that he was favouring one hand over the other. The king came forward with Queen Isabel to greet his brother, and the new bride stood back. Her clothing was simple, but the dark woollen cloak accentuated her clear skin and her grey-green eyes.

Connor lifted the girl down from her horse, and she curtsied before the king and queen. Joan gathered with the rest of them and heard him introduce the woman as his bride, Aileen. The child was his daughter, Rhiannon.

There was a moment of fleeting shock on King Patrick's face before he masked it and welcomed them both. Isabel smiled at the young girl and held out her hand, bringing her over to meet Liam. Aileen followed, and they walked inside the castle.

A pang caught at Joan's heart when she saw the young family. There was such love between them, she could not hide her own envy of the life she wanted to have.

'Go and join them,' Ronan urged. 'I know you're wanting to know more.'

She did, but didn't feel she ought to indulge her curiosity since they were strangers. Even so, Ronan departed to join the men who were carrying wood up the hill of Amadán. After he left, she could not help but look back at him, wondering what other talents he had hidden from everyone else.

Chapter Three

For a few hours, Ronan was glad to disappear into a crowd of men who did not know he was a prince. He could stack wood on the bonfires, and the hard labour took his mind off the troubles brewing. But it could not banish his thoughts of Joan.

He never should have kissed her that day. The impulse haunted him even now. He'd expected her to kiss like a maiden, innocent and sweet. Instead, she had ignited a fire within him, making him want to consume her. He had avoided all women since his brother's death, but the abstinence had come back to haunt him. Joan's mouth tasted of forbidden sin, of a woman who was born to be seduced.

And worst of all, she wanted a child. The very thought brought back the memory of his nephew's death. No, he could never grant her that. It wasn't even fair to ask a betrothal of her—not when her only desire was to become a mother. Better to let her go, to let her love someone else.

Perspiration lined his skin as Ronan stacked a final

log upon the bonfire. In the distance, the sun was setting, and the sky grew streaked with red and orange. Already he had decided to take a small group of MacEgan soldiers back to his lands, to scout out his stepbrother's forces and determine what to do next.

The problem was, he had no idea how many of his men had remained loyal to him. Odhran had hired mercenaries, but it was impossible that such a small number of fighters could take control of Clonagh so easily. What advantage did they have? Or did his people *want* Odhran to be their king?

You were never meant to rule over Clonagh, came the whisper of his conscience.

Neither was Odhran.

A heaviness weighed upon his shoulders, but Ronan tried not to dwell on his past mistakes or the disappointments he had brought to his father. All he could do was move forward, trying to restore the rightful ruler. But he remembered the years of trailing his brother, trying to gain his father's approval. He'd watched as King Brodur had rested his hand on Ardan's shoulder, telling him all there was to know about the Kingship. There had been pride in his father's eyes.

Pride that had never been there for Ronan.

A familiar ache spread out within him, stretching the emptiness of regret. Saintly Ardan was always meant to be the heir, never him. And though Ronan had tried to bring honour to their family name through his fighting skills, Brodur had seemed disinterested.

A hard knot formed in his throat at the thought of his father's fate now. He didn't know if Odhran was ruthless enough to harm Brodur. Though they had their differences, he hoped his stepbrother had merely deposed the king.

What had become of his people since he'd left them a few days ago? Were they unharmed? Or had Odhran punished those loyal to the king? He prayed that his father was still alive somehow, though it was unlikely. The question was what to do now.

After the bonfires were prepared and ready to be lit, Ronan followed the men back to the keep. All around him, the children held carved turnips hanging on slender pieces of rope. They had not lit the lanterns yet, but he saw the MacEgans gathering within the inner bailey. He overheard a child whining, 'It's dark. Why did we put out the fire?'

The mother shushed her son and said, 'All hearth fires must be put out. We will light them tonight from the Samhain bonfires.'

Just as the woman had predicted, the lights were extinguished everywhere. Ronan followed the crowd of people, and the king and queen had gathered with them in the dim twilight. The king's brother, Connor MacEgan, was seated beside his new wife, who had been crowned with a garland of flowers. Her daughter also had flowers in her hair, but it was the sight of Joan that drew his attention once more. Ronan didn't know if it was her white gown, but he never failed to find her within a crowd, though today she stood near the back, as if to avoid notice.

'My brother has returned to us,' the king announced in a loud voice. 'And he has brought his wife Aileen with him, along with his daughter Rhiannon. We have many reasons to celebrate on this Samhain night, and I am glad they are with us.'

He stretched out his hand and pointed in the distance towards the large stacks of wood atop the hill of Amadán. 'Let us light the fires and begin our celebration.'

The king gave the signal to a man mounted on horseback. 'Go.'

After a short time, the rider reached the piles of wood and started the fires, setting them ablaze. The bonfires burned in the darkness, while a cheer resounded from the people.

Then the rider returned with a torch and dismounted. He knelt down before the queen, and she lit a candle from the torch. Dozens of candles were passed out to all the folk, and one by one, they lit their wicks until there was a sea of light within the castle walls. It was beautiful in an ancient tradition, binding them together.

Ronan had held the same ritual with his own clan, last year, on behalf of his father. Seeing it here at Laochre only strengthened his resolve to bring peace to Clonagh and his people. With any hope, they would celebrate Imbolc in the spring, free from Odhran's rule.

An old woman received a large ewer of water from a priest and poured some of it over the threshold leading to the Great Chamber. The priest murmured a blessing over the holy water, protecting Laochre from any evil spirits that might wander this night.

Ronan moved through the people, making his way towards King Patrick and his brother Connor. When he reached them, Connor came forward to greet him. 'We met a few years ago, Ronan.'

He gripped the man's forearm, and Connor did the same, but with his left arm. At this close distance, he saw that the man's hand was heavily scarred, and it appeared as if the injury had not healed well. When Connor saw the direction of his gaze, he shrugged. 'My hand was crushed, and Aileen did everything she could to save it. Thanks to her, I still have a hand.' His face softened at the mention of his wife.

'She must be a skilled healer.'

'There is no one better. I brought her here to meet my family and to stay a while.' He sobered a moment. 'I was sorry to hear about your brother's death. Ardan was a good man.'

Ronan nodded, forcing back the ache of guilt. 'He was.'

'Patrick tells me that you are in need of soldiers to reclaim your kingdom.'

'I intend to take a scouting party back to Clonagh soon. You are welcome to join us, if you like.'

'My fighting days are at an end, I fear.' Connor held up his mangled right hand. 'But I can offer strategy, should you need it.'

'My strategy has not been working well thus far.' Ronan explained about the betrothal Rhys de Laurent wanted to make between himself and Joan.

'Neither of us wants to marry, but I could use her brothers' men.'

At that, Connor thought a moment. 'Do you like her well enough, Ronan?'

'I do,' he agreed. Joan was different from any other woman he'd met, and the other maidens seemed like foolish girls by comparison. He thought of her smile when they had carved turnips and her teasing manner. There had been an ease between them, as if they had been friends for a long time. But it contrasted with the way her hands had slid over his skin during the bath she'd tended. On that night, she had aroused him deeply in a way he had never expected.

He'd kissed her in an attempt to satisfy the cravings she'd conjured. He'd wanted to unravel that innocence, finding the true woman beneath it all. But instead of fulfilling the urge, it had only awakened it.

'Then you should consider a marriage,' Connor said. 'A Norman alliance would only help your people.'

But Ronan answered, 'I cannot wed just now. Better that Lady Joan should choose another man as a suitor.' One whose kingdom hadn't fallen apart, who had a better life to offer. Even if he did change his mind about marriage, he knew she would be unhappy. He couldn't imagine siring a child after all that had happened. And he didn't want to see Joan's smile fade into misery. It wasn't fair to her.

For a long moment, Connor stared at him. 'I will talk with my brothers and learn what we can do to help. But you ought to reconsider an alliance.'

'She believes she is cursed,' he told Connor. 'Every man she was betrothed to has died.'

'Do you think it's true?'

Ronan shook his head. 'Likely a terrible coincidence, nothing more. No one was trying to kill the men. The last one died before she even arrived. But she is still afraid.'

Ronan glanced across the gleaming candlelight to where Joan was standing. Her veil had slipped back to reveal her long dark hair. In her white gown, she captivated him, even though it was unlikely they would ever marry.

'I will do what I can to help,' Connor offered.

But Ronan doubted it would be enough.

Later that night, after the feasting, Joan picked up a sleepy-eyed Liam and returned the boy to the queen's arms. She followed the people into the Great Chamber where the hearth had been lit from one of the bonfires. The king's brother was seated upon a low stool, and there was a large crowd of men, women, and children gathered around him. Trahern was an enormous beast of a man, with a beard and shaggy hair. But there was a jovial air about him, as if he enjoyed being the centre of attention.

Joan didn't understand all the words of his stories, but she enjoyed the rich timbre of his voice and the spellbinding nature of the tales.

The queen drew her closer and gestured for Joan to sit upon a stool. 'Trahern is the greatest bard in

Éire,' she boasted. 'Listen and he will tell you about Brian Boru or the goddess Danu.'

'I don't speak Irish,' she reminded the queen.

'Trahern speaks both languages and will translate. He does it for me and for my guests,' Queen Isabel answered.

Joan took her place upon the low stool and gathered near the others. Trahern welcomed the people and began a tale about a woman who bore a child who was stolen by the fairies.

'Niamh was heartbroken over the loss of her daughter, but the fairies gave her a changeling in place of the child. From the moment she held the babe, she knew it was not hers. To be certain, she touched the child's hand with an iron nail, and the babe shrieked as if burned.'

Joan leaned in, caught up in the story. Idly, she reached for the iron cross hanging around her throat. Though she was a Christian, she did believe in fairies and otherworldly things. Someone handed her a goblet of wine, and she took a sip. The servants kept returning to her side to refill it, though she had no wish to drink too much.

'Niamh took the changeling to the Hill of the Fairies and pleaded with the queen to give back her child,' Trahern continued. 'She slept upon the hillside, and when she awakened, an old woman was seated beside her. She begged to share in her morning meal, and because she was kind-hearted, Niamh gave her a piece of bread and a drink of mead from her horn.

'After the old woman ate and drank, there came

a blaze of light. Niamh was frightened and shielded herself and the changeling from the enchantment. The old woman's grey hair turned to gold, and her rags were replaced with a beautiful gown of silk. "You have shown kindness to me and to my own child. For that, you shall be rewarded." The fairy queen reached out and took the babe, touching the child's forehead with her thumb. And the child, too, was transformed and returned to her mother. But time passes differently within the realm of the fairies, and the baby had now grown into a beautiful young girl. Before Niamh could take her daughter home, the fairy left a streak of gold within the child's hair, so she would always know that she had been touched by the queen.'

When the tale ended, Joan was startled to realise that her cheeks were wet with tears. She swiped them away and started to rise from her stool.

A hand pressed against her shoulder as she did. Joan knew without looking that it was Ronan. She didn't know what he wanted but was pleasantly surprised to see that he was carrying a trencher of food.

'I thought you might be hungry,' he offered.

'I am famished.' She smiled at him and took her wine goblet with her. The room swayed a moment, and she wondered how many cups of wine she had drunk.

Ronan guided her towards one of the trestle tables where she could sit. He gave her the trencher, upon which he had placed a selection of roasted mutton and beef, boiled goose eggs, and turnip greens, along with hot bread. Joan tore the bread in half and handed him the larger piece, while she ate the other. They shared the trencher, and she noticed that he seemed distracted but said nothing.

The doors to the Great Chamber remained open, and outside, she could see the gleaming candles. Several children roamed around with their turnips holding small stubs of candles inside. She smiled to see their excitement. 'It was kind of you to bring me food. I hadn't realised how hungry I was.'

'You seemed to enjoy Trahern's story. He is well known across Éire for his tales.'

Joan agreed and smiled. 'I think the king must have asked him to distract all of us with the entertainment while the food was being prepared.' She finished eating and wiped her hands, feeling a sudden awkwardness descending between them. A servant filled her cup again, and once the maid had gone, she lowered her voice. 'I cannot possibly drink any more wine. I'm already dizzy.'

Ronan took her cup and drank from it, but his eyes locked upon hers. His gaze passed over her veil and her face, down to the iron cross that rested upon her bosom. She didn't understand his interest, and decided to meet his gaze frankly with one of her own. 'What is it?'

He drained the silver goblet and set it aside, steepling his fingers. 'Nothing, really. But I was thinking that my older brother would have liked you,' he said, reaching for the wine again. 'He was a good man. Saint Ardan, I used to call him.'

She took the goblet from him and drained the rest. 'Are you trying to tell me you aren't a good man?'

His green eyes grew heated. 'What do you think, *a stór*?'

'I think there is more to you than people see,' she predicted. Any man who would ride for two days, barely stopping for food or rest, put the needs of others before his own.

She reached for a piece of bread at the same time as he did, and their hands touched. She curled her fingers around the bread and teased, 'I'll fight you for it.'

His hand pressed into hers, and she felt the touch warm her skin in a way she wasn't expecting.

'I'll let you win.' He lifted his hand away, and she offered him some.

With a mischievous look, she added, 'Because you know I would defeat you. Never stand before a hungry woman and her food.'

He did smile at that, and the intensity of his green eyes made her cheeks flush. Ronan truly was an attractive man. And it wasn't merely that she'd had too much wine. She found that she rather liked him.

When she returned the smile, he warned, 'I wouldn't do that.'

'Do what? Smile?' She didn't understand what he meant.

He refilled his wine glass, but she would not let him do the same for her. 'If you smile, every man in this place will want to wed you.'

Her smile did fade at his remark. 'Don't even tease me about that.' She folded her hands together and regarded him. 'I know I sound foolish. But I really did want to be married. If this curse were not upon me, I would have wed any man my brother chose.'

His tight expression softened. 'You wouldn't have wanted any of those men.'

'You're wrong. I am not hard to please. All I want is a man who is loyal and hardworking, one who can protect me and my children.' She took a bite of bread and wiped the mutton grease from her fingers. With a knowing glance, she added, 'Preferably one who would give me a child. I know I am older, so perhaps not as desirable as a younger woman.'

'There is nothing wrong with you, *a stór.* Younger women are empty-headed and too impulsive.'

'Whereas older women are simply…old.' Joan pushed her wine goblet aside. She had never lain with a man and undoubtedly her skin would not be so firm and delicate as a maiden of fourteen. Or what if she was barren? The very thought brought a pang of disappointment to her heart.

Ronan reached out and took her hand, leading her from the table. She wasn't quite certain what he wanted, but she went with him. Outside, the celebrations continued, and several men and women wandered off together in pairs. The night held a sense of enchantment, as if spirits truly did roam the world. Or perhaps it was the effects of the wine she'd drunk.

Either way, she watched the dancing from the stairs of the keep and was surprised to see many of the men and women wearing masks. Ronan stood behind her with his hands resting upon her shoulders.

It left little doubt that he was protecting her, though she still did not understand why he was granting her his attention.

'The people are disguising themselves to hide from the evil spirits,' he explained. 'It is said that time stands still on this night while darkness surrounds the earth.'

'You don't believe that,' she said quietly, turning to face him.

'I believe there is evil in this world,' he answered. 'And goodness to fight against it.'

She saw the shadow of grief in his eyes and understood that he was speaking of his people. 'You will get the men you need, Ronan. I will ask my brothers to help you and the MacEgans, as well.'

He lowered his hands from her shoulders, and she walked alongside him amid the crowd of people. 'I have no doubt we can take back Clonagh. But I need to understand how my father lost his throne in the first place. I will leave with a small group of men to learn what we can.'

Though she understood the need to discern his enemy's strengths and weaknesses, it was dangerous. For a moment, she had the foolish thought that he might not return. A chill passed over her, and she shivered.

'Do you want to walk by the fires?' he suggested. 'You're cold.'

She nodded, and he kept his hand at the small of her back as they approached the bonfires in the distance. The hill of Amadán was not large, but they walked up the path where others had gathered around the flames. She warmed herself, trying not to imagine the worst.

'Be careful when you return to Clonagh,' she warned. 'Do not let your enemies see you.'

He rested his hand upon her waist. 'Are you afraid I could die?'

She turned to face him and nodded. With a wry smile, she added, 'I am cursed, after all. We don't know what effect my presence will have on you.'

'Would you be sorry if I were killed?' His voice held a deep timbre, one that felt almost like a caress.

Her heart tightened, but she nodded. 'I would.' She had known him for only a little while, but she could not deny her own interest. Not only because he was handsome and she had enjoyed his kiss—but also because she sensed far more beneath this man. He had the talent of an artist and the skills of a warrior. 'We are friends, are we not?'

He traced the outline of her jaw, and a sudden rush of sensation filled up her skin. His green eyes held her captive as if she were the only woman left in the world. 'You should kiss me farewell. In case I don't return.'

She glanced around but saw that the only other MacEgans had begun to walk down the hillside. They were alone for the moment. Even so, she wondered if it was wise to do so. Both of them had drunk too much wine, and she felt certain that was why her blood thundered within her veins. She rested her palms against his chest and felt the echo of her own heartbeat beneath her fingertips. His hands threaded into her hair, and he stared back at her.

'I am not going to marry you,' she said quietly. 'I don't want you to die.'

'I'm not going to marry you, either,' he answered. 'Because I will not give you a child.'

His mouth lowered to hers, and the moment their lips touched, the fire inside her blazed. A thousand prickles of sensation slid over her skin, and her breasts ached when he pulled her close. Never in her wildest imaginings could she have guessed that a man could make her feel this way. She yearned for his touch, wanting so much more. But he would never give her what she truly desired.

His tongue slid within her mouth, and he seized her hips, pressing the hard ridge of his erection to the juncture of her thighs. She gasped, and the aching need intensified until she wanted more. Her breathing grew unsteady, and when she stared into his eyes, she saw the face of a conqueror.

Samhain was a pagan ritual, as old as the stones that lined the hill. Here, there was a sense of magic in the air, of a moment when the veil between earth and spirit seemed to part. For a moment, she hardly cared that this man was little more than a stranger. He kissed her deeply, until her lips grew swollen and bruised.

Joan was glad that her brothers were not here, for never would they allow her to be tempted by a man who did not want to wed her. Nor would they want her to indulge in her own desires. She was meant to remain a virgin, to wed a powerful lord and bear him children.

But she knew she could never marry any man. The unfairness of it all knotted up into anger. Were it not for this curse, she could have been married three times over.

He pulled back from the kiss, and Joan tried to calm her breathlessness. She looked him in the eye and demanded, 'You will return.'

He traced the edge of her cheek. 'I will. But the king has asked me to delay our journey one more day.' There was a note of tension in his voice as if he didn't like waiting. 'And I am also escorting you back to your brother's fortress at Killalough. You will travel with us when we depart.'

Joan had not expected to return to her brother's estate, though she should have. Rhys and Warrick would want to know what had happened between them, and they might offer soldiers to help at Clonagh.

And yet, the thought of travelling with Ronan made it impossible to still her beating heart.

Joan was surprised to see Ronan waiting for her after she broke her fast the next morn. 'Have you any plans for this day?' he asked.

She didn't know what he meant by that. 'None thus far.'

'Good. Then we can go out riding to the coast. I thought you might wish to see the island of Ennisleigh.'

Her gaze narrowed, and she managed a smile. 'Or did you mean that *you* wish to see the island?'

'I do, yes,' he admitted. 'And the MacEgan king will allow it if he believes I am taking you to see it. You are his guest, after all. It also gives me something to do while I wait for the men to be assembled.'

'So I am to be your reason for exploring.'

'If you're willing.' He offered his arm to her, and she decided there was no harm in it. The early-morning sky was a rich blue, and it might be an enjoyable way to pass the morning.

'All right.'

Ronan ordered horses for them while Joan asked a servant to pack a basket of food and drink. She tied the provisions to her horse before they rode out of the castle grounds.

At first, he kept the pace slow until they were out in the open fields. Then he turned back and asked, 'Are you a skilled rider?'

In answer, she nudged her horse faster and let him try to keep up. The wind made her hair and veil stream behind her as they rode towards the coast. Ronan caught up and guided her towards a pathway that led down a hillside. He slowed his horse down to a walk, and she did the same. Nearby, there was a place to tether the horses and fresh water for them to drink. Ronan unfastened the bag of provisions and took it with him.

'We have to walk down to the water's edge,' he explained. 'Connor told me to leave the horses here. There is a boat we can take to the island.'

She hadn't expected that they would actually row across the narrow inlet to the island, but he appeared eager to reach the shore. It reminded her of her brothers when they had tried to row a boat once, and she smiled at the memory.

The boat was tied to a small pier, and Ronan held the small vessel steady while she climbed inside. The water was relatively calm, and he took his place by the oars.

She bit her lip, and as he pulled through the water, he remarked, 'Is there something you find amusing?'

'I was thinking of my brothers. We were visiting our uncle once, and he let us explore the lake in a small boat.' A slight laugh escaped her, and she confessed, 'Warrick rowed in one direction, and Rhys moved his oar in the opposite way. They rowed us in circles, all the way across the river.' She had laughed so hard that day, her sides had ached.

'Do you want to try?' he offered, holding out one oar. She hadn't thought of it at first, but she picked up her skirts and sat beside him. When he pulled back, she mimicked him, and the oar came out of the water with a splash. Joan laughed again and saw the gleam of amusement in his eyes.

'I don't suppose I'm very good at this.'

'Try again,' he urged, and within a few moments, they found a rhythm together. She used both arms to pull back the single oar, and they moved swiftly through the water. When her arms grew weary, he let them drift for a time. It was peaceful on the water, and she enjoyed the moment of freedom.

'It sounds as if you were friends with your brothers,' he remarked.

'When they weren't trying to torment me, yes,' she said. 'Rhys cut my hair once, and I put toads in his bed.' She sent him a sidelong glance. 'He deserved it.'

'Remind me not to cut your hair,' he said drily.

'You would come to regret it.' For a time, they rowed in silence, and she felt at ease in his presence. Though she didn't know why she was confiding in him, she continued. 'My brothers and I grew closer after our father remarried. His new wife, Analise, was terrible.' The memory of the woman haunted her still. Though Joan had been sent away at the age of eight, she had heard about the infant daughter born to Analise within the year…and the horror that had followed.

'Why was she so terrible?' Ronan asked.

Joan paused a moment, pushing back the aching sadness. 'Analise murdered her infant daughter and blamed Warrick for it. I never saw my sister alive… only her grave, after she was buried.'

Ronan stiffened, and his jaw tightened. For a moment, there was a flash of pain in his eyes that she couldn't read. He gripped his oar, his knuckles white upon the wood. Then he murmured, 'I am sorry.'

Joan let out a sigh. 'For many years, my father despised Warrick. I tried to help my brother as best I could, but it was difficult. It took many years before our father could admit that he was wrong.' Her voice grew softer, remembering Edward's illness. There was a chance he might not recover, but she had made her peace with him. As had Warrick.

'It's better now between them,' she admitted. 'My

father finds comfort in his grandchildren, and Warrick has Rosamund, whom he adores. They are happy together.'

She didn't bother to hide the wistfulness in her voice, for she envied her brother's joy. With a rueful smile, she added, 'You see? Sometimes there can be a good ending to a story.'

But Ronan's tension had not dissipated. She sensed that there was a nerve she'd touched, though he answered, 'Sometimes.'

Though she wanted to ask him about his brother, she decided that it would only bring up bad memories. Instead, she changed the subject. 'Have you been to Ennisleigh before?'

'No. The king does not allow many visitors there. It appears to be a ruined fortress, but he has many soldiers hidden there who can attack invaders before they even reach the coast.'

'Then why did he allow us to come?' She held on to the edges of the boat, enjoying the morning sunlight.

'I told him it was your wish to see it. The king granted your request.'

She eyed him with a rueful smile. 'Why would King Patrick believe I would have any interest in seeing the ruins?'

'Because the queen convinced him that you might reconsider a betrothal if we spent the afternoon together.'

She narrowed her gaze in a teasing look. 'Well,

that's not going to happen, is it? You would rather be alive than dead.'

'Indeed. But I saw a chance to see the island, and I took it.'

She was somewhat distracted by his firm muscles as he rowed. 'Why would the queen believe that I would change my mind about marrying you?'

He shrugged. 'A few MacEgans saw me kiss you last night.'

Her cheeks warmed at the memory of it, and she looked out at the water. 'I had too much wine. And it was just a kiss, nothing more.' If she kept telling herself that, it might eventually be true.

'You never would have kissed me without the wine,' he said drily.

'Of course not.' *Liar*, her conscience chided. What woman wouldn't want to kiss a man who looked like Ronan? She stole a glance at his sensual mouth and decided that the man had talent when it came to kissing.

But it was best to change the subject. 'So you mean to see the ruins and then return to Laochre?'

'Yes. If you've no interest, you can stay in the boat.' They were nearing the opposite side of the inlet, and he slowed the pace.

'It sounds as if you used me for your own gains,' she accused with a smile. 'I won't be staying behind in the boat while you go off inspecting the ruins.' Now that they were here, she *was* interested in seeing the island. She was enjoying every moment of freedom from her overprotective brothers and father.

There was a sense of adventure here that she had never known before.

'As you will.' Ronan slowed the pace of the oars and then stepped into the cold water, dragging the boat on to the sand. He helped her out, carrying her to dry land as if she weighed nothing at all.

'I will pretend to show interest,' she said, not bothering to hide her teasing. 'And I won't tell the king if I am bored.'

His mouth curved in a smile. 'I will try to keep you entertained.'

The afternoon was one of the most surprising he'd ever experienced. Ronan led Joan through the ruins, and she jested with him at every opportunity.

'Oh, my heavens, look at that,' she breathed, pointing to a pile of stones. 'It's like nothing I've ever seen before!' With a brilliant smile, she turned back to him. 'Thank you so much for bringing me here. These rocks…they are simply breathtaking.'

Ronan fought back his own amusement. 'You are most welcome. And there is something else you might wish to see.'

He guided her towards one of the walls overgrown with vines. 'What do you think of that?'

She exclaimed a cry of exultation at the sight of the crumbling wall. 'It's simply perfect. Those vines are stunning. How can I thank you for bringing me here, Ronan?'

One of the Ennisleigh soldiers eyed them with confusion, as if he were uncertain whether she was serious. Ronan shook his head and waved the man on.

Then he rested his palm against her spine. 'It's everything you ever wanted, wasn't it?'

'It was,' she breathed. Her sides were shaking with laughter, and she broke away from him, hurrying up the winding stairs.

'Those stairs don't lead anywhere, Joan,' he warned. The second floor of the fortress was missing, and there was no roof at all. But when he reached the top of the steps, he found her doubled over with mirth.

'Did you see the soldier's face?' she chuckled. 'He must have thought I was mad, admiring the ruins.'

'Well, it *was* an attractive pile of stones. And the wall was quite majestic.'

She laughed again, and he couldn't help but join her. Gods, but it had been so long since he'd laughed. He couldn't even remember the last time.

'I must admit, this day was nothing like I imagined it would be,' she said, wiping away a tear while she struggled to regain her composure. 'I did enjoy myself, Ronan.'

He rested both hands on opposite sides of the staircase, watching her. She was so different from the other women he'd known before. So many had flirted with him, offering themselves in return for his favour—whereas Joan was adamant in avoiding marriage.

His gaze fixed upon the curve of her mouth. He had tasted those lips last night, and right now, he imagined claiming them again, pressing her back against the stairs.

'Why do you always wear white, Joan?'

Her smile faded. 'You know the answer to that. It's my way of avoiding the evil spirits.' She paused a moment, her mood turning pensive. 'When I wore the colours of purity, it seemed to appease the people of Montbrooke. I think some of them believed I might be a witch after what happened to my bridegrooms.'

He unfastened her veil, wanting to see her dark hair. 'What happened with those betrothals wasn't your fault.'

'But the men are all dead. What else can I believe?'

He had no answer for her. Yet in this moment, he found himself wanting to push back her fears. He liked this woman far more than he should. 'You should believe that you will find the right husband one day.'

For a moment, her blue eyes centred upon him, and he felt an unexpected tightness in his chest. He didn't understand it, nor did he want Joan to believe that there was any hope of him becoming that husband. When she understood his silent answer, her smile faded and she averted her gaze.

At last, he pulled away, helping her up. 'Are you hungry?'

She nodded. 'I am. Let us eat outside where we can look at the sea.'

Ronan guided her back down the stairs and retrieved the bag of food from where he'd left it earlier. They departed the fortress and walked along the outside of the ruins where grass had grown over the crumbling walls. To an outsider, Ennisleigh was nothing of value, a ruined pile of stones upon a tiny island.

But inside the fortress, there was a treasure of weapons, arrows, and supplies for war. Ronan was fascinated by all of it, for it gave the MacEgans a distinct advantage over their enemies. There were twenty soldiers here, stationed at every angle surrounding the island. They could see any enemy approaching by sea, and from the top of the ruins, there was a small platform where they could see enemies on land. Several piles of brush and wood were at the top of the tower, and signal fires could be lit quickly to alert the men at Laochre of danger.

'You look intrigued by their defences,' Joan said, spreading out a cloth with the food. 'Do you approve?'

He nodded. 'I may use some of their ideas with my own people. There is a roundtower not far away that we could use as a place to keep watch.'

She offered him a cup of ale and some cheese. He took it and ate, though he was still distracted with ideas about his own defences.

'Are you thinking about your invasion?' she asked.

He forced his attention back to her and nodded. 'We will choose the MacEgan soldiers this day. But we are not going to invade until I know which of my men betrayed us. I will not risk the lives of innocent people.'

The mood had grown sombre between them, and he almost regretted it. For an hour, he'd forgotten his troubles and had enjoyed spending time with Joan.

'I will talk with my brothers on your behalf,' she said. 'I believe I can convince them to help you.'

'And if they refuse?'

She eyed him for a long moment. 'Then you will have to marry the King of Tornall's daughter.'

Ronan left the *donjon* with Connor MacEgan after they had both finished their evening meal. Connor had selected a group of fighting men, and he wanted Ronan's approval. As they walked towards the training grounds, Connor said, 'I noticed that you spent the day at Ennisleigh with Lady Joan.'

'I was interested in the fortress,' he answered. 'Your defences are impressive.'

Connor's gaze turned knowing. 'I have been talking with my wife Aileen about Lady Joan. If it is your wish to wed her, we may be able to help you.'

Ronan had no intention of it, but he decided there was no harm in hearing what Connor had to say. 'What do you suggest?'

'You should take time to court her,' he said. 'Aileen noticed that she wears no jewels—only that iron cross. Or perhaps she might want a new gown.'

Ronan knew the cross was from Joan's attempts to keep away fairies and evil spirits. And she didn't seem interested in adorning herself. Jewels and gowns were not the way to win her agreement to this betrothal. 'She wears the gown and cross by choice.'

And yet, she had been fascinated by the carving he'd done upon the turnip. If he wanted to gain her interest, he suspected that was the way.

When they drew closer to the training ground, Connor's daughter Rhiannon approached shyly. He offered his hand, and she held it. 'Good eventide, *a inion.*'

She murmured a reply, and Connor leaned down, whispering another question in her ear. Then he smiled and turned back to Ronan. 'I asked my daughter what she thought you should give to Lady Joan to win her heart. She suggested a kitten or a young pup.'

Ronan smiled at the young girl and nodded his approval. 'It's not a bad idea.' A warm, living creature to love might suit Joan very well indeed. From the bright-eyed excitement of the girl, Ronan decided to enlist Rhiannon's help.

'Will you help me choose?' he asked the girl.

Rhiannon nodded and put her hand in his. Her utter trust caught him like a fist to the heart, and the pang of guilt squeezed tightly around him. He pushed back the emotions, for this was not the time to let the past interfere. Instead, he squeezed the young girl's palm and asked her to select an animal that she thought would suit. In the meantime, he and Connor would choose the men who would accompany him to Clonagh.

The young girl raced away, and Connor remarked, 'Rhiannon is a sweet girl. You can trust that she will choose the right gift for Lady Joan.'

He acknowledged the remark with a nod and told Connor that he would compensate them for the animal. He hardly knew why he was giving Joan a gift, when there would never be a marriage or betrothal between them. But then again, a genuine friendship had begun between them. He wanted to offer her something—even if it could never be the baby she wanted.

A hardness tightened in his gut at the thought of a child, along with the memory of Declan's death.

It was your fault, his conscience reminded him. If he had watched over the boy more closely, Declan never would have wandered off.

God help him, he couldn't forget Ardan's anguish or the raw cry of pain at seeing his son's limp body. It was the worst moment of his life, and Ronan would have given up his own life if it could have brought his nephew back. He didn't deserve a wife or a child of his own...not after his own sins of neglect. He despised himself for what he'd done. And now, it seemed wrong to find happiness of his own. Not after what Ardan had suffered.

But he could not deny that he'd enjoyed the time he'd spent with Joan. Her humour and warmth had brightened the darkness inside him. If circumstances were different, he might have considered her for a wife. He couldn't remember the last time he'd laughed, and for one moment, he had set aside the grief.

Rhys and Warrick de Laurent had given him three days to win Joan's agreement. But Ronan had pushed aside the idea of marriage, without any desire to pursue it.

Now, he was starting to wonder. He had to do whatever was necessary to restore Brodur to power and free his people from Odhran's reign. And if that meant a new alliance formed to save their lives, he might not have a choice.

It was startling to realise that he was not so opposed to the idea of marriage any more. There might be a way to set boundaries, to make Joan understand why he could not sire a child. He had offered her a false betrothal earlier, one to benefit both of them. Was it still possible?

He dismissed the thought as soon as it came. Breaking a betrothal was nigh impossible, even under these circumstances. Then, too, he doubted if he could end the betrothal and give Joan into the hands of someone else. He didn't want to imagine her yielding to another man. The thought of another suitor touching her made him clench his fists. Whether he'd intended it or not, he wanted Joan for his own.

But if it were a real union, he knew he would never be able to maintain a celibate marriage. Not after the way she'd kissed him. The very thought of the way she'd responded to his touch was deeply arousing. He wanted this woman badly…and the answer to his problems lay before him—all he had to do was wed her. He was beginning to reconsider it.

Ronan joined Connor, and they both inspected the men, looking for the strongest fighters. One adolescent caught his attention, a young man who was shorter than the others but had begun to develop more powerful muscles. His dark hair was cut short, and he fought with a ruthless air.

'What about him?' he asked Connor, pointing towards the lad. 'He's young but seems hungry to prove himself.'

Connor's expression hardened. 'He is our brother, Ewan. And you'll have to ask Patrick if he is ready.' The man's tone suggested that he did not think so.

But the young man defeated three others before a more experienced soldier brought him to the ground. Even then, Ewan stood and brushed himself off, showing no sign of fatigue. If anything, he appeared eager to continue.

'If Patrick gives his consent, I want him to join us,' Ronan said. 'Along with the four men over there.' He remembered what it was like to be fighting for respect, wanting to gain the approval of his peers. And Ewan MacEgan did have the strength and skills.

Connor kept his expression neutral. 'We will see.'

A few moments later, Rhiannon came hurrying forward. Her hair was in disarray, the unbraided strands hanging across her shoulders. 'I found him for you. I tied my ribbon around its front leg so you would know which one I chose.'

'And what did you choose?' Ronan asked.

The young girl smiled shyly. 'It's a surprise. Something very special.'

He didn't press her for the answer, but asked, 'Do you think Lady Joan will be pleased?'

Rhiannon nodded. Connor rested his hand on his daughter's shoulder and smiled. 'I'll bid you luck. But I do trust that Rhiannon chose a good gift.'

At that moment, Ronan saw Lady Joan descending the stairs. The gift would give him the means to broach the subject of an alliance between them. 'Thank you for your help.'

He took his leave from the pair of them and walked towards Joan. She approached him and ventured a smile. 'Did you pick the soldiers you wanted?'

'Most of them,' he agreed. 'Will you be ready to travel to Killalough at dawn?'

She nodded. 'And as I promised, I will speak to Rhys and Warrick on your behalf when we arrive.'

He nodded, though he doubted if her brothers would agree since there was no betrothal. At least, not yet. At the moment, he did not need her brothers' men, since all he intended to do in the next few days was scout out Clonagh's defences. But afterwards, it was critical to have enough men to ensure the victory.

'Rhiannon seemed excited when I saw her just now,' Joan said as they neared the stables. 'Did something happen?'

He slowed down and admitted, 'I asked her to help me choose a gift for you.'

'A gift?' Her brows furrowed. 'For what reason?'

'To bribe you,' he said smoothly. 'I have every faith that it will be nearly as exciting as the pile of rocks at Ennisleigh.'

'That's not possible,' she answered wryly. 'But have you seen the bribe?'

'I have no idea what she selected—only that she tied her ribbon around it.' He decided to refrain from mentioning that it was an animal.

Joan appeared intrigued by the idea and followed him towards the stables. Inside, it was dark, and it smelled of hay and horses. Ronan wasn't entirely certain what they were looking for, but he imagined that one of the dogs had given birth. Or perhaps it was a cat. Yet, he saw no smaller animals within the stables.

'I don't see anything,' Joan said at last. 'Do you think it's in one of the stalls?'

'I truly don't know. I suppose we'll find out together.'

Her face brightened at the prospect, and they continued searching. When they reached the last stall, Joan gave a slight cry. 'Oh, my. Look, Ronan.'

Inside the stall, one of the mares had just given birth. She was cleaning her baby, and a blue ribbon was tied to the foal's front leg. The foal wobbled towards its mother, and Joan's face was alight with wonder. 'Is it a filly or a colt, do you think?'

Ronan tilted his head, 'It looks like a filly.'

'Look at how beautiful she is,' Joan breathed. 'I couldn't possibly take her from her mother until she's older, but she's a wonder.'

'Better than rocks?' he teased.

'Much better.' Joan embraced him on impulse, but when she tried to pull away, he held her waist a moment longer. In the darkness of the stable, she froze, resting her palms on his chest. He leaned his forehead upon hers, breathing in the scent of her. For this single moment, he pushed back the past and concentrated on her.

Although she was not a young maiden, there was an innocence about her—a goodness that drew him closer. He wanted to tempt her, to drive her past the boundaries of virtue until she surrendered to him. But he was torn between desire and obligations.

'I know I shouldn't accept this gift, Ronan,' she whispered. 'It isn't right to take the filly from the MacEgans.'

'Connor gave his daughter permission to choose,' he murmured. 'I see no harm in it. I will reimburse them for the animal.'

'Thank you.' She rested her head against his heart, and for a moment, he savoured the touch of her embrace.

'I enjoyed spending the day with you, Joan,' he said quietly. 'I've had few reasons to smile in the past few months.' He stroked back her hair, and she didn't pull away.

'I enjoyed it, too, Ronan.' She braved a smile, but he could see the rise of emotion in her eyes.

'I have been thinking…' he began, feeling foolish. 'About marriage, that is.'

She paused, her expression turning curious. 'What do you mean?'

'I know that you have no wish to wed,' he said, 'but—'

Before he could finish, she suddenly cut him off. 'That isn't true at all. I would very much like to be married.' She drew back and stared into his eyes. 'If I could break the curse, I would welcome a marriage and a family of my own.'

Before he could continue, Joan went on, 'But if I become your betrothed, you could die. And I cannot let that happen. No matter how I might feel about you.'

Her words pierced him like a spear, at the realisation that she did care for him. It felt as if the ground had shifted beneath him. This woman was willing to give him up to save his life. He couldn't remember the last time anyone had treated him like a man of worth.

She stepped back, and he saw the devastation on her face. Without a word, she turned and fled.

Chapter Four

After she left the stables, Joan's mind filled up with worry. She could not forget Ronan's embrace or his kiss. The yearning made her feel uneasy, for she knew she should not develop feelings for this man.

But a part of her knew it was too late. If he were struck down at Clonagh, it would wound her heart. She liked Ronan, and his presence had pushed away the cloak of loneliness that she had worn for so many years. With him at her side, it felt like she had set aside the shell of herself, filling up the empty spaces within. Her brothers supported a match between them, and she had sensed that Ronan was going to ask her to reconsider a betrothal. She couldn't answer that—not unless she could break the curse. And there was no way to know if that would ever happen.

Ronan had said they would leave on the morrow at dawn, and he would escort her to Killalough. The thought of facing her brothers was intimidating, for they would want to witness a betrothal on her behalf.

Though she had told Ronan she would convince them
to offer soldiers, she knew in her heart that they would
not grant them—not without her promise to wed.

But even if she did find a way to lift the curse,
Ronan had refused to sire a child. She could not understand why, for he was the sort of man whom she
could easily imagine as a father. But whatever the
reason, it was an invisible wall between them—one
she could not ignore.

When she returned to the *donjon*, Queen Isabel invited her to join the other ladies in the solar. Young
Liam and Rhiannon were seated at the far end of the
chamber.

'I am glad you could join us,' Isabel greeted her.
'The men are gathered together, discussing their
strategy.'

Joan chose a seat beside Aileen. The dark-haired
beauty smiled warmly at her, but she could not speak
the Norman language. Isabel translated on her behalf.

'Aileen said that your gown is beautiful,' the queen
remarked.

Joan thanked her and then mentioned Rhiannon.
'Your daughter is beautiful as well. She helped Ronan
choose a gift for me, and will you tell her that I loved
it?'

Isabel translated for both mother and daughter,
and the little girl brightened. Joan then turned back
to the queen. In a low voice, she said in the Norman
language, 'I understand, if I cannot accept the filly.'

The queen dismissed her fears. 'Ronan will compensate Patrick for the animal. You needn't worry.'

They continued to talk while several of the women embroidered linen. Joan picked up some mending and occupied herself while they spoke in Irish. It didn't bother her that she couldn't understand them, for it allowed her thoughts to drift back over the day. She had truly enjoyed herself with Ronan, even if they were simply sharing a meal amid the ruins. And she could not deny that she was attracted to him. Each time he drew near, her heart beat faster, and she longed for his touch.

She was starting to care for this man and it would hurt to let him go. But her defences were crumbling, and she knew not how to reinforce them.

'Joan, I am sorry we have been neglecting you,' Queen Isabel said. 'Aileen was telling us of how she and Connor were reunited after many years. I will translate as she tells us what happened.'

Joan did want to hear the story, but asked, 'Is it true that he did not know of his daughter until recently?'

After the queen translated, Aileen nodded. Then she began her tale, and Isabel relayed it back to Joan.

'At the feast of Bealtaine, I took my friend's place as the goddess Danu in the Sacred Marriage,' Aileen said. 'I lay with Connor that night in the darkness, and we conceived Rhiannon. After he left, I did not tell him of the child, and I married an older man instead. He took care of me for a time until he died a few years later.'

Aileen's face turned wistful. 'Rhiannon is my only child thus far, and never do I regret how she came into my life. But I am so thankful that Connor became my husband.' Her face shone with joy at the thought.

The young woman's revelation struck Joan in a way she hadn't thought of. Aileen had lain with Connor in secret, never revealing herself to him until years later. It made Joan wonder what sort of courage it took to reach for the man she wanted.

The idea was so forbidden, her mind could not relinquish it. Though it was sinful, she envisioned a night with Ronan in her arms, and her skin prickled with anticipation. She did desire him, and each kiss tempted her more than the last. When he had kissed her, he had responded with his own need.

The very idea of seducing him shook her to the bone.

'You're very quiet, Joan,' the queen remarked. 'Are you all right?'

She nodded. 'I've just been feeling troubled, that's all.'

'If you are unwell, Aileen can help,' the queen offered. 'She is a skilled healer.'

They didn't truly understand…but then, how could they? Joan's face was burning, but she admitted, 'It's not truly a healing matter. It's about a…a family curse. I need to find a way to break it, or else I can never marry.'

Instead of chiding her or accusing her of foolish beliefs, the queen seemed to consider the problem with all seriousness. 'To break a curse, you may wish to consult a wise woman. Our healer, Annle, knows enough of the Norman tongue. She has served me for several years now, and I trust her.'

It might not do any good. And yet, what other choice did she have?

Joan murmured her thanks, though she was frustrated with herself for remaining passive all these years. Her previous efforts to avoid the curse had come to naught. Being a woman of virtue had done nothing to bring about her greatest desire, to conceive and bear a child.

Her gaze moved towards the children on the opposite side of the room. The look of utter joy on Liam's face made her smile as he stacked a wooden block on top of another before he giggled and knocked it down. There was nothing more heartwarming than the laugh of a child.

And all she had was an abyss of loneliness stretching ahead. Her father was ill and dying, and soon he would be gone. Her brothers had moved away, leaving her to care for him, now that his wife Rowena had passed on. The stone walls of Montbrooke were closing in on her like a prison with no doorway. At least if she bore a child, she would have someone to love.

Today, she had glimpsed a very different life. She had laughed and enjoyed herself with Ronan. For one afternoon, she had put aside her fears and simply lived her life as she wanted to. God help her, she never wanted to go back to the isolated existence she had known. Here, she had freedom like she had never experienced before. And she didn't want to lose that.

Somehow, she had to speak with this wise woman and learn if there was any way to break the curse.

It was later that evening when Joan found the elderly woman, Annle, in a small dwelling that smelled of rosemary and other dried herbs. The wise woman had white braided hair, and she was holding a mortar and pestle.

'Queen Isabel said I could find you here,' Joan began. 'Do you understand the Norman language?'

The healer gave a nod. 'I do, yes. Our queen believed everyone here should learn the language, because of the Norman invaders. It was safer for all of us.'

Joan was relieved to hear it. And yet, she had no idea how to ask the woman for what she wanted. She hardly knew the answer herself. The only clarity was her resolution to break the curse. Ronan had spent so much time with her, she was terrified that he would face death when he returned to Clonagh on the morrow. And if there was a charm or method to prevent it, she would not hesitate.

'The queen thought…you might be able to help me,' she began. 'There is a curse upon me, one that prevents me from marrying. Every man I have been betrothed to has died.'

The healer set aside her mortar and pestle. Her expression held sympathy. 'Many men die, my lady. But it does not mean there is a curse.'

Joan met the woman's gaze evenly. 'For me there

is. And I have to end it tonight. I will pay any price if it can be done.'

Annle studied her for a moment. Her gnarled face was thoughtful, and she enquired, 'Is there a man who has caught your interest? Someone you wish to marry?'

A flush of embarrassment spread over her cheeks, for Joan nearly admitted yes. She had grown to care for Ronan very much, and there was no question that she desired him. His kiss had left her breathless and wanting more.

Neither of them had wanted a marriage in the beginning. Now, she wondered if there was any hope of having a different life.

'There is…someone,' she confessed to Annle. 'But if there is a curse, I don't want to endanger him. He is leaving on the morrow, and there may be a battle. I am afraid of what could happen.'

The old woman waited for her to elaborate, but Joan couldn't bring herself to say more. She already felt foolish enough in seeking help.

Finally, Annle spoke. 'There are no herbs or remedies that will lift a curse. Yet, if he is the man you wish to wed, there are ways to bind him to you.'

Joan didn't know what to think of Annle's answer. 'I do not want him to be harmed when he leaves. I cannot let it happen—not if there is a way I can protect him.'

'Do you believe he will die if you do not lift the curse?'

Joan nodded. 'I am certain of it.' Somehow, she had to end this misfortune. Whether or not she was promised to Ronan, she did not want her curse to shadow him.

'And how much would you sacrifice to save him?' Annle asked quietly.

'I will do whatever I must,' Joan answered. He was a good man and did not deserve to die. 'What must I do to ensure his safety?'

The healer set aside her mortar and pestle, her expression unreadable. 'The sacrifice will be great. But it will bind him to you beyond this world. The only question is whether you want him badly enough for it to succeed.'

A sudden sense of foreboding slid within her veins, but she forced herself to ask, 'What must I do?'

'You must go to him this night, and surrender your innocence,' Annle answered. 'Take his body inside yours, and his spirit will be caught within you. Then the curse cannot touch him, because his essence will be bound to yours. And if he is a man of honour, he will wed you to save your virtue.'

For a moment, she could hardly breathe. *I cannot.*

How could she even imagine such a thing? She knew nothing of seduction, and the price was far too great. She wanted to break the curse, not force Ronan to lie with her.

Her mind spun with the implications. If she came to Ronan in the darkness, he would resent her for it. He might believe she was trying to steal a child from him against his will. This was wrong in so many ways.

Yet, earlier, he had started to speak of a betrothal

once more. She had cut him off, believing it was impossible. But what if she was mistaken? What if she could find a way to break the curse and seize a life with Ronan? Was that not worth the risk?

The idea of seducing him was both terrifying and arousing. There could be no turning back if she did as the healer commanded.

'What if he does not desire me?' she asked the healer. 'I know naught of men or how to offer myself.'

The old woman's wrinkled face stretched into a smile. 'I can brew a potion for you that will make you alluring to him. But it can only heighten arousal and any feelings he may already have. If he does not want you, there is nothing I can do.'

The very thought of using a potion to seduce a man terrified her. Joan could only imagine him refusing to drink it or refusing to lie with her. It would be humiliating.

'Will he know what is happening?' she asked. She didn't like the thought of forcing herself upon him against his will. It needed to be his choice, despite the risks.

'He will know, but if he has feelings towards you, he will not care.'

Joan closed her eyes, trying to decide what was right. 'If I do this, it will make him furious.' He might cast her out, ending the friendship between them. And she didn't want to imagine losing him.

The healer reached for basil, chamomile, and lavender. 'If you please him, he will forgive you.' She added a few more unfamiliar herbs and began mixing them in a stone mortar. With the pestle, she ground them together. 'You will need a strong wine. Soak this mixture in half a cup of wine until you are ready. Then add a heated wine to mask the flavours. He will still taste them.'

'After he drinks it, will he need to lie down?' She felt foolish for asking. 'Will it cause him to sleep?'

Annle laughed lightly. 'He will not be wanting to sleep, my lady. But you should go to him wearing only your cloak. The moon will be full tonight. Unclothe yourself and kiss him within his chamber. Do not speak, but offer your body to him, and touch him as you will.'

'I don't know what to do,' she admitted, feeling ashamed.

But the healer grew serious. 'Once you have aroused him, you will place his shaft within your womanhood and ride him. Take him swiftly, and you will find what you seek.'

'And afterwards, the curse will be broken?' Joan ventured.

The healer stared at her for a moment, a slight smile on her face. 'Yes. I believe it will be.'

Ronan stared outside the window of his chamber later that night. The wagons were packed for Joan's return to Killalough, but she had been acting strangely since he had seen her an hour ago. She seemed nervous and had been twisting at the iron cross around her neck. When he asked her what was wrong, she had insisted that it was nothing. But her face had flamed at the question, and he did not press for more answers.

It was dark, save a single candle burning beside his bed. Ronan had closed the window in his chamber to keep out the chill of the night air. All the preparations had been made, and he had arranged to take six MacEgan soldiers as an escort to Killalough. Patrick had forbidden him to take his younger brother, despite Ewan's arguments.

Ronan hoped to add more men if the de Laurent lords would agree to help. He already knew they expected a betrothal, but unless Joan changed her mind, that would not happen. Still, he had sensed a difference in her today. It truly did seem that she might reconsider a marriage with him, though she was afraid of the curse.

Ronan stripped off his armour and tunic when a knock sounded at the door. It was late, and he was not expecting anyone. His hand moved to the dagger at his waist, and he kept it there when he opened the door.

A serving girl stood at the threshold, holding a tray. Her hair was covered by a veil, and she wore a shapeless grey cloak. She kept her face averted and held out a goblet and ewer of wine. His suspicions went on alert, for he had not ordered wine.

'Who sent this?' he asked, wary of the young woman's presence.

She gave no answer but took a step into his chamber and closed the door behind her. Her refusal to speak struck him as unusual. Instinct warned him that this servant might be a threat, but the longer she stood there, the more he sensed something familiar about her.

'I did not ask for wine,' he said.

Again, she did not speak, but set down the tray and poured wine into the goblet, holding it out to him. Her actions were not those of a servant at all, but of a woman who did not fear a prince's orders.

In the darkness, he could not see her face, but the familiar scent of flowers struck him like a quarter-staff to his gut. It was Joan. Why was she here, and what did she want? It was clear that she was trying to disguise herself, but he saw through her efforts.

Ronan took the goblet and lifted the cup to her lips. 'You drink first.' Though he doubted it was poisoned, he wanted to see her reaction. If there was anything in the cup that was out of the ordinary, she would taste it first.

The woman hesitated but obeyed. When she held out the cup to him again, he took it and drank from the goblet, never taking his eyes off her. He tasted the warmed wine, and the flavour held many spices with a hint of cinnamon and cloves. She took the goblet from him and set it down.

Ronan waited, trying to understand what she wanted from him. A warmth seemed to catch within his gut, spreading out like a flame. It was not at all unpleasant, but it felt relaxing. For a moment, it was as if his troubles slid away, leaving nothing but her.

When he heard the soft rustle of fabric falling to the floor, he realised that Joan was offering herself to him. Why would she do this? Earlier, she had refused to even consider a betrothal and had cut him off before he could speak. But now, it seemed that she wanted something else. Every suspicion tightened within him.

Before Ronan could order her to leave, Joan reached for him. Her arms wound around his neck, and she pressed her bare breasts to his chest. Her skin was cool, and the unexpected skin upon skin sent a bolt of desire through him. He wanted to cup her softness, to torment her swollen nipples. Damn her for this.

He could not stop himself from kissing her, but this time, he became the hunter and Joan his prey. She yielded to him, and he invaded her mouth with his tongue. She gripped his neck, her fingers sliding into his hair. Ronan kissed her hard, wanting to show her that he would not be led astray. She would not command him.

He had already told her he would not grant her a child. Did she honestly believe she could convince him otherwise? She might be an innocent, but there was no denying that there was another side to Joan de Laurent—a wild woman who responded to his touch, desiring more.

She continued to kiss him, running her hands over his shoulders. Her touch ignited his senses, hardening his shaft. And though he had no intention of granting her wish, neither would he turn her away. Not yet. She had begun this wicked game, but he intended to win it.

Her skin was like silk, and he explored her with his hands, moving down to cup a breast. He stroked the erect tip of her nipple, and she gasped as it hardened.

'You like that, don't you?' he murmured in Irish. He was not about to reveal what he knew. Instead, he decided to tempt her more, to show her the pleasure that could be between them if she accepted the betrothal. He lowered his mouth to her breast, suckling the tip, and she moaned, arching her back against him.

'That's it, *a stór.*' He rewarded her by lifting her into his arms and taking her to the bed. He left his trews on, but laid her down gently.

It was then that he realised the effects of the wine. Somehow, it intensified the desire he was feeling, and from her reaction, he guessed it had done the same to her. He brought the goblet to her and helped her sit up. When he pressed it to her lips, she hesitated, but he urged her on. She had brought this potion, and he wanted her to experience the full effects of the wine.

After she had drunk from the goblet, he laid her back down and spilled a little of the wine upon her bare skin. She gasped again, but he silenced her when he began to drink it from her body. His tongue moved over her skin, around the curve of her breast, back to the nipple again.

The potion affected him deeply, and his shaft grew thick like an iron rod. He had no control over his body's response, but he intended to make Joan fully aware of what she had done.

He suckled her hard until she opened her legs to him, her breathing coming in quick gasps. He did the same to the other breast and moved his hand to her inner thigh, stroking the soft skin. As he tormented her other nipple, he moved his palm to her heated centre and was rewarded with the damp seam of her opening.

'*Dieu,*' she whispered, and he slid a single finger inside her.

Joan didn't know when she had lost command of herself. She had paid the wise woman for the potion, which Annle had claimed would deepen Ronan's desire and fill him with lust. But never in her wildest imaginings had she believed she would have to drink it, too.

Her skin was heightened with such sensitivity, she felt as if she would burst into flames. The heat of his mouth, coupled with the gentle stroking of his hand, was taking apart her mind and her heart until she was at his full mercy.

Then he positioned his thumb upon the hooded flesh and began to caress her as his mouth laved her breast. The rhythm of his fingers mimicked the motion of his tongue, and she began to imagine how it would feel to have his shaft within her. She wanted him desperately, craving the invasion that would come.

Joan wanted to command him to remove his clothes, but she could not speak Irish. Worse, she had been unable to stop herself from the single word that had escaped her. She feared that Ronan had heard it and would question who she was. If he learned the truth, she didn't doubt he would send her away. The sense of urgency deepened within her, and she threaded her hands through his hair, lifting her knees to allow him full access. She needed him to claim her, to finally break the curse.

But instead, Ronan lowered his mouth to her stomach, trailing a path towards the dark triangle of hair between her legs. With both hands, he cupped her hips and lifted her to the edge of the bed. Then he knelt down and tasted her intimately.

The shocking sensation was so bold, she nearly came off the mattress. A guttural cry tore from her, and she gripped the bedcovers, unable to understand the rush of need.

His tongue entered her, flicking over her sensitive flesh, until she could no longer grasp a coherent thought. Her body was rising higher, seeking *something* with such desperation, she could not quite understand it.

He spoke in Irish against her, and she wanted so badly to answer him, but she did not dare. Instead, she rocked against him, fighting back against the rising wave of pleasure.

And then he switched into the Norman language. 'I know why you came to me. But I will not give you what you seek. Not until betrothal vows are spoken.'

Shock reverberated through her. She had tried so carefully to disguise herself, to come to Ronan in the darkness without speaking. And yet, somehow, he had guessed.

She could not think of what to do now, for he slid a

finger inside her and pressed against the walls of her opening while his tongue worked her. A hot sensation caught within, spiralling her upwards until she arched hard against him. She was nearly sobbing from the pleasure, until it broke apart and she rode the storm of intensity. Her body trembled from the coursing pleasure, but Ronan only held her as she shuddered.

Never in her life had she imagined she would feel like this. But he kept his word and did not touch her any more. A sense of panic mounted inside her, for the curse was not broken. She had to do something to bind him to her, or else he might be killed when he returned to Clonagh.

Her heart bled at the very thought. Though she had not known him for very long, she could not deny that she had feelings for Ronan.

She sat up from his bed, her heart pounding. He rose and went to retrieve her fallen garments. There was no question that he meant to send her away. But she could not allow it. Not yet.

Though it was the greatest risk, she stood before him and took the gown. Then she let it fall from her fingertips to the floor. Without knowing where she got the courage from, she reached for the ties of his trews and unlaced them. Her warm hands slid down his backside, and he went rigid.

She waited for him to command her to leave, but when she reached around to his erect manhood, Ronan closed his eyes and let out a rough breath of air. Her palm curved over him, and she marvelled at his length and size.

'Joan,' he groaned. But the words were not a demand—they were a plea.

She took him by the hand and guided him to the edge of the bed where he sat down. She explored his muscled body with her hands, relentless in her need to bring him pleasure. Her hands moved down to cup him intimately, and she kissed him, refusing to let him protest. She got to her knees and rose up, guiding his shaft to her opening.

Fear gripped her, but she knew there was no choice. This would break the curse and protect him. Gently, she tried to ease him inside, but his length was too large.

He had gone motionless, his green eyes staring at her in the candlelight. 'I will not help you, Joan. This was never meant to happen between us.'

She knew that. He would expect her to give up in humiliation, knowing she had failed. For a moment, she questioned her decision, wondering if she was truly forcing him against his will. In the darkness, she waited, giving him the chance to push her back.

But Ronan *did* appear to find her touch pleasing. Her heart beat faster when he reached up, lightly touching her hips. His erect shaft rested against her wetness, and when she moved against him, he let out a hiss of air, pulling her closer. His actions and his words were utterly at war. And so, she decided to try again.

Joan pressed his shoulders back, guiding his palms to her breasts. He did caress her nipples, and a surge of wetness bloomed between her legs. Slowly, she rose up and claimed the tip of him. Annle had told her to ride him, and she remembered the rhythmic rise and fall of a horse trotting. She tried to duplicate the same motion, bouncing against him. His eyes were closed, and he groaned, pulling at her hips to thrust inside. There was a slight pain as he breached her, but she took him a little deeper.

She could not sheathe him fully, and so she leaned forward. Ronan took her nipple in his mouth, and his palms went to her hips. He moved against her as she thrust downward, and a cry escaped her when their bodies were fully joined.

This was forbidden, and her brothers would be furious with her if they learned of it. But she wanted to believe it would break the curse and bind them together.

He grew still once more, but this time, she rose and thrust against him until he was buried deep inside her. She didn't quite know what was expected now, but it felt good to ride him. The erotic sensation of arousal washed over her again, and she began to quicken the pace.

He let out an exclamation in Irish when she squeezed him hard within her depths. The shock of her own needs pulsed within, and she began to pant as she rode him. The rush of mounting desire caught her, and she hardly recognised her own voice as she took his body inside hers. Ronan gripped her hips, thrusting to meet her until she trembled violently against him, the waves of pleasure causing her to convulse against him. He groaned and turned her to her back, penetrating a few more times before he collapsed on top of her.

Their heartbeats merged, and her legs were tangled around his waist as the aftershocks took her. For a moment, he remained buried inside her, but there was tension in every part of him.

At last he spoke. 'Clothe yourself, and return to your chamber,' he commanded. 'We leave at dawn.'

Ronan hardly spoke to Joan at all during the ride to Killalough. She didn't look at him, nor did she speak. It was as if she had conjured an enchantment over him last night, seducing him with a potion of wine.

But from the moment she had dropped the cloak, revealing her body, he had been lost beneath her spell. His body still ached with arousal, though his mind was filled with frustration over what she had done.

Why had she surrendered her virginity? Was it an attempt to steal a child from him? If that was her plan, then he hoped to God she had not succeeded.

But he did intend to use this to his advantage.

No longer would he allow her to deny a betrothal between them. After this night, he would never surrender her to another man. Joan was his, and he intended to claim her as his wife. If she dared to refuse, he would tell her brothers what she had done. And now, he would have all the soldiers he needed.

He'd barely slept at all, dreaming of her touch and the way she had trembled in his arms as she found her release. Her skin had been silken, and he had marvelled at her beauty. Never had he imagined she would be so responsive, so easy to pleasure. He was a bastard for touching her so intimately, drawing out her release until she nearly screamed from the force of it. And God above, she had pleasured him, too, riding him until he had lost himself in her arms.

He wanted to prove that he was not a man who could be so easily manipulated. But she was a stubborn woman intent on getting her way. Her shoulders were held back, her gaze fixed upon the road ahead as they travelled together.

They would reach Killalough before nightfall, and Ronan intended to speak with her brothers to arrange the betrothal. Joan would have no choice but to agree after the intimacy they had shared.

There had been a time when he had not wanted a marriage—but now, everything had changed. And to his surprise, he didn't mind at all.

As they continued riding through the clearing, her face was furrowed with worry. Ronan asked, 'What is it?'

Joan's face flushed, but she confessed, 'I am trying to decide what to tell my brothers when they ask if we are betrothed.'

He slowed the pace of his stallion. 'We will tell them to draw up the necessary documents. Our betrothal will be signed and witnessed this night.'

Her expression faltered. 'I have not yet agreed to this, Ronan.'

He reached out and took the reins of her horse. 'You agreed to it when you entered my room last night. From the moment you bared yourself to me.'

Her face flushed crimson, and her blue eyes turned downward. 'I did it to save your life from the curse—that was the only reason.'

'I don't believe you.' Ronan lowered his voice. 'You enjoyed the way I touched you. You had every opportunity to stop.'

'The wise woman said the curse could be broken if I...if we...'

Her words trailed away, but he understood her meaning. 'If you lay with me,' he finished.

She nodded mutely. 'I hoped you would not recognise me.'

'I knew who you were from the first moment you came to me.' His voice was husky and only brought back memories of that night.

'I have never done anything like that in my life, Ronan,' she murmured in a pained voice. 'It's not the woman I am.'

He knew she had been a virgin—there was no question of it. But if she truly believed it was a means of breaking this curse, then it explained why she had seduced him.

Her cheeks were flushed with embarrassment, but it only heightened her beauty. He had not forgotten the delicate softness of her skin or the way she had responded to him. Though he had been with women before, she was like no other.

Joan met his gaze, and whispered, 'I was not trying to trap you into a marriage with me. I only meant to protect you.'

He kept the reins of her horse and increased their

pace. 'You will tell your brothers that we are going to wed.' In this he would brook no arguments. There was no going back now.

She closed her eyes and shook her head. 'If you do not wish to marry me, I will not force the matter. I could easily become a bride of the Church.'

He drew his horse even closer. 'You were meant to be a wife, Joan. Especially after what happened between us last night. Don't lie to yourself.'

Her face burned with a blend of humiliation and the flare of her own arousal. But she averted her gaze, as if to avoid his anger.

His thumb stroked the inside of her palm, and he reassured her, 'There *is* no curse. Only your fears.'

Anger flared in her blue eyes. 'You're right, I am afraid.' She spurred her horse onwards, and he tightened his hold on the reins.

'Why would you be afraid?'

'Because you do not believe me. I know I sound like a madwoman. But you don't *know*. For one or two suitors to die might have been a coincidence. But three men? I won't take that risk again. Not with you.' Her eyes gleamed, and he was struck by her unshed tears. 'I needed to break this curse, no matter what it cost me. I was weary of watching men die for my sake.'

His own anger softened when he realised she was overcome with her own emotions. She genuinely blamed herself for their deaths and thought that she had to prevent his as well.

He gentled his tone. 'I am not going to die, Joan.'

But she said nothing more. Instead, she rode alongside him, shielding her feelings in a frozen mask.

Ronan watched over her as they continued their ride towards Killalough. Though she kept her head held high, it was only a façade. When he glimpsed her face, he saw a tear sliding down one cheek.

Never had any woman wept for him. Ronan hardly knew what to say or do. Finally, he tried to console her. 'It will be all right, Joan.'

But she refused to look at him. 'Will it? I'm not so certain any more.'

'We will make the best of a marriage between us,' he said. It was all he could offer her.

'A marriage without children?' she countered.

In this, he would not relent. He did not want to be a father—not after Declan's death. Despite Joan's heartfelt wish, he could not agree.

'If need be,' he answered.

'And what if I refuse?' she said coolly. 'I have said already that I want a child more than all else.'

'You will agree to the marriage,' he said softly, 'or I will tell your brothers that you surrendered your virtue to me.'

Frustration and humiliation coursed through Joan during the remainder of the journey. How could Ronan demand this of her? She had wanted to save his life, and in return, he intended to imprison her within a marriage with no possibility of children.

Her actions ensured that she could not walk away from Ronan or deny the betrothal. Her brothers would be furious with her choice, and she could not tell them what had happened.

How had it come to this? She had mistakenly believed that offering her innocence would break the curse. But there was no sense of peace within her, no sense that the bad luck had been lifted away. After she had given herself to Ronan, there was naught to calm the storm of emotions—instead, she felt more confused than ever. It was as if she had lain with him out of desire instead of her hope of protecting him. She had enjoyed every moment in his arms, but now, he was cold and unyielding in his demand for a true betrothal. His anger held a note of vengeance, and she knew not how to ease the tension between them.

They arrived at Killalough by nightfall. Joan gritted her teeth as servants took their horses and led them into the Great Chamber. Ronan rested his palm against the small of her back, and his touch was possessive. There was no doubting what he meant to say to her brothers.

Warrick sat at the high table upon a dais beside his wife, while Rhys stood waiting for them at the bottom of the steps. Her older brother approached and embraced her lightly before greeting Ronan. 'I am glad to see you are both well. Have you come to a decision, then?'

'We have,' Ronan answered. He took her hand, and when he squeezed her fingers, there was no doubting his silent command. 'We will draw up the betrothal agreement tonight.'

Joan wanted to argue, but the firm pressure on her hand was a warning not to speak. Yet she had no intention of remaining silent. 'I have terms of my own to add to the betrothal,' she told her brothers. 'We can discuss them later, after we dine.'

Ronan leaned in to her ear. 'And what terms are those?'

As they followed her brother towards the dais, she murmured, 'I will tell you later.' She was not about to reveal her own demands until the time was right. If he intended to force her hand, then she was not about to back down from her own wishes.

'Come and join us at the table,' Warrick said, gesturing for them to sit beside him. He introduced Ronan to his wife, Rosamund, who was expecting another child. Rosamund's face appeared pale, as if this new pregnancy had not been easy on her. She cradled one infant while a nursemaid held the other. Joan sent her a sympathetic smile, her heart softening at the sight of the babies.

Ronan bowed in greeting. 'My lady.'

'It is my pleasure to meet you,' Rosamund answered. 'Perhaps we can speak later, and you can share your wisdom with me about governing an Irish clan. The Ó Neills have no interest in learning our language, and it has been difficult to help them.'

Joan recognised Rosamund's offer as a way of building ties between them. If Ronan helped them bridge the challenges of the clan, it would bring them together as allies.

'I will speak with their leaders on your behalf,'

Ronan offered. 'There may be a way of meeting their needs and yours. But you must have someone here who can translate until you have learned the Irish language. And they must learn the Norman tongue in return.'

Joan noticed that her brothers said nothing of the translator they already had. It only confirmed her suspicions that they were trying to draw Ronan in, bringing them together.

'The difficulty is that our home is in England,' Rosamund admitted. 'We need to appoint a chieftain to govern on our behalf. But choosing the right man will be a challenge when we cannot converse properly.'

'I will speak with your men later this night and learn what I can,' Ronan agreed.

'Good,' Warrick answered. 'I have a few men who may suit as chieftain, but I would welcome your opinion.'

Ronan nodded and accepted a trencher of food from a servant. He sat beside her, and though he hardly spoke at all, he seemed fully aware of her presence. His hard thigh pressed against hers, and it evoked a memory of the forbidden night they had shared.

His fingers brushed against hers during the meal, and Joan was startled by her body's awakening. Never in her life had any man made her feel such a strong response. It was as if she remembered his hands moving over her bare skin, and she yearned for more. She veiled her reaction by taking a sip of wine.

'I am glad to hear that you have agreed to this

betrothal, Joan,' Rhys said at last. 'It seems that my daughter Sorcha was right.' To Ronan, he added, 'She predicted that Joan would marry a prince, but our father did not believe it.' Then he turned back to her. 'You said that you had terms of your own before you would agree to the betrothal. What is it you want?'

Ronan's hand moved to her leg beneath the table in an unspoken warning. Joan paid it little heed, for she had to lay down her own expectations. She would not wed a man who intended to take her brother's soldiers and ignore her desires. If she was forced into marriage, she would demand that he fulfil his end of the bargain.

She faced both brothers. 'I want a child of my own. I am not as young as most maidens, and I dare not wait very long.'

Ronan squeezed her knee, and she caught the silent message: *Don't do this.*

But *he* was the one who seemed to want a celibate marriage. She could not agree to a union with no promise of ever having children. It would be heartbreaking.

'If I do not conceive a child by Yuletide, I will annul the marriage,' she finished.

Ronan's hand tightened over hers, his green eyes turning to stone.

Her brothers appeared discomfited by the condition. 'Joan, Yuletide is not a reasonable length of time.'

But Ronan intervened and said to her brothers, 'If

you will excuse us for a moment, Joan and I need to talk about this further.'

In other words, he was going to try to talk her out of it. But she added, 'While I speak with Ronan, you may decide how many of your men you will send to Clonagh.'

She stood from her place and kept her hand in Ronan's. From the firm grip of his hand, there was no doubting his anger. He had tried to force her into this marriage, but she would not go meekly—not unless he yielded to her own wishes.

They walked outside the main *donjon* and into the inner bailey. But instead of choosing a place to speak, Ronan led her outside the gates.

They walked only a few paces before he stopped. 'Why would you even speak of an annulment?'

'Because you have said that you will not give me a child,' she answered. 'How can I marry a man who will not grant me the one thing I long for most?'

He stood back from her, his hands at his sides. 'I cannot be a father, Joan. It's not something I want.'

'Why?' The word blurted forth before she could stop it. She tried to soften it, saying, 'Help me to understand.'

He grasped her waist and stared at her. It seemed as if he were trying to decide whether to speak. She didn't push but simply waited. His green eyes held a blend of anger and grief. Finally, he admitted, 'Because I am to blame for my nephew's death. Both my brother and his son would still be alive if it weren't for me.'

There was such ragged pain in his expression, she could not say anything. 'I have no desire to ever have children of my own,' he finished. 'Not after what happened to them.'

'I am sorry.' But even as she spoke, she knew the words would not heal his wounds. Instead, she rested her hand upon his shoulder a moment before he pulled away. The guilt weighed heavily upon him, and it bothered her that he would not accept comfort. She couldn't imagine what had happened but did not ask. It could only bring back harsh memories, and her heart ached for his loss.

'Now, the only one left in my family is my father.' His tone remained leaden. 'I may have lost him, too.'

Joan's heart bled for him. 'We will do all we can to save Brodur.'

His expression turned shielded. 'Then you must agree to the marriage offer as it stands. I need your brothers' men to fight back.'

Her lips pressed together as she considered it. Ronan wanted a marriage in name only, with no hope of children. He had lost his kingdom, and until he regained it, there was nowhere for them to live. She understood that all his concentration rested on freeing his father from captivity and restoring the throne. Marrying her was a means to an end. And if she agreed to these terms, it might save his kinsmen—but it would consign her to a life without the child she wanted.

She knew he would still invade Clonagh, with or without her brothers' men. He would fight his enemies, and if there were not enough men to help him, he would die. That was a fact, regardless of whether she agreed to wed him. If she refused the betrothal, her brothers would not help him at all. The blame for his death would lie on her shoulders.

'I cannot agree to those terms,' she said quietly, 'but I will delay signing a betrothal agreement. My brothers will still send men to help you win back Clonagh, since they believe you have my consent for a marriage.'

It was the best she could offer to Ronan. A part of her was deeply afraid that it would not be enough. She prayed she had broken the curse and that he would be safe during the battles ahead. Although they were not formally betrothed, she worried that he could be hurt, simply by being so near to her. It would be wiser to close off her heart and steel herself against the inevitable danger. But whenever she looked at Ronan, she saw a man stronger than any other. The intensity of his gaze, and the way he made her heartbeat quicken, touched her like no one else.

She had lived her life in fear during the past few years, only to lose every man she had been betrothed to. She didn't want to lose him, too. Yet, she could not imagine a marriage where he shielded himself, refusing to share her bed. It was an impossible arrangement.

In his eyes, she saw a man who would sacrifice everything for his family. He would surrender his own life for his father's. She admired his loyalty and strength of will. But only time would reveal whether the curse was broken and whether they could have a true marriage between them.

Chapter Five

One day later

It was well before dawn, and Ronan had gathered a dozen soldiers to accompany him to Clonagh. His emotions hardened with anger towards his step-brother Odhran. He knew not what he would find this morn, but he prayed his father would be alive. Tension knotted in his stomach as they approached his homeland. The autumn air was frigid with a hint of ice in the wind. The horses walked in silence as they approached, and frost coated the ground.

Rhys and Warrick had accompanied him, along with the other MacEgans who had travelled with them this far. There were a dozen men total, enough to surround the fortress and to survey its defences, but not enough to attack.

This day, his intention was to observe his enemy and learn Odhran's weaknesses. He needed to understand why such a small group of rebels had gained control of the Ó Callaghans. Once he learned the truth, he intended to destroy those who had stolen his father's throne.

He had no doubt of the danger. If any of them was discovered spying, they could be killed by Odhran's men. Ronan could only hope that he would never be forced to kill one of his own kinsmen.

They left their horses tethered by the stream so they could continue their approach on foot. 'When I give the signal, I want you to split off and surround the ring-fort,' Ronan commanded. 'There will be no bloodshed. I need to know how many men are guarding Clonagh and whether they hold any prisoners. If any of my people are in danger, I want to know immediately.'

He explained which men would go in each direction and insisted, 'Stay hidden, and do not fight unless you are in danger. I want only information this morn. Tell me if my father is still alive, and find him if you can.'

He continued leading the group of men towards Clonagh. The horizon had transformed from a deep purple into a softer rose as the dawn approached. Ronan stopped walking, for they were reaching the outskirts of the fortress. He raised his hand in a silent signal, and the men began spreading out around the perimeter of the fortress. There were only a few moments more until dawn, and the men lowered to the ground, keeping their position hidden.

Ronan moved towards the back of the ringfort where there was only one guard. There was a broken section of the fence, near the bottom, that he had intended to repair before he'd learned of Odhran's treachery. He peered through the broken wood and counted six men who were lighting outdoor fires. There was no sign of his father, and none of the women had left their homes. There was only the thick cloak of silence, and he knew not what that meant. While there were no signs of violence or a struggle, he was uneasy about the surroundings.

There were a dozen guards surrounding the fortress, and his instincts warned that something was wrong. Ronan rested his hand upon his sword hilt, waiting for the rest of the people to emerge. When no one did, he realised that he could get no answers by remaining in the shadows. He had to infiltrate the fortress and find out the truth.

The sun had nearly risen, and he remained on the ground, creeping towards one of the men. He had nearly reached him when one of the guards spied them. The soldier shouted out a warning, and within seconds, torches were lit all along the walls.

Ronan cursed and unsheathed his weapon. There was no point in secrecy now. To Warrick he commanded, 'Take the men back. I'll stay behind to ensure that you get them out alive.'

'You cannot fight them all alone,' Warrick argued. 'It would mean your death.'

But fighting wasn't his intention. 'I know this fortress well. I have a better chance of slipping away than any of you. Now go!'

The men retreated, disappearing into the shadows as they ran back to where their horses were tethered. Ronan moved towards the gates, his sword drawn. A sudden calm descended over him as he prepared to fight. He was badly outnumbered, but he knew these men. In his heart, he didn't truly believe they would try to kill him.

When he charged towards the first attacker, he recognised one of Odhran's mercenaries. The soldier swung his sword, but Ronan had no shield to block it. He ducked, and the blade sliced through empty air. As he dodged the man's weapon, he spied an archer climbing up the gate tower, preparing to shoot at Warrick's men. He had to reach the archer before the man could loose any arrows.

Ronan needed to end this sword fight quickly. He struck hard against his enemy's blade and gritted his teeth when the man's sword slashed his side. He shut down the pain, refusing to let the wound stop him. No doubt Joan would worry over him later, and he concentrated on thoughts of her as he fought. He wanted to win back Clonagh and bring her here to rule at his side. The thought strengthened his resolve, and he continued to lash out, even while moving towards the tower.

Once he neared the ladder, he quickened his pace, barely avoiding another blow. Behind his attacker, he saw one of his former friends, a man who had once fought alongside him. Darragh didn't move, but simply watched the fight.

It infuriated him that his friend's loyalty had dissolved after so many years. Why would his friends turn against him? Ronan had been willing to sacrifice everything for them, and now, they would not even lift a hand to help him fight.

'When did you become Odhran's traitor?' he snapped at Darragh.

At that, his former friend turned and walked away. Ronan poured his anger into the battle and slashed at his assailant's stomach, ending the fight.

He ignored the blood seeping through his tunic and sheathed his sword. The pain was a searing ache, but he hurried up the ladder. He strode towards the archer and ripped the bow free of the man's hands. 'Leave them,' he ordered.

For a long moment, he stared at the Ó Callaghan guards in disbelief of their betrayal. 'Where is my father? Did you kill him?' he demanded. The only answer to his question was silence. But several men lowered their faces as if in shame. Rage flooded through Ronan, and he continued, 'Or did you want Odhran as your king?'

Again, they said nothing. But each of the men met his gaze with a hard look. Once again, Ronan was convinced that all was not right. He had not seen the familiar sights and sounds of the morning, with people talking among themselves as they carried out their tasks. Instead, it felt as if the clan was merely going through the motions of everyday life.

The women had kept out of view, and so had the children. Which meant that it was dangerous for them to leave their homes. There were few mercenaries visible, and another realisation took root. 'He's keeping hostages, isn't he?'

At that, one of the men nodded. Before Ronan could question them further, a roar sounded from the opposite end of the fortress. He saw more armed men approaching, and his time was running out. There was no alternative but to leave once again.

'I will return with an army,' he promised. He tossed the bow aside and climbed down the ladder. When he reached the gates, he saw Darragh standing with a waiting horse. Ronan had no time to wonder why, but he mounted the gelding and urged it into a hard gallop. There were no arrows fired towards him, nor did anyone follow.

He rode hard through the meadows, questioning what he had seen. There was no trace of violence, no sense of suffering—only the men's confirmation that he was right about hostages.

But then, Darragh had given him a horse to aid his escape. His former friend had not helped him fight, but neither had he abandoned him to die. The gesture sobered him, making him wonder why these men were so afraid to act against Odhran. The only man who had dared to attack was the lone mercenary. Not one of his own people had raised a weapon against him—and that gave him reason to hope.

Ronan joined the others near the place where they had tethered their horses. Joan's brothers were waiting, and as soon as he drew near, Warrick demanded, 'What happened? You're bleeding.'

'It's nothing.' He refused to dwell on the wound, though he was starting to feel light-headed. 'They let me go. We'll talk more when we get further away from Clonagh. Odhran's men might still pursue us. I don't want to take that chance.'

Yet, his clansmen had not immediately followed. It was as if they had held back, unwilling to fight a battle that wasn't theirs.

Ronan rode among the men for the rest of the day, turning over the matter in his mind. Though he had hoped to gain insight about his enemy, he had found only more questions. Odhran had hostages and was using them to control his kinsmen. Likely the women and children from what he could tell.

By nightfall, Ronan spied the gleam of torches in the distance, surrounding the walls of Killalough. His head ached from the exertion of riding, and his ribs burned from the wound. The world was spinning, and he needed to rest and treat the injury. He knew he had been bleeding for hours, but the frigid cold had helped him push back the pain.

Ahead, he spied Joan waiting, along with a few other women. The moment she saw him, she came running towards him. Yet when she reached his side, her image blurred. A ringing sounded in his ears, and he attempted to dismount. The moment his feet hit the ground, his knees sagged.

He was hardly aware of what Joan was saying, but there was terror in her voice when he collapsed to the ground. Ronan put his hand to his side, and it came back soaked in blood. He wanted to tell her that it was nothing, only a slip of his enemy's sword, but he couldn't bring himself to speak.

His last image was of Joan's stricken face as darkness closed around him.

* * *

'He's not dead, Joan.'

Her brother, Rhys, was trying to speak in a calm voice, but his words did nothing to allay the dread rising within her. He said something about Ronan being wounded in a sword fight, but all she could remember was the blood. No one could lose that much blood and survive, she was certain. Tears stung at her eyes, and she followed her brothers into one of the guest chambers. They carried Ronan inside and sent for the healer, but her mind was crying out with fear.

No, he hadn't died yet. But perhaps it was because she had not yet signed the betrothal. Inside, she felt numb, horrified that she had been wrong about breaking the curse.

The healer was shaking her head and speaking in Irish, pointing towards the door for them to leave. Joan understood that there were too many people in the room. She stood and guided her brothers towards the door. 'I will help her. Leave us,' Joan ordered. She had the right to be here at Ronan's side.

Warrick pressed a hand to her shoulder. 'It was just a small wound, Joan. He will heal quickly.'

But he didn't know that. No one did.

Joan raised her chin and stared hard at her brother. 'I will stay with him.' She didn't want to hear false reassurance. Her heart was already beating swiftly out of fear, for she knew the danger of a fever. One wound could end a man's life, and Ronan's battle had only begun.

Once the men were gone, the healer removed the

bloody tunic, revealing a jagged wound across his ribs. Though it wasn't deep, it had bled for a long time. The stubborn man hadn't even bothered to wrap it.

Her emotions ran wild between anger that he hadn't taken care of himself and fear that the curse would come upon him. Joan reached out to touch him, but he didn't respond. He seemed completely unaware of her presence, and fear doubled within her.

The healer handed her a basin and motioned for Joan to go and bring back water. She took it and filled the basin. Though she tried to remain calm, her hands trembled when she passed the water to the healer. She wanted to ask the woman so many questions. Would Ronan live? How bad were his wounds? But she could say nothing at all.

The healer washed Ronan's wound and bandaged it. Joan sat beside his pallet on the floor. She smoothed back the hair at his forehead, so afraid that he would grow feverish. Though she knew the woman would not understand her words, she asked quietly, 'Will he live?'

The healer's gaze was kindly, and she reached out to squeeze Joan's hand. Then she rose from her place beside Ronan. She mixed up some herbs and placed them in a wooden cup. Then she poured boiling water over the herbs to steep into a tea. She placed it on a low table nearby. Then she sent a questioning look to Joan, and Joan nodded, understanding her meaning. 'I won't leave him.'

The healer brought over more water and a linen cloth. She touched Ronan's forehead and soaked the linen in the water before wringing it out to place upon his head. The healer gestured towards the cup and pointed to Ronan. It was clear that the healer wanted Ronan to drink the tea, and Joan nodded, pointing back at the cup. 'I will ensure that he drinks it.'

The healer's expression curved in a gentle smile before she left them alone. Once she had gone, Joan studied Ronan's unconscious form. 'I warned you this might happen,' she said softly. 'But you didn't believe me.'

With a sigh, she arranged the linen across his forehead. Though she had wanted to hope that she had broken the curse, it did not seem possible now. He had been harmed with the mere suggestion of a betrothal.

Joan took his hand in hers, feeling such guilt. No matter what choice she made, it brought danger upon him. If she turned away and refused to wed him, her brothers would not send men to aid his cause. Or if she stayed, it was likely he would die in battle. 'I cannot be the cause of your death,' she whispered as an unwanted tear slid down her cheek.

She never should have let herself have feelings for this man. It hurt so badly, she felt as if a blade had sliced her in half. A dark fury boiled within her that Fate would curse her so. She had never done anything to deserve this, and she wanted to rage against the heavens for the misfortune.

She wept in silence for the life she wanted but could never have. Why could other women love a man and bear him children? Why not her?

You should leave Ronan, her conscience urged. *If you care enough, you should let him go to save his life.*

But she didn't know if she had the courage to walk away. For now, Joan could only sit beside him and pray that he would recover from these wounds.

She caressed his hand with her thumb, so worried about him. But she was startled when his fingers curled around hers in a gentle squeeze.

'Ronan, are you awake?' she asked.

'No.' His voice was rough, heavy with pain, and he winced.

Despite his discomfort, her eyes welled up with tears of thankfulness. At least he was starting to awaken. Joan squeezed his hand in return, trying to gather command of her emotions.

'You were wounded at Clonagh,' she told him. 'The healer tended you, and she left a tea for you to drink.' She had to release his hand to get the tea, and found that it had cooled. 'Here. This should help you feel better.'

She raised the cup to his lips, and he tried to drink. From his expression, she guessed that the herbs tasted bitter. But he did drink half of it before he turned his head aside.

'What did you see at Clonagh?' she asked.

He was silent for a time before he admitted, 'It was strange. I saw nothing at all. There was no violence, no evidence of suffering.'

She put the cup down. 'Did it seem that your kinsmen were happy?'

He shook his head. 'There was very little noise. No

children or dogs roaming around. One of Odhran's men attacked me, but no one else did.' He told her about Darragh giving him a horse and allowing him to escape.

'It sounds as if Odhran is controlling them in some way,' she said. 'What about your father? Did you see him?'

'There was no sign of him. I think he must be dead.'

The heaviness in his voice revealed his unspoken sorrow, and she moved her hand to his forehead. 'I pray he is not, for your sake.'

He let out a rough sigh. 'I need to speak with your brothers to learn what else they saw. I know we can take back the fortress with our combined forces, but I believe Odhran is holding hostages. We must be careful in our attack.'

She nodded, and he caught her hand in his. For a moment, he looked into her eyes. 'You've been crying, Joan.'

She saw no reason to deny it. 'You frightened me. I was so afraid you would die.'

'But I did not.' He reached up and cupped her cheek. 'I'm still alive.'

She took comfort from his touch, knowing that he wanted her to believe in him. He had survived the battle.

Deep within, a fragile wisp of hope took root. Was it possible that she *had* broken the curse? Would he have died otherwise? She laced her fingers with his, praying it was possible.

'I am so glad,' she whispered, meeting his green eyes. She squeezed his hand and released it as she stood. 'I will go and find food for you. Get some sleep for now.'

She would try to talk with her brothers about sending more men, though she knew not what they would say. But in the end, she would do whatever was necessary to protect Ronan.

Ronan awakened with a jolt to the sound of an infant screaming. For a moment, his lungs constricted with fear as he thought of Ardan's son. But then, Declan had been three years of age, not a baby. It took Ronan a moment to realise that he was staying at Killalough, and the crying child must be one of Warrick's twins.

He tried to calm his racing heartbeat to fall asleep once more. And yet, the sound of the wailing infant remained outside his chamber. He closed his eyes, but sleep would not come. The sword wound on his ribs throbbed, despite the poultice and bandages. The healer had given him more tea to prevent a fever, and she had returned twice more to check on him.

But he could not fall back to sleep this night—not with the noise of a sobbing child.

Ronan rose from his sleeping pallet and opened the door. He saw Rosamund walking up and down the hallway with two babies in her arms.

'I am so sorry,' she apologised. 'I think the twins are getting teeth, and both of them are in pain.' She bounced her daughter, who had her fist in her mouth and was bawling. 'How is your wound, Ronan?'

'It will be well enough in a few days.' He leaned against the wall, feeling unsettled by the presence of the babies. Rosamund clearly had her hands full, and Warrick was nowhere to be seen.

When her son began to wail, Rosamund handed the infant to him. 'Could you take Stephen for a moment while I settle Mary?'

She gave him no choice but to hold the boy. For a moment, the infant appeared confused, and then he started fussing. Ronan shifted the baby's position until he held him on the opposite side, facing Rosamund. 'There's your mother, lad. She's gone nowhere.'

The infant lowered his mouth to Ronan's hand and began gumming at his finger. What was he supposed to do now? He couldn't recall a time when an infant had attempted to gnaw at him before.

'Perhaps you should send for Warrick,' he offered. 'I fear I might drop your son.' He had tried to have little contact with children, especially after what had happened to Declan. But it seemed as if Fate was forcing him to face the past. He was deeply conscious of how small the infant was, how helpless. And he cradled the boy closer, as if to protect him.

'Is your wound hurting you?' Rosamund asked.

'It's bearable.'

He waited for her to reclaim the boy, but instead, Rosamund smiled warmly. 'Warrick is walking along the fortress walls to inspect our defences here at Killalough. He will be back soon enough, if you can stand to hold the baby a moment or two longer.' She eyed her son. 'Warrick felt the same way as you when he held Stephen for the first time. But you won't drop him. I trust you.'

While she likely believed she was being reassuring, her words were a spear that thrust through his heart. Ardan had trusted him once, and his son had died from it. He didn't deserve anyone's trust.

But before Ronan could hand the infant back to Rosamund, he felt the small body growing slack against him. For a moment, he feared the worst, only to realise that the boy had fallen asleep. The baby's head rested against Ronan's forearm, his mouth still sucking at his finger.

'You have a good hand with children,' she murmured. 'Thank you for your help. Will you follow me back to my chamber where we can put them in their cradles?'

Ronan wanted nothing more than to give the boy back to Rosamund, but she offered him no other choice. While he followed her, she said, 'I am so happy for Joan and you. You don't know how lonely she was for so many years. It was terrible what happened with the men she was betrothed to.'

'It was,' he agreed. 'But that is in the past now.' Though he knew it was late and Joan was asleep, he almost wished she could have stayed. He was glad of her presence, and it had soothed him.

'I think you will make a good marriage between you,' Rosamund said. 'And I hope you have many children.'

He couldn't even grasp the idea, for it sent a cold chill of fear through him. But he said nothing at all.

Rosamund stopped in front of her chamber and pushed open the door. He followed her inside, and she showed him where the two cradles were. He was careful not to disturb the boy as he laid him on his back.

'Thank you for your help,' Rosamund said. 'I am sorry for disturbing you from your rest.'

He gave a noncommittal nod and bade her a good night before he returned to his chamber. His ribs were aching, and he still felt restless, his mind too preoccupied to sleep. Instead, he searched through a bag of his belongings and withdrew a carving knife and a bit of wood. He leaned back against the wall and let his mind drift as he shaped the wood with the blade. He thought of Joan and her desire for a child.

She would make a good mother, just like Rosamund. He could easily imagine her walking with a fussing infant, soothing the child at her breast. But God help him, he didn't know if he could give Joan a baby. He wasn't meant to be a father. He wasn't at all the kind, patient man Ardan had been. Too often, Ronan had let other distractions keep him from his duties.

When he thought of his brother, he remembered Ardan lifting Declan on his shoulders while the boy squealed with delight. Sometimes he tickled his young son, and the burst of laughter had made Ronan smile.

An empty ache caught him, as he wondered if he could ever be the man his brother had been.

His blade moved over the ash wood, flicking chips

and curls to form the shape he wanted. It was a simple design, but one that would suit Joan well.

Over the next hour, he distracted himself from the pain by wielding his blade against the wood. And when it was finished, he hoped she would be pleased with it.

Then he turned his attention to another gift, this one for Rosamund's babies. He chose a few thin pieces of wood and shaved the edges until they were soft and round. Last, he bored holes within each one, stringing them along a bit of twine. When he shook the twine, the wood rattled. He imagined young Stephen shaking the rattle and gumming the round bits of wood.

After he had finished with the gifts, he wrapped them up and set them aside. It was only an hour or so before dawn, but the work had helped occupy his mind. He lay back upon his pallet, imagining Joan's face when he gave her the carving.

Though he knew not if she would like it, it was something he could offer of himself.

Over the next few days, Joan avoided the conversation she needed to have with Ronan. His wound was healing, and he'd gone to speak with several of the Ó Neill men to help her brothers choose a chieftain.

Though she could not understand his Irish words, there was an air of command about Ronan, as if he knew exactly how to speak with the men. She studied those who wanted to lead, judging them by their stance and her own instincts. There seemed to be an agreement of some kind, and soon, all the men dispersed.

Ronan caught her watching and came to join her. 'We will hold competitions tonight. Those who want to become chieftain must voice their claim and engage in contests until we have chosen the strongest and wisest from among them.'

'And what if you have a man who is wiser but not stronger?'

He nodded towards the people. 'Each man will have a wooden bowl. The people will place one stone in the bowl, and whichever bowl holds the most stones will be their chieftain. But I have told them that they must abide by the wishes of Warrick and Rosamund, since the land is theirs.'

'My brother will allow them to keep their traditions,' Joan said. 'Warrick knows how much it means to them.' And she trusted that the people would choose the best man to lead.

She was about to step back when, to her surprise, he lifted away her iron cross. 'I have something for you.' From a fold of his cloak, he withdrew a new wooden cross. The edges were smooth, and the grain of the wood was set in two different directions to create a subtle design.

'Did you make this?' she asked.

He placed the new cross around her neck and then rested his hands on her shoulders. 'I did. You seemed to like my turnip. This will last longer.'

Knowing that he had carved the cross himself brought a pang to her heart, and she braved a smile.

'It's perfect, Ronan.' She traced the edges of the wood that were silken. 'Better than the iron one.'

'Iron is cold. Not like you at all.' He took her hands in his.

'Thank you.' She squeezed his palms, and he held her hands a moment longer. 'Are you feeling better now? Your wounds are healing well?'

Ronan nodded, his palms warm against hers. Being with him was a risk to her heart. He made her want to be with him as his wife, to push back the years of loneliness and make a different future. But the days ahead would be dangerous, and she prayed he would survive the battle to come. *Let him be safe*, she prayed.

He released her hands, and she touched the wooden cross again. 'It's beautiful, Ronan.'

His green eyes locked upon hers, and she grew vulnerable to his gaze. He seemed to see deep within her, and her wayward heart faltered.

To distract herself from the worry, she said, 'I promised I would meet with my brothers. I will see you at the evening meal later.'

Rhys and Warrick stood on the far end of the fortress, and she seized the opportunity to meet with them. She hurried towards her brothers, and when she reached them, she was slightly out of breath. Rhys sent her a sidelong look. 'Is something wrong?'

'I came to ask you for a boon,' she said quietly. 'I want you to promise that you will send men to help Ronan. No matter what happens.'

Her brother's face tightened. 'And what do you mean by that, Joan? Has he harmed you in any way?'

She shook her head. 'I care about him very much, Rhys. And when he came back wounded... I was so afraid he would die.' Even now, her heart ached at the thought of Ronan's injuries. He was improving with each day, but it didn't diminish the tightness in her gut at the thought of him fighting again.

Warrick came to stand beside Rhys, and he let out a sigh. 'I know you believe in the curse, Joan, but it is time to put it behind you.'

'I want to believe it's over,' she murmured, 'more than anything. But I need a little more time.'

'Time for what?' Rhys asked.

'I want to delay the betrothal until I can be sure Ronan will survive this battle. I beg of you, send the men to help him.'

'I will not endanger the lives of my men because you cannot make up your mind,' Warrick said.

'It's not about making up my mind,' she insisted. 'I just want to be certain the curse will not take him from me.'

'All men face death in a battle,' Rhys said. 'It has nothing to do with a curse. In your heart, you know this.'

She wanted to believe it. But though she was trying to set aside the past, her fear for Ronan was more real than the curse. When he had been wounded the last time, the pain had struck her to the bone. She couldn't bear to think of it.

'I want him protected when he goes into battle,'

she insisted. 'I won't let him risk his life without enough men to guard him.'

'Warrick and I came to an agreement last night,' Rhys continued. 'We will gladly send the men Ronan needs to retake his lands and restore his father to the kingship. But only if you marry him.'

She started to refuse, but he cut her off. 'If you do not wed Ronan before he goes to battle, he will return to Clonagh with only the MacEgan soldiers he brought with him. We will do nothing.'

'Why would you turn away from him?' she demanded. 'After he has tried to help you find a chieftain for Killalough?'

'Because you want a husband, and he is willing. If you agree to the marriage, we will send three dozen men. If you refuse, we will send no one.'

'You would sentence him to die, if you abandoned him,' she argued.

'No, you would,' Rhys countered.

Her brother's accusation burned her to the core. She wanted to rage at him for putting her in such an impossible position. This was about more than a curse—it was about dominion. Her brothers intended to bend her to their will, until she had no choice but to acquiesce.

Emotion clogged her throat, and she faced Rhys. 'I cannot take that risk.'

Her brother only shrugged. 'His life is in your hands, Joan. The choice is yours.'

Chapter Six

That evening, the men gathered in the centre of Killalough for the competitions. Three of the Ó Neills had been chosen to compete as chieftain. Ronan sat beside Joan, who had been quiet most of the day. He was pleased to see her wearing the wooden cross he'd carved, yet he sensed that something was troubling her. Even her brothers had been evasive.

'Are you all right?' he asked.

Joan nodded, but he noted the flush on her cheeks and the tension in her stance. For a time, she didn't speak, but kept her attention upon the contests. At last, she ventured, 'Who do you think will win the contests?'

'Possibly Bertach. He won the wrestling match earlier.' Ronan's interest was not on the competitors but on Joan. He didn't like seeing her so troubled.

'Strength doesn't always make a good leader,' she remarked. 'Wisdom is better.'

'It can be,' he agreed. Though Bertach had seemed intelligent enough when he'd spoken with the man.

'But the people will not respect a man who cannot fight.' She said little, and he could tell that she was distracted this night. 'Which of the men do you prefer?'

At that, her gaze shifted to him. There was a flare of interest in her eyes—almost as if she was thinking of him. Then abruptly, she masked it. 'I don't know. They are all strangers to me.' She thought a moment and added, 'You should ask them questions to test their knowledge.'

It was a sound idea, and he agreed with her. 'I will ask the *brehons* to give them a series of tests to determine which man can make sound decisions.'

She nodded, but it still seemed as if her mind was preoccupied. Although her brothers had drawn up the betrothal agreement, she had delayed in signing it. Ronan understood her reasons, but time was running out.

He took her hand in his and said, 'I intend to return to Clonagh to speak with Odhran. I will ask about my father and negotiate for his release if he is still alive.'

She appeared uneasy by his declaration. 'Do you think that's wise when you were wounded the last time? It will be dangerous.'

He agreed with her, but he had no intention of going alone. 'I will have a dozen men with me. We will not attack, unless there is a need.' Though he had wanted to attack Clonagh with full forces, her brothers had cautioned him against it. They had advised him to seek help from his loyal kinsmen and try to free the hostages first. Else, Odhran would likely kill every prisoner.

Joan paled, and she shifted her gaze towards Rhys and Warrick. 'You've only just recovered from your wounds. How can you leave so soon?'

'I must know why my own people are being held hostage.' There were too many questions, and he needed to understand what control Odhran held over the Ó Callaghans.

'I don't want you to go back.' Her voice was soft, laced with fear.

'I have no choice, Joan.'

She closed her eyes and nodded. 'I know. But I cannot help but worry.' Her blue eyes were filled with concern, and he squeezed her hand in reassurance.

'There is something else.' He caressed her hand with his thumb, knowing she would not like this. 'Your brothers have agreed to send more men with me. But they are demanding that we wed before I go.'

Her face blanched, and she started to shake her head. 'I cannot, Ronan.'

'Are you afraid of becoming my wife?'

'You know why I am afraid,' she answered. 'The last time you went to Clonagh, they nearly killed you. I don't want you to be hurt.'

He stared hard at her, and for the first time, he wondered if she would ever agree to a union between them. 'I lived through the last battle, Joan. Have faith in me.'

She closed her eyes. 'I want to believe that the curse is broken. Or that it was never real. But the truth is, I cannot send you off into battle without feeling as if my heart is being torn apart.'

She met his gaze, and in her eyes, he saw the gleam of unshed tears. 'I would rather walk away from you and save your life than risk losing you. I care for you, Ronan.'

Despite her claim, he suspected another cause of her turmoil—that she had no faith in his fighting skills at all. Anger and frustration swelled up within him, and he needed a way of releasing the tension before he spoke words he didn't mean.

He strode away from her and went to join the men competing to become chieftain. They were preparing to fight with colc swords, and he seized one, intending to join in. The fight would let him release the pent-up anger, and it would reveal which of the three men had the greatest skills in swordplay.

'Who will fight me?' he demanded. 'I want to see your skills with a sword.'

Bertach stepped forward, his own weapon in hand. 'I will fight you.' He picked up a shield, and someone tossed Ronan one to use.

He gave Bertach no time to prepare but lunged at the man, swinging the sword hard. Bertach raised his shield to deflect the blow and struck in retaliation. Their swords clanged together, and Ronan lost himself in the fight.

With every blow, he fought back against the doubts Joan held. He would return to Clonagh, even without her brothers' men if need be. It was dangerous, yes, but he would never turn away from his people if they were imprisoned.

Perspiration lined his skin, and he was pleased

with Bertach's fighting. The man defended himself well, and he was quick on his feet. It felt good to fight, and Ronan quickened his pace, testing Bertach's reactions. The man was breathing hard, but he kept up his endurance.

Ronan was about to strike again, when a blur of motion caught his attention. A woman screamed, and he jerked his head to see a small boy running towards them.

'Da, don't let him hurt you!' the boy called out, just as Bertach's sword swung hard.

Ronan reacted out of gut instinct, throwing up his shield and shoving the child out of the way.

'Danu...' Bertach breathed in shock. His sword was embedded in the wood of Ronan's shield, only inches from where the child had been.

The boy was sobbing, and Bertach dropped his weapon, gathering the child in his arms. Ronan left both his sword and shield and walked away. His hands were trembling, and his mind replayed the boy's actions over and over. Had he not thrown up his shield, the boy would be dead, killed by his father's own hand. Dimly, he heard Bertach's wife weeping as both of them embraced the child.

Ronan couldn't bring himself to see them. Instead, he trudged out of the gates into the open fields. The sun was sinking lower, covering the grasses with golden twilight. He needed to be alone, to push back the ghosts of the past.

But then he heard the sound of footsteps behind him. When he turned, he saw Joan silhouetted by the torches. She appeared as shaken as he felt. 'Ronan, where are you going?'

He didn't know, nor did he care. Instead, he turned his back on her and continued striding through the fields. A few sheep grazed nearby, and he wandered towards the rocky hillside. There was an outcropping halfway up, and he decided to climb it.

It shouldn't have surprised him that Joan followed him, but she doggedly trailed him until she reached the same stony plateau.

'You saved his life,' she murmured. 'They want you to return so they can thank you.'

He sat upon the limestone and stared off at the horizon. 'If he is alive, it's enough for me. I don't need their thanks.'

She sat beside him, adjusting her white skirts upon the stone. For a time, she waited for him to speak. Then he said, 'You needn't stay here, Joan. Go back to the others.'

But she didn't move. 'You're thinking of your nephew, aren't you?'

His thoughts were bound up tightly within him, and he had no desire to share them. It was easier to close himself off, to pretend as if nothing had happened. And yet, she already sensed the turmoil within him and had not hesitated to join him.

He didn't know why, after she'd refused to accept him as her husband. Though she claimed that she cared for him, she had little trust that his battle skills could overcome her prophetic fears.

'Perhaps you were given a second chance this day,'

she offered. 'Were it not for you, the boy would have died.'

Though he knew she was only trying to reassure him, the words did nothing to allay the guilt he carried. 'There were no second chances for Declan.'

Joan reached out to his shoulder, and her gentle touch was a silent invitation to tell her the rest. He didn't want to reveal any of it, but he sensed that she was not passing judgement upon him. There was only quiet understanding in her gaze.

'Declan drowned because I was too distracted to watch over him.' He made no effort to hide the self-loathing in his voice. 'My brother Ardan was in a council meeting with my father and the other leaders of our tribe. I didn't attend that day, because I had no interest in their conversations. Instead, I was with Declan's nursemaid.' He gritted his teeth, wishing he had never flirted with the young woman. 'While I kissed her, the boy wandered off. After Declan went missing, I tried to search for him.'

Ronan clenched his hands together, feeling the tension knotting within him. He waited for Joan to speak or ask questions. Instead, she continued to rest her hand against his shoulder.

'When Ardan and my father learned what happened, they joined in my search. But it was my brother who found his son in the river.' The memory of Ardan's anguished face haunted him to this day. 'Declan had fallen through the ice and drowned. Ardan pulled his body out.'

'I am so sorry,' she murmured. 'It must have been terrible for both of you.'

He stood, for there were no words to describe the grief or the guilt. 'I will blame myself for his death every day for the rest of my life.'

She held out her hand, and he helped her up from the limestone. He was half-expecting to hear her agree with him, but she simply kept his palm in hers. 'It was a terrible accident.'

'Ardan was in the freezing water for too long,' Ronan admitted. 'He caught a fever and died a sennight later. First, he lost his wife in childbirth and then his son. After Declan died, he lost the will to live.'

The stricken look on Joan's face mirrored the emotion in his heart. He could hardly return the embrace when she moved into his arms. She held him close, and he breathed in the scent of her hair. He didn't deserve the comfort, but her arms around him seemed to fill the empty holes of loss.

He drew back and saw the sorrow in her eyes. 'And now you know why I will never sire a child. Not even for you.'

Joan didn't know what to say to him after such a revelation. The weight of such grief was crushing, and she couldn't imagine how Ronan had endured after his brother had died. This was a man who was punishing himself for being alive after losing his loved ones.

Now, she understood his need for redemption. This was why he had to rescue his father and restore Clonagh. He could never live in peace until he had atoned for his sins. His face was ravaged with pain, and she held back her own tears.

'You should go back,' he said at last. 'Your brothers will be worried about you.'

'Walk with me,' she urged. 'I don't want to return alone.' Though she made it sound as if she needed him to protect her, the truth was, she didn't want *him* to be alone right now.

He shadowed her on the walk back to Killalough, and she felt the heaviness of his mood. Now she understood why he did not wish to have children of his own—it was not because he disliked them. He was afraid of being unable to protect them.

He had allowed his own fears to overshadow the truth, just as she had. Ronan had asked her to set aside her fears, to wed him and trust that he would be strong enough to fight and survive. Perhaps it was time to try.

With each step, a new clarity emerged. Avoiding marriage would not necessarily keep Ronan safe—but it would bind her in loneliness. She could not protect him by walking away; it would only endanger him more.

Although he did not wish to sire children, she understood now that it was born of his own guilt. In time, he might face his fears and overcome them—just as she had to. She wanted to heal his invisible wounds, for despite his past mistakes, he was a good man and she would not turn away from him.

The decision calmed her, and it felt right. Marrying Ronan was the only way her brothers would send men to help. And no matter what happened, she cared deeply for this man.

When they reached the fortress, Bertach came forward with his wife and son. He gripped Ronan's hand, and spoke rapidly in Irish. Joan didn't doubt that the man was thanking him for saving his son's life. One by one, the people surrounded him, until she was separated from Ronan.

Her brother, Rhys, came to stand beside her. Joan glanced up at him. 'I will wed him before he leaves for Clonagh.'

'Are you certain this is what you want?' He rested his hand upon her shoulder in silent support.

'It is.' Not only did Ronan need her brother's men, but he needed her. She would not turn away from him.

'We will sign the betrothal documents this night,' Rhys said. 'And you may speak the vows afterwards, if you wish.'

'The wedding will happen on the morrow,' she corrected. She wanted time to make it into a celebration, even if it was only a small feast.

'I am glad you came to your senses,' Rhys said. 'It will be a good marriage, Joan.'

She wasn't certain about anything right now, but she was not going to let anything happen to Ronan. 'Send word to me when it is time for the documents to be witnessed and signed. I will go and prepare myself.' She excused herself from her brother and walked inside the keep.

Her thoughts were spinning inside her, the emotions shifting between fear and a glimmer of joy.

Though she resented her brothers' interference, she understood that they saw this as a means to an end. They wanted her to be wedded to a man she cared for.

Ronan wanted to marry her, too, and she now understood why he never wanted a child. It was a fierce ache within her, being torn between this man and her deepest desire. If she married him, she might not ever have a baby.

And yet, giving him up was far worse. He had come into her life, giving her reasons to smile. Whenever she saw Ronan, her heart gave a leap. If she spent the rest of her days with him, would that not fill the loneliness inside?

There was so much danger ahead, but she pushed it back. She wanted to relinquish her fears, to set aside all thoughts of the curse. It lingered in her mind, but she told herself not to dwell upon it. As she passed a maidservant, she gave orders for a hot bath to be sent to her chamber. Her nerves were fraught with uncertainty, but she would do everything in her power to ensure Ronan's safety.

There was no other choice.

The betrothal was signed and witnessed now. There was no turning back.

Joan met Ronan's gaze, and a sudden ripple of awareness slid through her skin. She grew conscious of every feature—his dark blond hair, those intense green eyes. This man would become her husband, and their lives would join together. She didn't know what thoughts were going through his mind, but his stoic demeanour suggested that he regretted telling her how his brother and nephew had died.

'You will wed in the morning,' Warrick told them. 'My wife will make the arrangements. Afterwards, our men will accompany Ronan to Clonagh while my sister remains here with us.'

Though Joan understood why she had to stay behind, she wished she could travel with them. 'Could I not stay back at the camp, away from the fighting? Once we take Clonagh, my place is at Ronan's side.'

'It's safer here,' Warrick responded. 'Before we attack, Ronan wants to meet with Odhran and his father's wife, Eilis. We will join him and learn what we can.'

She didn't like that idea at all. It was entirely possible that Odhran had already killed King Brodur and would seek to harm Ronan as well, since he was a threat to his stepbrother's reign.

At that, Ronan touched his hand to her spine and leaned in close. 'It is better for you to stay here where you are protected.'

The heat of his palm slid through her skin. She met his gaze and saw that he had closed himself off to her. Whether it was regret at his confession or preparation for the battle ahead, she did not know.

But everything would change between them tonight. She had her own war to wage, this time to win his heart.

'May I speak with you alone?' she asked.

Ronan nodded, and she excused herself from her brothers, leading him down the narrow hallway towards her chamber. She opened the door, but he hesitated a moment. 'We can speak outside.'

She ignored him and stepped through the doorway. 'We are betrothed now, Ronan. It matters not that we are alone in my chamber.'

He stepped inside but kept the door open behind him. The room was small, with hardly more than a single bed and a stool. There was only one window, and it was shuttered. 'What did you want, Joan?' he asked quietly.

Her heart was thrumming within her chest. She had worn her best white gown, and the wooden cross he had carved hung between her breasts. 'I wanted to speak with you before you leave on the morrow. Will you close the door?'

He did, and she came to stand before him. 'I know you blame yourself for Declan's death. And it was a terrible accident. But your brother would not want you to go on living like this.'

'Ardan is dead, and so is Declan. I won't forget that it was my fault.' There was a stony resolution in his voice, the wariness of a man who would not forgive himself.

'No, you won't ever forget,' Joan said softly. 'But you can go on with your life and honour their memory.' She reached out to take his warm hands, trying to gather her courage. There was another reason for bringing him here. She wanted to reassure him that she would stand by him even as he went into battle.

She pulled the ribbons from her hair and let the braids fall free. His expression tightened at the sight, and she could tell that he wanted to leave her. And yet, he didn't move.

'I wanted you to know that I will keep my word. I will wed you in the morning, as I promised,' she told him.

'Will you?' His tone was soft, but with the barest hint that he didn't believe her. 'You said earlier that you were afraid I would die in battle. You refused to marry me because of the curse.'

She recognised his suspicions. He couldn't possibly understand why she had changed her mind, for they had not spoken since he'd revealed what had happened to his nephew.

'I know,' she murmured. 'But I was wrong to let my fears dictate my life.'

A hardness edged his face as he confronted her. 'Why did you ask me to come here, Joan?'

Her cheeks flushed, and she gazed downward. 'I thought you should know the reasons why I changed my mind.'

'Did you?' His voice was resonant and seductive. 'Or was there something else you wanted?' He slid his hands around her waist and drew her close. Her hips pressed against his, and her body immediately responded to the hard ridge of his arousal. Never had she forgotten the night she had seduced him, but there was an undercurrent beneath his behaviour that she didn't understand.

He was trying to drive her away, possibly to frighten her. But she knew that Ronan would not hurt her, no matter what he might say.

His hands moved to her hips, and her breath shuddered as he moved against her. 'You believe the curse will fall upon me in battle, and I will die. But before I leave, you intend to steal a child from me.'

'No.' Her face constricted, and she stepped back from him in shock. 'That wasn't my reason at all. I only wanted to talk to you. We've barely spoken since you told me about your brother and nephew.'

'I don't need your pity, Joan.'

Nothing could be further from the truth. 'It wasn't pity, Ronan.' She swallowed back her tears, not knowing how to dispel his anger. 'I care about you. And the reason I refused to wed you earlier was because I thought if I left you alone, you would live.' She fought to keep control of her emotions. 'I couldn't stand back and let the curse fall upon you, Ronan. I watched three of my suitors perish. I couldn't endure it again.' This time, the tears did fall, and misery cloaked her. 'Not with you.'

'You have more faith in that curse than you do in me.'

'I've lived with it for so long,' she said wearily. 'I was only trying to protect you.'

He stepped back and rested one hand against the wall. 'I don't need protection from a curse that doesn't exist.'

But then she sighed and raised her chin. It was time that he heard her own confession and learned the truth. 'I was seventeen years old when my father betrothed me to Sir Robert Fitzkellen. He was a warrior, like you.' A half-smile faltered at her mouth. 'I was so young and full of dreams. I never imagined they would bring his broken body to me. He was killed in battle.'

His expression remained steady, but he said nothing.

'I hardly knew him,' she admitted, 'but I wept for the life I thought we would have together. He was a good man with a kind smile.' And though they were strangers to one another, she had grieved for him.

'What of the others?' he asked.

She clasped her hands together. 'The second died of illness. I didn't know him either. But after each man died, it took away a piece of my spirit. I felt responsible somehow, even though I know I couldn't have changed it.'

Joan smoothed the edges of her white skirts. 'I know I must seem foolish to you. Always wearing white. Behaving like a woman afraid of evil spirits. But how else do I fight against an enemy I cannot see?' Her voice seemed to catch in her throat. She didn't know what to say or how to make him understand the truth. 'We will be married in the morning,' she said slowly. 'I have said I will do this, for I am trying to put the curse behind me.'

'But you still want a child.'

She nodded, unable to deny it. 'I will wait, if I must.'

'Do not wait on me,' he said. 'It will never happen.'

The coldness in his voice was borne of tragedy, and she steeled herself against it. He had not forgiven himself for the loss and was trying to push her away. The pain caught in her gut, twisting deeply.

'If you do not want me as your wife, then say so,' she told him. 'I would never force myself upon you.'

In the dim light of the candle, she saw the shadow of his loss and grief. He reached out to trace the outline of her face. 'I shouldn't want you as my wife.'

There was a darkness in his voice, but his hand moved down her throat and he cupped her face. 'But I crave you every moment of every day.' He let his hands move to her waist, and her skin erupted in sensation.

'You weaken me with every breath.' He bent to kiss her, his mouth stealing a taste of her. She rested her hands upon his shoulders, not knowing what to say or do. 'And I would kill any man who tried to take you from me.'

Never in her life had anyone looked at her the way Ronan did. And she couldn't have stopped herself from kissing him if she'd tried.

Chapter Seven

Joan tasted the salt of her own tears as Ronan's mouth covered hers. She wound her arms around his neck, welcoming the hard length of his body as he pulled her to stand before him. His heated mouth tempted her, and she yielded, opening to him as his tongue traced her lips. When he entered her mouth, her fingers dug into his hair.

He's going to die, her mind warned. *Just like all the others. You cannot stop it.*

But she refused to listen to the echoes of past fears. And it was that determination that drove her, pushing back the boundaries between them. She needed this night with Ronan. For these last few hours, she wanted to feel whole instead of the shell of a woman.

'You are going to wed me on the morrow,' she commanded as she drew his fingers to the laces of her bliaud. 'Swear it.'

'I will wed you on the morrow. This I swear.' He fumbled with the tunic he wore and lifted it over his head, baring his skin to her. Then he slid her gown over her shoulders, exposing her shift. For a moment, he stared at her, as if memorising every curve. 'But when we lie together, I will only pleasure you. There can be no child.'

A tremor caught her heart deep within, but it was all he could give. For now, it would have to be enough.

Joan met his penetrating gaze while she let the shift fall to the floor. The cool night air brushed against her bare skin, and she was conscious of the unspoken desire rising between them.

'You're beautiful, Joan.' Then he bent to her throat and kissed the pulse point. Gooseflesh rose over her body, and she drew him to her. She wasn't afraid of Ronan after the first forbidden night she had offered herself to him—only of what would happen when he left her.

The wooden cross he'd carved hung between her breasts, and he reached out to it. Ronan brushed the erect tip of one nipple, then the other. Sensation flooded through her, echoing between her legs. She took a deep breath, trying to gain command of herself.

Ronan removed the carved necklace from her throat and drew her to lie back on the bed. The coverlet was soft beneath her bare skin, and for a moment, she felt the rise of nerves. He commanded, 'Close your eyes, Joan.'

She obeyed and felt the gentle touch of his hands upon her skin. Her body grew more sensitive, and when he drew his palms lower, her nipples tightened. His knuckles brushed over one breast, then the other. He slowed down, circling her curves. The erotic sensation made her grow moist between her legs, and when he rubbed his thumb over her nipple, she gripped the coverlet and arched against him. He did the same to her other breast, and lingered upon the cockled tip for a moment.

It was an exquisite torture, and she felt her body tremble as he drew his hand down her legs and at last between them. Though he did nothing more than touch her mound with his palm, she felt the rising of her own arousal. This man was the only one she had ever desired. Never would she allow anything to happen to him.

When he stopped, she sat up and opened her eyes. Her body felt alive, and she rose from the bed. 'Let me touch you, Ronan.'

He removed the rest of his clothing, letting it fall to the floor. Her skin warmed at the sight of his erect shaft. He captivated her with his hard lines and his body.

'Lie down upon the bed,' she whispered. 'Close your eyes.'

He did, and she drank her fill of his muscular form. Slowly, she drew her hands over his throat and down his taut pectoral muscles. His fists tightened at his sides, and she caressed his arms, watching for his response.

He was so rigid, holding himself so tightly, she wondered if this bothered him. When she drew her hands over his stomach and arousal, he flinched. His green eyes opened, and she froze at the carnal heat in his expression.

Ronan grasped her by the waist and laid her back upon the bed. His hands moved over her bottom, grasping her hips. On instinct, she parted her legs, and he moved his hand between them. She inhaled sharply when his fingers caressed the wetness there. It conjured up the fierce memory of the first time he had pleasured her. And she closed her eyes, feeling the familiar ache of desire.

But this time, she did not want to be the only one feeling this way. She needed to share it with Ronan, to make him feel the same way she did. And so she grasped his hips, tracing the hardened muscle. She drew her hand slowly to his shaft and then took him in her hand. His smooth skin was rigid, and when she grasped him, he froze.

'Joan, you—' His words broke off when she stroked upwards. The slick head of him intrigued her, and she rubbed her thumb there, watching as his face tightened.

In silent answer, he slid a finger inside her moist depths, stroking her in the same way. Her knees nearly buckled, and she held on to his waist with one arm, still keeping her hand upon his erection.

Ronan lay on his side upon the bed and faced her. He lifted her hip over his and continued to stroke her. She squeezed him gently and drew her palm up and then down against his shaft.

'My God, that feels good,' he murmured. He slid another finger inside her but kept up the pressure of his thumb against her hooded flesh. She struggled to keep from moaning, but it was difficult to keep her control. He knew exactly how to touch her, how to draw out the swollen sensations burgeoning inside.

And then he lowered his mouth to her nipple. The pressure of his tongue suckling against her was too much to bear, and she did cry out. No longer could she concentrate on bringing him pleasure in the face of this. She arched as he stroked her with his hands between her legs and his mouth upon her breast.

Tremors built up inside, and she guided his manhood between them, to her wet opening. He slid against her entrance but went no further. Then, he kissed her other breast, and her fingers dug into his shoulders.

She looked into his eyes and saw the fervour of his gaze. 'I want you inside me, Ronan. Just as before.'

'Don't ask me for that.' Instead, he thrust against her, and the ridge of his erection made her gasp. He continued the rhythmic strokes until she cried out with her own delight. Even without him inside her, he was driving her towards the edge of fulfilment.

'Don't move, Joan,' he warned. He drew back enough to move his thumb back to the place of delicious torment. He stroked her, evoking the same familiar pleasure until her breathing grew unsteady, and she felt herself rising to his call.

'Touch your breasts,' he commanded.

She felt uncertain but obeyed, drawing her fingers over the sensitive wet tips. When she pinched them gently, she felt a surge of lust building within her. This time, Ronan thrust inside her with his fingers, and she felt the caress deep within her. She was shaking from the intensity, unable to think or breathe, as a shimmering sensation took root and grew.

Then suddenly, he grasped her hips and began to thrust against her, his shaft pressing upon the sensitive flesh. She felt his body where his fingers had been, and she quaked beneath him, lifting her knees. As he thrust, he captured her mouth, and she held him close, feeling the moment when her body surrendered, spasming around him. The sudden release made her wrap her legs around his waist, and he growled, seizing her hips.

'I'm sorry,' he gritted out.

She encircled his shaft with her palm, squeezing gently. He groaned as she moved her hand up and down in a relentless rhythm. He shuddered when his own pleasure came roaring upon him, and she revelled in watching him come apart, spilling his seed upon her stomach. He slid against her a few more times before he collapsed on top of her.

Her heart was racing, her body slick with perspiration. She held no regrets at all for this night with Ronan. There was a chance that he might not survive the battle at Clonagh, and she sent up a silent prayer to all the gods for his safety.

But even as he tucked her into his arms, drawing her into sleep, Joan could not push away the uneasiness of the danger that lay ahead of him.

In the early morning, Ronan was aware of Joan's presence in the bed. For the first time, he had slept deeply. It was as if her presence brought him peace, pushing away the nightmares of the past.

Though he had not intended to touch her, there was no denying the feelings she had evoked. God help him, he wanted her even now. He had lived with the jagged edges of suffering for so long, he hardly knew what it meant to feel this sense of contentment.

She had brought him here last night after signing the betrothal, wanting to talk to him. He knew she wanted a child desperately, and she'd said she was willing to wait. But like a bastard, he had cut her down and had sworn it would never happen.

Her face revealed her vulnerability, and he was struck with the realisation that he *wanted* to wed Joan. Though he did not deserve a woman like her, she had somehow drawn herself into his life.

He imagined Ardan's quiet smile and what he would think of Joan. His brother would have teased him about her, claiming that she was too virtuous to wed someone like Ronan. But he had a feeling Ardan would have liked her.

He had lived beneath the crushing weight of guilt for so long, he had not known peace. Not until this night. But he did not delude himself into thinking he could remain celibate with Joan. She haunted him, tempting him with the beautiful curves of her body and her smile.

God help him, he didn't know what to do. He was torn between desire and upholding his vow not to have children of his own.

He pushed back the turmoil of thoughts and concentrated on what would happen now. He would take back Clonagh and save his father. Only then could he put the past to rest. The thought centred him, giving him strength.

Joan awakened and sat up, holding the bedcovers to her body. 'You must go, Ronan. My maid will be here soon enough to prepare me for our wedding.'

He knew it and rose from the bed to fetch his discarded clothing. Once he was dressed, he turned back and saw her struggling with her own garments.

He went to help her with the bliaud. His hands lingered upon the laces, and he grazed the tip of her breasts with his knuckles. She gave a slight intake of air, but he held her waist a moment longer.

'I will leave for Clonagh immediately after our wedding celebration,' he said. 'I have delayed it far too long.' Once he had retaken the fortress, he could bring her back to live with him there.

'You don't have to avoid me, Ronan.' There was a fragile coolness in her voice, but he pushed past it.

'I am not avoiding you,' he corrected. 'I will send for you as soon as I can.'

Her face softened into a sad smile. 'Will you?' Her tone said she didn't believe him.

'When it is safe for you to join me,' he clarified. But he didn't know when that would be. He was trying to force his thoughts back to the battle plans and away from the alluring woman in front of him. He needed to turn his attention back to the Ó Callaghan tribe for they needed him the most.

'I will come for you,' he assured her. 'You belong to me now, Joan.'

At this moment, he wanted nothing more than to press her back into bed and love her again. Last night had bound them together, and he could never let her go.

'I pray to God that you will be safe,' she said, her eyes filling with tears. She drew him into her arms, holding him close.

The moment she kissed him, he felt the force of her need. Nothing in the world could have stopped him from touching her again, and the softness of her tongue was his undoing. He kissed her hard, threading his hands through her hair. Joan yielded sweetly, her body pressed close.

When he drew back, he said, 'I will see you at the wedding.' Then he kissed her once more before he departed.

The door closed behind him and Ronan walked down the narrow hall towards his own chamber. There was no turning back for either of them, but he wanted to wed Joan, despite all the risks. No longer was this marriage about acquiring soldiers for war. Instead, there was a greater purpose and a new life that awaited him.

He centred his focus on the first problem—winning back his father's throne. If he accomplished this task, it would restore his honour and offer redemption for the mistakes he had made.

And perhaps he would one day be worthy of siring a child.

* * *

'I expect you to uphold the bargain you made,' Joan told Rhys and Warrick. Though she believed her brothers would send soldiers to help Ronan, she wanted to ensure that the men accompanied him this day to Clonagh. The morning sky had cleared the clouds from the night before, and she had seen the faint outline of the moon disappearing as the sun rose.

Joan paled when she suddenly realised how much time had passed since she had been at Laochre. The sight of the moon unnerved her, for it reminded her that her woman's flow had not yet come. A sudden tremor of anticipation flooded through her with a hope so fierce, she could hardly bear it. She tried to tell herself that it was far too soon to know, but it gave her a reason to dream. It might not be real.

And yet…what if it were?

'We will uphold the terms of the betrothal, as long as you wed Ronan,' her brother said. His gaze narrowed upon her, and Joan forced her attention back to Rhys.

'I will marry him, as I have said. But he intends to leave for Clonagh after the wedding celebration.' She sent a pleading look towards Warrick. 'You must send all your men to accompany him.'

Her brother gave a nod. 'They will…but only after you speak your vows.'

'I have already said that I will.' But from the harsh expression on Rhys's face, she sensed there was something more that he had not said. Before she could ask anything further, Warrick's wife Rosamund approached.

'I will help you choose a gown and prepare for the wedding,' she offered. 'Will you come with me, Joan?'

She allowed the woman to lead her away, feeling uncertain about what lay ahead. When she was alone with Rosamund, she asked, 'Why is Rhys so angry?'

The young woman shook her head. 'You needn't worry, Joan. He will be satisfied once you are wedded.'

She was beginning to wonder if her brothers had learned that Ronan had come to her chamber and stayed all night. It was entirely possible. Her thoughts were distracted as she followed Rosamund down the hallway, but abruptly, she saw her brother's wife blanch and stop walking. For a moment, she remained in place and took a shaky breath.

'Are you all right, Rosamund?' Joan asked. 'Should I fetch Warrick?'

'No, no. I'll be fine. It was only a sudden pain.' She offered a weak smile and added, 'I never thought I would be pregnant again so soon. Neither of us expected it. And though I should be used to it after the twins, sometimes it hurts badly when the babe is stretching my skin.'

Rosamund took another deep breath and then began walking again. 'We will go and choose your gown now.'

'I will wear white, as I always do,' Joan said. Since Ronan was about to return to battle, she was taking no chances.

'Are you certain?' Rosamund asked. 'I have a red bliaud that would be lovely against your dark hair. Or perhaps a blue one?'

She shook her head. 'No colours.' At least, not until Ronan returned victorious from battle.

'What would you like prepared for your wedding feast?' Rosamund asked. 'I will give the orders now, and the cooks will arrange whatever you like.'

'Ronan intends to leave for Clonagh afterwards,' she said. 'I don't suppose it matters what we eat. Anything the men like will be good enough.'

Rosamund stopped at that. 'Joan, this is your wedding. It should be a celebration that you will remember for years to come.'

She understood that, but she also recognised that Ronan was feeling uneasy about it. And so, she admitted, 'A feast and a lively celebration would make Ronan feel uncomfortable. After all the tragedy his family has suffered, he blames himself.'

At that, Rosamund seemed to understand. 'And he will not stop until he has freed his father from captivity.'

'Yes. But we can have another celebration after he returns.' Joan followed Rosamund into the chamber where a steaming tub of water awaited her. The thought of a hot bath was wonderful, especially given the cold wintry air.

'I will arrange a simple feast, then,' Rosamund promised. 'And I think you will be pleased by it.' She promised to send a maid to help with her bath and departed the chamber, leaving Joan alone.

As she undressed and stepped into the tub, she tried to push back her fears. She would marry Ronan today, and they would be happy together.

She rested her hands upon her flat stomach, praying that it would be so.

Ronan stood within the courtyard, awaiting Joan. He had dressed in a borrowed tunic, and both Rhys and Warrick stood on either side of the stairs leading from the main keep. The people of Killalough had gathered together to witness the wedding, and there was an air of anticipation. The new chieftain, Bertach Ó Neill, had helped arrange the celebration.

The air was so cold, Ronan could see his breath forming clouds. The hard ground was frozen, and frost coated the grass. They waited longer, but there was still no sign of Joan. Warrick had promised that his wife Rosamund was assisting her with wedding preparations, but there was still the possibility that Joan was hesitant to wed.

A faint sound caught Ronan's attention, and he turned towards the guard tower, wondering what it was. A split second later, he heard the warning from the captain.

'To arms!' the man shouted.

Ronan echoed the command to Warrick's soldiers, seizing a shield from one of the men and unsheathing his sword. He didn't know what the threat was, but he would help the men defend Killalough.

He was surprised to see the Norman soldiers spread out in even formations. Men with spears took the first line, while swordsmen took the second. It was clear that the men were well-trained and prepared to fight.

When one of the younger Irish boys seized a shield, Ronan grabbed him by the arm. 'Go and keep the women inside. Defend them, if need be.' The boy's eyes widened, but he nodded and hurried up the stairs.

Ronan didn't know what enemy they faced, but he joined with Warrick and Rhys. A dozen men surrounded the gates, preparing for the charge that would come. The men at the tower called out their enemy's position, and Ronan steeled himself for the fight ahead.

Chaos erupted from within when men emerged from one of the outbuildings. Beside him, Warrick uttered a curse. 'They didn't seal off the souterrain passage.'

They had no choice but to split their forces in half. 'Take the Norman soldiers to defend the gates,' Ronan ordered. 'Give me the Irishmen, and we'll push them back.'

Warrick agreed, and Ronan ordered the Ó Neills to join at his side. A gleam of white caught his eye, and he saw Joan standing at the doorway. Her hair was crowned with flowers, and terror filled her eyes. A moment later, the same boy Ronan had ordered to protect the woman pushed her back inside, closing the doors.

Thank God.

He could not risk anything happening to her or to Warrick's wife Rosamund. As he poured himself into the fight, he let his mind go still while his sword cut down the raiders. He didn't know any of the men, but he suspected they were Irish mercenaries—possibly hired by Odhran.

He lost all sense of time, and his muscles burned as he pushed back the enemy. This was supposed to be his wedding day to Joan, but instead, there was blood and violence. And when the last of the men had finally retreated, he saw Warrick and Rhys near one of the wounded assailants.

Ronan stepped forward to question the man. 'Why did you attack Killalough? Who sent you?'

The man spat out a mouth full of blood, clutching his wounded stomach. He had taken a sword to his gut, and there was no hope for him.

'You are going to die this day,' Ronan said quietly. 'Your wounds cannot heal, and you know it. The question is whether you want to end your suffering now or endure the pain.'

The man closed his eyes and then said, 'We were hired to weaken your forces.' He coughed again, and pleaded, 'End it. Please.'

Ronan rested the tip of his sword at the man's throat. 'Who hired you?'

'A man named Cearul.'

At Warrick's questioning look, Ronan shook his head. He didn't recognise the name, but like as not, the man had not given his true name.

'Tell the Normans to go back to England,' the dying man gasped. 'They have...no place here.' With that, he closed his eyes. Ronan attempted to question him further, but there was no answer. And so, he granted the prisoner mercy, ending his life in one swift stroke.

He joined Warrick and Rhys, helping to move the wounded men inside. It was clear that this had indeed been the men's goal—to wound, not to kill. He counted at least thirteen men who were wounded severely enough to be unable to fight and three others who had died.

'Do you think we have other enemies, beyond your stepbrother?' Rhys asked him.

Ronan shook his head. 'I still believe this is Odhran's doing. Or perhaps Eilis.' He didn't trust the queen at all, and she might have more power than he had anticipated. But attacking Killalough and wounding his soldiers was an act of war—one they could not deny.

'We will meet with Bertach and some of the others,' Warrick suggested. 'Tend the wounded, and decide what to do.' Their healer was already organising the Ó Neills, while several men carried the injured into a nearby outbuilding. Although none of the Norman soldiers had died, they would now have to delay their attack because so many of them were wounded.

'Though I regret to say this, we should wait another day or two for your wedding, out of respect for those who died. It would be ill luck to marry upon a day such as this,' Rhys replied. 'And Joan has enough fears, as it is.'

It was for that reason that Ronan had wanted to

have the wedding. She might be afraid of the curse once again.

They walked up the stairs and Warrick pounded on the door, demanding that they allow them entrance. Once they opened, Ronan was startled to see Joan and Rosamund with spears in their hands.

The moment she spied Warrick, Rosamund dropped her spear and ran into his arms. He held her close while she embraced him. Joan remained frozen in place, her face pale and afraid. But when Ronan took a single step towards her, she followed Rosamund's example and let the spear fall. He took her by the hand and guided her away from her brothers, knowing that she was holding her feelings together by a thread.

Without a word, he brought her up the spiral stairs that led to the second floor. The moment they were alone, she threw herself into his arms and held him, weeping softly. 'I have never been more angry in my entire life.'

Ronan wasn't quite certain what to make of that. When she pulled back, her face was red from crying, and she admitted, 'After all we have been through, I was so afraid. And when they *dared* to attack us on the day of our wedding, I was ready to join in the fight myself.'

Without waiting for an answer, she held him again, resting her face against his heart. And something shifted within him as he smoothed her hair back. 'We will marry a few days from now, Joan. Your brothers will arrange it.'

'No. It will be today.'

It was not what he was expecting, and he drew back. 'Rhys believes we should wait, out of respect for the dead.'

'I will no longer live in the shadow of fear,' she said. 'Delay the celebration if you must, but this day I will be your wife and put the past behind us, once and for always.'

In her sapphire eyes, he saw that she would not be dissuaded from this. And though he knew it was unwise, he understood her reasons. 'Are you certain this is what you want, Joan?'

'I am.' She squared her shoulders and offered a rueful smile. 'I did not wear all this wedding finery for naught. And neither did you. Will you speak with my brothers, or shall I?'

He took her hands in his. 'I will make the arrangements.'

Joan could not deny that she was afraid. Although she had made the decision to marry Ronan, there was no doubting the unrest on his face. His plans to invade Clonagh had been disrupted by the raid, and while he should have been pleased that she had agreed to the marriage, there was a shadow of discontent in his expression.

Her brothers, Warrick and Rhys, had arranged for a private wedding in a small chapel within the fortress. Rosamund held her twin babies, and Warrick and Rhys stood behind them, as if they were sentries on guard.

Joan held Ronan's hands and spoke her vows, but

she was deeply aware of the lingering tension of the earlier attack. Her bridegroom was distracted by the events of this day, and she wondered if she should have listened to him and delayed the ceremony.

But the truth was, she wanted to marry him. No, it wasn't the sort of wedding she had envisioned—in the aftermath of a battle—but she had no regrets about choosing Ronan. His strength and goodness attracted her, and she welcomed a union with this man.

The priest gave a short Mass after they were wedded, and when it was done, Ronan kissed her. The warmth of his mouth was fleeting, but it was a promise of something more. Her cheeks flushed at the brief touch.

Her brothers offered their good wishes, and Rosamund promised, 'We will enjoy a feast in a few days. I will see to it.'

Despite the circumstances of the wedding, Joan could not deny the feeling of joy rising within her. She was amused that her brothers were eyeing her new husband as if they didn't entirely trust him.

Rosamund then turned to Warrick. 'Shall we escort them to the bedding ceremony?'

Her brother nearly choked at the suggestion, and he shook his head. 'Forgive me, but that is something I have no desire to witness.'

Her cheeks flamed crimson, but Joan admitted to her brother, 'We...already consummated the betrothal.' It might have been weeks ago, but her brothers didn't need to know that.

Warrick turned murderous, but Ronan held his

ground. 'It matters not. We are wedded now, and the marriage cannot be undone.'

Before her brother could say a word, Rosamund put her hand in his. 'Good. Then there is no need for us to interrupt your wedding night.'

Ronan escorted Joan from the family chapel and was about to lead her to their chamber when she stopped him. 'Could we spend some time away from Killalough? It's still light outside. We could go riding.'

But he shook his head. 'After what happened earlier, it's not safe. There could still be men watching the fortress.'

'Oh.' Her mood dimmed at that. She wanted to lift his spirits, to find some way of celebrating this wedding together. An idea came to her, and she said, 'Would you come with me somewhere else? Inside the fortress, that is?' She took his hand in hers and led him towards the stairs. Ronan didn't seem particularly eager, but she had her own plans in mind.

Joan guided him through the Great Chamber and towards the doors leading outside. It was colder than she had anticipated, and a few sparse flakes of snow drifted downward, illuminated by the torches. She led him towards the kitchens and said, 'I thought we could have a small wedding feast.'

Ronan seemed somewhat confused but followed her inside. Joan asked the cook and the maids to leave them to dine alone, and they were met with knowing smiles.

'What would you like to eat?' she asked her new husband. When he shrugged, she said, 'I know what we should do. You can choose what you believe I would like to eat. I'll do the same for you.'

'If you wish.' He took a wooden bowl and started looking on the far side of the kitchen while she took the closer area. She thought about what she had seen him eat in the past and chose a selection of mutton and cheese. But when she opened a small wooden box, she found a delicate crust dotted with honey, crushed nuts, and spices. Carefully, she broke off four pieces of the honeyed cake and then turned to join him at the wooden table.

There was only one chair and one stool. Joan set down the food she'd chosen for him in front of the chair, and then pulled the stool beside him. To her surprise, when she sat, the stool was so low her forehead met the edge of the table. She eyed Ronan and grinned. 'Well, this won't make it easy to eat.'

In response, he pulled her to sit on his knee. 'You will sit here, *a stór*.' He held her with one arm while he offered her a piece of bread. It was soft with a crisp crust, and she broke off a piece for him.

'You're right, I do like bread.'

She gave him some of the roasted mutton, and when he gave her some of the meat, his thumb brushed against her mouth. And suddenly, the atmosphere shifted from one of dining together to a sensual moment. She grew aware of his hard thighs and the touch of his fingers against her mouth as he fed her a piece of salmon he had selected. She offered him some, but he shook his head. 'I don't like fish. I never have.'

She countered by giving him the honeyed cake. When her fingers were sticky, she licked one. Ronan's mouth lifted in a seductive smile as he took her fingers and licked off the rest of the honey.

Heat flooded through her, and she felt an aching emptiness between her legs. Her breasts grew uncomfortable against the silk of her bliaud, and she understood that she had begun a battle of her own. He turned her to straddle him, and his green eyes were dark with desire. Joan glanced at the door, uncertain of whether they might be interrupted by a servant.

'Have you…finished?' she managed to ask.

His hands moved up her bare legs to her bottom. He palmed her and squeezed gently. 'I've barely begun, Joan.'

She felt her body go liquid at his words, and he unlaced her bodice, his hot breath upon her skin. When she was bared to the waist, his hands moved to her inner thighs.

'Someone might walk in,' she whispered. But when his mouth fastened upon her nipple, she could think of nothing but the drowning sensation of him. 'We shouldn't do this here.'

'You belong to me now, Joan. And I will pleasure you whenever I want to.' With that, he slid two fingers inside her, stroking her intimately. There was a faint smile on his mouth. 'Do you want me to stop?'

'N-no.' Her fingers dug into his shoulders as he caressed her. 'But I want to return to our chamber.' The danger of discovery heightened with every moment, and she needed to be alone with him.

His green eyes were hooded with desire, and he lifted her into his arms. Though her gown was still undone, she managed to cover her breasts. He gave her his cloak, and she used it to hide herself while he took her away from the kitchens.

Ronan crossed the inner bailey and returned to the keep. Flurries of snow drifted down upon her, but she felt only the heat of desire for her husband.

When they reached the spiral stairs inside, Ronan lowered her to stand. Joan clutched the cloak around her as she hurried up towards their chamber.

The moment they were alone inside, he barred the door and took her in his arms, kissing her as if he could not get enough. The cloak fell to the floor, and he ripped the laces of her gown free, hurrying to take it off. She helped him remove his tunic and trews until at last he lifted her up and tossed her back on the bed, naked. A laugh caught in her throat, but it immediately quieted when she saw the intensity in his eyes.

'I am going to touch you all night long,' he swore. 'Until you can no longer bear it.'

He lowered his mouth to her bare breast to suckle her. She let out a gasp, feeling the molten heat of his mouth upon her. But this night, she intended to pleasure him, too. She reached down between them and palmed his erection, squeezing his length.

Ronan muttered beneath his breath in Irish, and she teased, 'Did you like that?'

In answer, he freed her other breast and tantalised her with his mouth. 'Did you?'

She fisted him gently and answered, 'Yes.'

It became a conquest of trying to drive each other past the edge. Though she was shaking from the force of her own arousal, she would not give in. Not until she had what she wanted.

She guided his rigid length to her entrance and held the tip of him there. 'Do you feel how badly I want you?'

The expression on his face was so tight, he seemed unable to bear it. 'You're so wet, Joan.'

'Come inside me,' she pleaded. 'I don't care if you spill your seed outside my body. But I need you to join with me.'

There was a moment of indecision on his face, and she kissed him. 'You need me as badly as I need you, Ronan. Join with me.'

The strain upon his body was so taut, she knew he was at the edge. Softly, she reached down and cupped him, stroking him.

With that, he thrust hard, filling her completely. She cried out with the shock of it, and her body trembled as he was deeply embedded. For a moment, he stayed there, not moving at all. But she arched her back, lifting her hips in small thrusts. She squeezed him within her depths, and he closed his eyes as if unable to bear the pleasure.

'You are mine, Ronan. As I am yours.'

At that, he began to withdraw and penetrate. The rhythm was slow and smooth, his thickness invading her fully. They did not speak of the impending battle nor of the risks ahead. For now, there was only the joining she had longed for.

'Joan,' he said roughly as he gripped her waist. She met his thrusts, embracing him within her depths as the echoes of pleasure rippled within her. Ronan took command and pulled her hips to the edge of the bed. He stood, holding her bottom as he entered and withdrew. The new position took him deeper, and a cry erupted from her throat as the white-hot pleasure seized her.

She felt every inch of him as he thrust, and her body shattered apart. But Ronan continued to penetrate, lifting her hips up. There was a desperation of a man well past the point of control. When she met his gaze, a sudden fear grasped her heart.

He was behaving like a man who did not expect to survive the war ahead. As if he were claiming the last moments with her before they disappeared for ever.

He continued to pump inside her until at last he growled and withdrew, spilling himself upon her belly. He collapsed beside her, and she held him close.

In a few days, he would leave her behind. But she could no longer stand back and let him go off to fight.

A premonition caught her with the fear that if she remained at Killalough, she would never see him again.

Chapter Eight

A sennight later

Although Ronan had hoped to leave sooner, he had to delay the battle because of the wounded men. Rhys and Warrick had convinced him to stay long enough for the men to heal, and they had promised to remain at Killalough to protect Joan. She had not been pleased about staying behind, but her brothers had given her no choice.

They had spent most of the day travelling towards Clonagh, and it gave Ronan time to think. He had sent word to Odhran that he wanted to meet to discuss the fate of Brodur. He hoped that somehow his father was still alive. Although Brodur had barely spoken to him after the death of Ardan, Ronan needed to make amends. Somehow, he had to free his father and restore him to the throne. But he could not do this until he knew what was happening within the fortress and where his people's loyalty lay.

It seemed as if his life had been turned inside out.

He had never intended to marry, and now he had a wife. Somehow Joan had woven her way into his life. She was not the shy, virtuous woman he'd envisioned. He'd expected her to be demure and quiet when they were alone. But she knew how to get beneath his skin, and only last night, she had awakened him with a kiss. She had aroused him in the dark, riding him hard until they were both sweaty and well pleasured.

His innocent wife had become sensual, and it was a physical ache to be apart from her. Each time he made love to her, it grew more difficult to stop himself from releasing inside her. Perhaps that was why she welcomed him into her arms every night, in the hopes that somehow a child would be conceived. Yet another part of him prayed it would never happen. He didn't know if he could watch her grow round with his child without remembering what had happened to his nephew.

Ronan forced the thoughts away when they reached the outskirts of Clonagh. There was a thin layer of snow on the ground, and several of his kinsmen guarded the gate. He spied others who were spaced at intervals around the walls. Although they held their weapons, they did not attack as Ronan drew closer. He had left most of the men encamped a few miles away while he travelled with only ten Norman soldiers. He intended it to seem as if he was here to negotiate for Brodur's release, not to attack. Right now, he needed to gather information and learn what had happened with the hostages.

As they rode within the gates, a heavy stillness

still cloaked the air. His intuition warned that women and children were imprisoned within these walls, but there was no proof. Yet, he could not deny the danger here, visible in the faces of the men who lined the pathway. Resentment was carved into their faces, as if they blamed him for this. And when he passed Darragh, his friend's face showed no emotion at all.

Ronan dismounted from his horse and gave it to a kinsmen, ordering the other men to do the same. He continued towards the centre of the fortress, surrounded on both sides by the armed Norman soldiers.

Odhran stood in front of his father's house with Eilis at his side. His stepbrother was clothed in a saffron silk tunic, and he wore a gold band around his forehead. His brown hair fell across his shoulders, and his beard was trimmed close to his face. The satisfaction on Odhran's face mirrored the queen's smug smile. Eilis appeared as if she was well pleased with the outcome of their rebellion.

Ronan continued to walk closer, though every muscle in his body was rigid with tension. It was a struggle to hide his hatred. Were it possible, he would have brought the Norman army here this very day, slaughtering his stepbrother and seizing the throne. But he could not do so until he knew the truth of what had happened here.

'Ronan,' the queen greeted him. 'I see you've come to accept your rightful king.'

He didn't even spare Eilis a glance. Instead, he stared hard at Odhran. 'Where is my father?'

Odhran paused, deliberately holding back an answer as he drew himself up to his full height. But Ronan still held the advantage of looking down on the man.

'He has gone into exile,' Odhran answered. 'I believe he travelled to Normandy.'

It was undoubtedly a lie. Ronan turned towards his people to see their response, but most had their heads lowered. It was Darragh who held his gaze a moment before his eyes flickered towards the hillside where hostages were kept. Ronan gave a faint nod towards his friend before he turned back to Odhran.

'And what if I don't believe you?'

His stepbrother shrugged. 'I care not what you believe. Your opinion holds no weight with me.'

'I am going to find him,' Ronan insisted.

'If you wish to travel to Normandy, do as you will. But do not return here. They do not want you.' Odhran gestured for two of the men to come forward. 'Your belongings are in this trunk. I give it to you freely as a sign that I mean only peace towards you, Brother.'

'We are not brothers.' Ronan's voice barely hid his rage. Then he turned towards his kinsmen. 'Do you truly want this man as your king?'

'We didn't want you,' came another voice. It was Darragh. The man reached out for the trunk and put it on his shoulders as he strode towards Ronan. It felt as if his friend had betrayed him in front of everyone, and it took an effort not to lash out.

'Take your belongings and go,' Darragh said loudly. 'We are content here, and Brodur is gone. There is nothing more for you.' When he reached Ronan's side, he muttered beneath his breath. 'I will meet you by the river later this night.'

Some of his tension dissipated, but Ronan gave no sign that he had heard the man. He took the trunk and handed it over to one of the Norman soldiers. Then he regarded Odhran. 'You will not remain king for long.' With that, he turned away but met Darragh's eyes briefly to show that he had understood the message.

At nightfall, he would have the answers he sought.

Ronan waited that night near the river as Darragh had asked. He knew his friend would not arrive until well after dark, and he ordered the remainder of his men to join them. They made camp by the water's edge, though he had forbidden them to build fires.

He held himself back from the Norman soldiers, setting up his tent on the outskirts. After they ate a cold meal of dried meat and bread, he retreated from the men. He dragged the trunk inside his tent, though he already knew what was inside: a few pieces of clothing, an extra pair of shoes, and most of his carving tools.

There was a block of wood that he'd begun to shape, with the barest hint of a face. He had never met his mother, and he had tried to envision her within the wood. Now, he found himself picking up the chisel and shaping it once again…only this time, it was Joan's face he carved.

He gripped the wood and fell into the familiar pattern of carving. The hours slipped away, and his hands were stiff, but he saw the clear image of his wife staring back at him in the wood. He would see her soon enough but wondered what news he would bring back to her.

She had slipped into his life seamlessly, and he could not deny that he was pleased with the marriage. Joan was steadfast and kind, fiercely loyal to those she loved. There was no doubt she would make an excellent queen for the Ó Callaghan people.

But it was his own capabilities that he questioned as a future king.

There came the sound of grass rustling outside his tent, and Ronan unsheathed a dagger as he stepped outside. When he saw Darragh standing with one of the Norman soldiers, he kept the blade in his hand.

'I am no threat to you,' his friend said by way of greeting. 'I am the one facing the greater risk.'

Ronan put down the dagger and gestured for the man to enter the tent and sit. He dismissed the Norman soldier and closed the flap behind him. Then he opened by asking Darragh, 'What happened at Clonagh?'

Darragh waited a moment and then said, 'Queen Eilis hired mercenaries to attack and imprison Brodur. After you left, those mercenaries seized nine of the tribe's children. My son Ailan was one of them.'

There was worry and anguish upon the man's face, and now, it became clear what Odhran's strategy was. By taking children as hostages, he had effectively imprisoned both parents.

'After they took the children, my cousin Leena

tried to save her daughter.' He closed his eyes, and his fists clenched. The familiar mask of grief washed over him, and he shook his head. 'They killed her as an example to all of us.'

It was far worse than Ronan could ever have imagined. To slaughter a mother attempting to save her child was an act of savagery. He didn't want to voice the question, but he had to know. 'And the child?'

Darragh lifted his gaze and stared hard at him. 'They slit her throat in front of everyone.'

Ronan expelled a curse. By the blood of Danu, he could hardly grasp such a thing. It was one matter to kill men in battle—but this went beyond anything he could envision.

'Not one of us will lift a hand against Odhran,' Darragh continued. 'We cannot risk the lives of our own children. And any man who would murder a little girl has no soul.'

'I am sorry,' Ronan answered. 'I swear to you, I will find a way to free them. No matter what happens.'

'I want to believe you,' his friend said slowly. 'But know this—we will do nothing to endanger the children. He keeps them close, in your father's house.'

'I need to know everything about his defences and the mercenaries among you,' Ronan insisted. 'Most of all, I need to know what he has done with my father.'

'The king is in chains,' Darragh said. 'No one can save him.'

'Where is he being held?'

'Underground, in the souterrain passage.' His

friend's face turned grim. 'He cannot survive for much longer. Not when the ground below is frozen.'

Ronan didn't know what to think of that, but time was running out. He needed to gather a larger army and impose a strategic attack. This had to be a swift, silent strike with no mistakes; else, the mercenaries would kill the children. It seemed wise to consult Rhys and Warrick, he decided. He could be back at Killalough by the following night.

His emotions tightened within him as he envisioned seeing his wife again. Though it had only been a short time apart, he missed Joan. It took an effort to force his thoughts back to the present.

'I need to bring back more men,' he said. 'Will you join us?'

Darragh shook his head. 'My place is here, for I cannot leave my wife unguarded. And I have to be there if there is any chance of freeing Ailan.'

'I will return within two days,' Ronan promised. 'And when I do, I vow, we will free the children first.' By breaking Odhran's hold upon the people, it would enable them to join in the fight.

'I hope to God we succeed,' Darragh said. 'We can't go on like this.'

'You won't have to.'

After the man had gone, Ronan picked up the wood carving tools to put them back in the trunk. To his surprise, he saw his father's ring inside. He didn't know how it had come to be there, but he slid it on to his finger.

Darragh had warned that Brodur was dying, imprisoned within a freezing chamber. The battle ahead would be fierce, and Ronan knew that the people would die fighting for their children…just as Ardan had.

A numbness settled within him, and there was no way to know if he could succeed in this. There was a very real possibility that he could die fighting for his people, just as Joan had feared.

He wished he could return to her, to steal every last moment in her arms. But if the worst came to pass, at least he would know that he had done everything he could to redeem himself for the sins of the past.

Joan awakened at night, feeling a rush of terror. Though it had been only a few days since Ronan had left, she had barely slept during that time. Her body seemed to be raging as if with a fever, and then the next moment, she was cold.

When she complained to Rosamund after breaking her fast, the woman only smiled softly. 'That happened to me when I was with child,' she said. 'I found that I was hot and cold all the time during the first few weeks. Of course, it's entirely too soon for that to be true for you.' But though she spoke in teasing, Joan had to turn away to hide her blush. For she *had* lain with Ronan several weeks ago.

Although he didn't want a child, she couldn't dispel the prayer that it could be true. Her courses still had not come, and it was possible that she had conceived on that first night she had offered herself to Ronan. He would be angry, but if it was true, she could only hope that one day he would forgive her and learn to love the baby.

She turned back to Rosamund and ventured, 'I had always heard that women felt sick during the early months.'

'Sometimes,' the woman agreed. 'But for this child, I did not feel sick until later. Some lucky women are never sick. You might be one of them.'

At this moment, Joan wouldn't care if she were sick every day. She could only hold fast to the fervent hope.

She followed Rosamund out of the Great Chamber, and up the spiral stairs to the solar. A fire was lit in the hearth, and Joan moved away from it, fanning herself with one hand. Though Rosamund sat and picked up her embroidery, Joan found herself feeling restless. 'I wish I knew what was happening at Clonagh.'

Rosamund drew her needle through a length of linen. 'Your husband will return soon, Joan.'

'And what if he doesn't? What if they took him captive?' Uncertainty wove threads of fear within her mind. She began to pace across the room, trying to calm her fears. Though Ronan had sworn he only meant to meet with his stepbrother and learn the fate of his father, she knew not if Odhran would uphold the peaceful negotiation.

Joan walked towards the window to stare at the falling snow outside. It was nearly Yuletide, and some of the women were carrying branches of holly and fir to decorate the keep. She rested her hand against her flat stomach, wondering if next year she would be holding her own child. *Please, let it be so. And let Ronan not be angry.*

She started to turn away from the window when she heard the familiar sound of approaching horses. Her heart gave a leap when she saw the men riding through the gates. She strained for a glimpse of Ronan, but it was too difficult to tell if he was there. Her brothers were already talking to some of the men, but she needed to know if her husband was all right.

'I think the men have returned,' Joan said, hurrying from the room. When she reached the spiral stairs, she slowed her pace only slightly. She crossed through the Great Chamber and pushed the doors open outside.

Joan started to run down the stairs, but her footing slipped on the snow, and she lost her balance near the bottom. Strong arms caught her before she could hit the ground. When she steadied herself, she looked into the eyes of her husband and felt a surge of relief. *Thank God.*

'Are you all right?' Ronan asked.

Joan threw herself into his arms, holding him close as she blinked back tears. 'I am so glad you're home.'

'As am I.' He took her arm in his and walked with her up the stairs. 'I would be glad of a hot meal, and then I will tell you what we've learned.'

'Were you successful in retaking Clonagh? And is your father alive?'

A tension passed over him. 'We are returning on the morrow, once I have spoken with your brothers about our strategy. My father is alive, but he can-

not last much longer where he is imprisoned underground.'

She tried to shield herself from the familiar fear,
telling herself that Ronan would have all the soldiers
he needed. But there was always danger within a battle. Every man risked his life, and her husband would
be no different. Yet, once again, he had survived the
danger, and she took comfort that he had returned to
safety. The curse, if there had ever been one, must
be over.

'How many mercenaries are still there?' she asked.

'At least a dozen that I counted. Perhaps more. But
they have another means of controlling our people—
they have their children as captives.' He told her of
what he'd learned, and her heart sank. If Odhran had
already killed one child, none of the parents would do
anything to risk the life of their own son or daughter.

'What will you do?'

'We'll have to initiate a surprise attack. But Odhran
will be expecting it, after our last meeting. The only
way to save my father and the children is if we can
slip in without anyone noticing.'

Which was impossible with an army of men. Joan
led him inside the keep towards the Great Chamber
where her brothers were waiting. 'You need the help
of your people inside the ringfort, Ronan. They could
keep Odhran's men away while you rescue the children and your father.'

He nodded. 'And when they are safely out, we attack.' She reached out to take his hand, caressing it

with her thumb. He squeezed her palm. 'It will be all right, Joan. I don't intend to die.'

'No one ever does,' she whispered.

That night Ronan lay naked with Joan in his arms, but she seemed quieter than usual. When he asked her about it, she said, 'I worry for your safety and that of your men when you return to Clonagh.'

'It will be dangerous,' he agreed, 'but Darragh will help us. If it means helping his son escape, I have no doubt he will do everything in his power to ensure that we succeed.'

'Odhran will be expecting you,' she said. 'And I know men might die during the attack. I just don't want you to be one of them.'

'I will be careful,' he swore. He kissed her, and she clung to him with more fervour than usual. Even when she embraced him, he sensed that there was something more, something bothering her.

'Good,' she murmured, falling into silence once more.

'What is it, Joan?' he asked. He had no doubt that she was deeply troubled by something. Surely, she had set her fears of the curse aside by now.

But Joan took his hand and brought it to her flat stomach. She held it there a moment, staring into his eyes. 'It's something else. Or perhaps, *someone* else.'

His mind spun with the implications, and a coldness gripped him. Denial rose to his lips. 'Joan, I don't think—'

But she rested her hand atop his. 'In twelve years,

my courses have always come when I expected them to. This was the first time they have not.'

He couldn't bring himself to speak. If it were true, it must have happened the first time they had lain together. He had been so caught up in her, seduced by that forbidden night, that he had shut out the consequences. Though he had known there was a risk of her becoming pregnant, he had wanted to believe that it hadn't happened.

'Ronan?' she prompted gently.

Panic boiled within him, and he hardly knew what to say except, 'How do you feel?'

'Nervous. Overjoyed. Terrified.' She smiled. 'Everything.' She drew her arms around his neck. 'It will be months yet before we know for certain. But this is what I've wanted all my life. And to think that this precious gift may be growing inside me—' Her voice broke off, and her eyes filled with tears. 'I know it's not what you wanted. But if this has come to pass, I pray you can one day accept it and find joy in our child.'

He held her, though his own response was a raw fear. No other emotions were possible right now.

'Will you not say something?' she whispered. He could hear the heartache in her voice, for she wanted him to share in her happiness. But all he could feel was a soul-wrenching sense that his worst fears had come to pass. He had already lost his nephew. Was he now meant to pay an even greater price?

'What do you want me to say?' The words came out bleaker than he'd intended.

She pulled back her arms from his neck, retreating. He knew he had cut her down, but his throat had closed off from anything else. It was fear that suffocated him, fear that Fate would punish him even more.

'You don't want it to be true, do you?' she whispered.

I don't deserve to be a father. But again, he could only remain silent. He could not lie to her and say that he was happy. When she continued to wait for an answer, at last he said, 'There is no man less suited to being a father than I. But what I want doesn't matter now, if you are with child.'

He heard a shuddering sigh in the darkness, as if she were crying. The sound pierced through him, reminding him that he was behaving like a bastard. He wanted to apologise, not wanting to hurt her feelings. But the thought of being a father numbed him with the chilling fear that he would never be good enough for them. Though it might already be too late, he didn't want to sire a child.

'I thought…in time, you might change your mind.' Her voice was broken, revealing the invisible wounds.

He couldn't. The death of Declan and his brother would haunt him until the day he died. He deserved no happiness of his own—not when he had destroyed the lives of the people he loved.

For a time, Joan lay on her side with her back to him. He longed to comfort her, but there were no right words to say. At last, she murmured, 'You must be careful when you fight at Clonagh. Come back to us.'

The stone of doubt weighed heavily upon him. And

this time, when he faced her, he admitted, 'You will make a good mother, Joan. Even if I don't return.' He drew his hand over her face and kissed her lightly.

He expected her to kiss him back and was fully unprepared for her anger. 'Don't even speak of it, Ronan. Don't even think of giving up. You must return.'

'I will try.' He rolled over and stared up at the ceiling.

Joan turned away from him, curling into a ball. He closed his eyes, knowing that he'd hurt her. He hated the thought of making Joan weep, but this wound was too deep and would never heal. If she was expecting a child, it was far better that she not rely on him. She didn't understand the hole inside him or that he would shoulder the guilt for ever.

She was waiting for him to speak, but he could only stare at the opposite wall. Better that she should hate him than to hold any feelings for him. He didn't want her to love a man like him.

He had failed so many people in the past year. And he knew not whether he could save Clonagh or be the right man for her. Failure lurked in the shadows, and he dared not reach for a happiness he didn't deserve.

Chapter Nine

Ronan and her brothers left at dawn with more men, but Joan could not relinquish the premonition that her husband would not return. She was restless all day, trying to take her mind off the invasion. Worse, every time she thought of his reaction to the possible baby, her eyes teared up. He had grown so distant last night. She had hoped that Ronan could put aside his past and share in her hopes, but instead, he had closed off his emotions. It hurt more deeply than she could have imagined, for he had every right to blame her. She could only hope that she wouldn't lose him.

Did he truly believe he wasn't coming back? Was he planning to sacrifice himself during this invasion, for the sake of his people? Horror filled her at the thought. But she knew how deeply the guilt ground against his conscience. He blamed himself for all of it. And the thought of waiting here for soldiers to bring back his broken body was too much to bear.

She had married Ronan because he had become her friend and because she had wanted to protect him. But now, there was so much more at stake. She had fallen in love with this man. She wanted to awaken beside Ronan and see affection in his gaze. She wanted him to share a life with her and to love her in return.

Joan refused to stand by and let him be martyred—not when she could gather forces from another tribe to help him. She caught sight of Rosamund's maid and ordered the woman to pack her belongings. She had no intention of interfering with the men's battle plans—she would stay far away from the fighting. But she intended to seek help from the MacEgans. They had sent men earlier, and now she would ask them for more forces. Yet, it would take time for a messenger to send word and for them to arrive at Clonagh.

She found Rosamund inside the keep. The woman was consulting with their new chieftain, Bertach. 'They should arrive by nightfall, but you will need to make room among your quarters.'

Joan came closer and asked quietly, 'Who will arrive by nightfall?'

'The MacEgan soldiers.'

At her surprised look, Rosamund added, 'I sent for them a sennight ago. You are not the only one whose husband is in danger.'

Joan was so relieved to hear that they had both come to the same conclusion about needing more soldiers. 'Do our men know about this?'

Rosamund shook her head. 'They are too proud to admit they could use more help. Queen Isabel promised me that if we ever needed more men, she would send them.' She studied the keep and added, 'The MacEgans can provide a distraction that will keep our husbands alive.'

The thought reassured her, but Joan still had no wish to remain behind. She needed to see Ronan with her own eyes when the battle was finished.

And when he had succeeded in saving his people, only then could she look towards building a life with him.

They approached Clonagh in the middle of the night. Ronan sent two men inside the fortress to unseal the underground souterrain passageway where his father was being held prisoner. Once the passageway was open, they could silently free the captives.

Rhys and Warrick had joined him, and each man took command of twenty-five other soldiers. Torches flared against the night sky, set in even intervals around the fortress. Ronan steeled himself for the battle ahead, gripping his shield in one hand. Time seemed to slow, and they waited for long moments by the souterrain passage before there was any movement at all.

Finally, Ronan pushed back the shrubbery, and he saw the stone moving away from the passage. It could only be unsealed from the inside, and he held his hand upon his sword until he recognised the faces of his men.

But his father was not among them.

'There was no one inside,' a soldier said. 'No sign of anyone at all.'

They had moved the prisoners, then. Ronan stepped inside the souterrain passage and motioned for six other men to join him. In a low voice, he commanded, 'The rest of you should encircle the fortress. I will give a signal and then you will attack.'

Rhys hesitated. 'If you only have six men inside, they could kill you before you can raise a signal.'

He knew the risk, but more men would draw greater attention. 'What do you suggest?'

'We could cause a distraction with twenty men near the front gates. Then you would have time to contact Darragh and find out where the prisoners were moved.'

It wasn't a bad suggestion, except that it would draw the greatest retaliation to those men. 'It's a grave risk,' he said. 'All of Odhran's forces would be directed there.'

'For a short time,' Rhys said. 'When your men are in place, we can attack from both within and without. But you must make haste.'

'Do not kill any of my kinsmen unless they directly attack,' Ronan ordered. 'I am trying to save them and their children.'

Rhys nodded and chose twenty men to accompany him. They moved towards the front gates while Ronan took his men inside the fortress. The tunnel was cold, the walls lined with stone. They did not light a torch for fear of being discovered. Instead, each man rested a hand on the shoulder of the one in front of him, with Ronan leading the way. When he reached the ladder, he climbed up, followed by each of his men. Inside the roundhouse, he saw a woman approaching the doorway. Her eyes widened at the sight of him.

'Where are the children?' Ronan demanded. 'We've come to get them back.'

'Odhran keeps them captive within his home,' she whispered.

He started to move towards the door, but she caught his shoulder, 'He knows you've come, Ronan. Be careful.'

'Where is my father?' he demanded.

'They moved King Brodur, but we don't know where they took him.'

And then he understood what Odhran had planned—a choice between saving his father or saving the children. If he chose the king, the people would turn against him for not protecting their offspring. If he chose the children, he would be responsible for his father's death.

It was an impossible decision, one he never wanted to make. But he knew what his father would want—for him to choose the future of their clan over a single man's life. A shadowed sorrow flooded through him with regret.

When the last of the men had climbed up the ladder, Ronan directed them to prepare for the fight. All they had was the element of surprise. It was the best they could hope for.

And if there was any means of saving both the

children and the king, he would do everything in his power to make it happen.

It was still dark when Joan rode alongside the MacEgan soldiers, her nerves fraught with anxiety. They had arrived near Clonagh at eventide, just as Rosamund had predicted. She was so grateful that her brother's wife had sent for the men.

'You shouldn't be here, my lady,' Ewan MacEgan told her. 'It's too dangerous.'

'I don't intend to go near the ringfort,' she said, 'but I need to know if my husband is safe.'

'She can wait with Aileen until the battle is over,' a male voice interrupted. Joan saw Connor MacEgan approaching on horseback with his wife and more soldiers. 'We will need help with any wounded men.'

Aileen drew her horse closer and dismounted. She had several baskets of supplies tied to the mare, and she greeted Joan with a smile. Joan inclined her head and returned a smile she didn't feel. Her heart was tangled up with worry.

'I didn't need you to take command,' Ewan said to his older brother.

'I've been fighting longer than you.' Connor flicked the reins of his horse and walked alongside him. Though Joan knew he was only being an over-protective brother, he was also undermining Ewan's authority. The adolescent was not tall, but he had clear strength and a stubborn quality about him.

Connor left four guards with them, and the men began setting up two tents for any wounded men who might be brought back. Aileen began untying her baskets from the mare. Joan helped her bring them inside the first tent. It felt awkward because she could not speak with the young woman, and more than once, she wished she knew the Irish language.

The healer built a small fire outside the tent and set out a pot to boil water. She brought out two wooden cups and added chamomile and mint to both. When the water was hot, she ladled it over the herbs to steep.

'Thank you,' Joan said when she took the cup of tea from Aileen. In truth, it felt good to sit down for a time. She had been feeling dizzy this morn, and her body ached as if her courses were about to start. Without thinking, she rested her hand upon her womb, to alleviate the pain.

Aileen studied her a moment, a slight smile on her face. Then with a questioning look, she rested her hand upon her own womb and asked a question in Irish.

Joan did not hide her smile and nodded. Aileen brightened and returned the smile, offering more words that sounded congratulatory. Then the healer busied herself, preparing for the wounded. She lit an oil lamp and placed it inside the tent while she set up her supplies.

Joan stood and helped Aileen sort through bandages. It felt good to be useful, and it helped keep her mind off the aching pain in her middle. As they worked together, Joan took a mortar and pestle to grind other herbs into medicines. Aileen pointed to different objects and began teaching her the names in Irish. In return, she gave Aileen the Norman words.

The darkness began to fade, bringing the faint crease of dawn on the horizon. But instead of bringing a rise of hope for Ronan's return, Joan's nerves only tightened. She prayed that her husband would be safe, especially with so many men to fight alongside him. But she hated the feeling of helplessness, for there was nothing she could do now.

A sudden pain struck her abdomen, and she inhaled sharply, resting her hand across her womb. It hurt so badly, dizziness washed over her, and she let out a slow breath.

Though she tried to hide it, a ringing sound filled her ears and the dizzy feeling grew stronger. She closed her eyes to steady herself, and when she opened them at last, she saw Aileen's concern.

'I'm all right,' she said, even knowing the woman would not understand her.

But then a sudden twisting pain struck hard, and she gasped, pressing her hand to the area. Aileen was at her side immediately, and her expression blanched.

Joan was so afraid, she could hardly bear it. It was indeed possible that she was in danger of miscarrying this child. Aileen helped her inside the tent and helped her lie back on the ground. The healer lightly pressed a hand to Joan's stomach in silent question.

Tears welled up and spilled on to her cheeks. 'I'm afraid,' she admitted. 'I don't want to lose my child.'

Aileen held her hand and brought over a small pillow which she placed under Joan's hips, elevating them. Then she drew Joan's feet atop a stone, as if to hold the unborn child in place. If only it were as simple as that.

God help her, what would happen when she had to stand again? The aching had not receded at all, and she could not remain like this all day. Panic snared her senses, and she rested her hands upon her swollen womb, as if she could calm the babe and keep it within her.

Aileen gathered other herbs, blending them into another type of tea. She gave Joan the new cup and bade her drink the hot liquid. She obeyed without question, though a part of her was desperately afraid. Her hands moved to grip the wooden cross Ronan had carved, as if she could draw courage from it. She prayed for the child and for his safety. Somehow, Ronan had to come home to her.

Aileen beckoned to one of the Irishmen and spoke with him, giving an order. Joan wasn't certain what it was, but the man hurried away, retracing the steps the other soldiers had taken. Perhaps he had gone to tell Connor, but Joan didn't want any distractions to interfere with Ronan's battle plans.

She wished Aileen had said nothing at all. But she could not dwell upon it, for at the moment, it felt as if someone were trying to split her skin apart.

Please let the baby be all right, she prayed. She was fully aware that this could be the last and only child she ever bore. Though she likely should not have come this far from Killalough, Ronan had needed the MacEgan men. She had to do everything in her power to help him.

She steadied her breathing, feeling such fear, it nearly consumed her. Over and over, Joan told herself that it would be all right. She only had to have faith.

But when she looked down, she saw the blood.

Chapter Ten

The soldiers moved with stealth through the fortress. Ronan kept searching for a sign of Darragh, but his friend was nowhere to be found. One of the women spied him, and her expression transformed into alarm. Ronan raised a finger to his lips and she remained silent. Slowly, he lowered his weapon and approached.

'Tell our kinsmen that they will not face any threat from us. We are here to free the prisoners, nothing more. Spread the word among the others that they must not attack.'

The woman's eyes filled up with tears, and she nodded as Ronan moved back into the shadows. He pointed towards the main dwelling and said, 'We will split our group and surround my father's house.'

But the soldier shook his head. 'It feels like a trap,' he muttered beneath his breath. 'They may be waiting for us inside.'

Though it was possible, Ronan saw no other choice but to encircle the structure. If the children were free, then his people would join him in overthrowing Odhran—he was sure of it.

He motioned for the men to split and move into position. 'Wait for the signal from outside the gates. When they sound the alarm, we move in.'

In the darkness, they kept near to the shadows of the outer wall. The bitterness of the night air was freezing, but Ronan felt none of the chill. Instead, he waited in silence.

He knew the dangers that lay in wait and there was no question Odhran wanted him dead. Ronan wasn't afraid to meet his own death, but he needed to free the prisoners first. It felt as if Fate had given him a second chance to redeem himself for losing Declan. If he returned the children to their parents, it would atone for his sins. And he might be able to reconcile himself to a new future with Joan. A sudden pang struck his heart as he thought of the child. It was too soon to know, but if he survived this battle, he wanted to be a man of worth. Someone his son or daughter would be proud of.

As he moved forward, he couldn't deny the soldier's premonition that something didn't feel right. It was entirely too quiet. Even if his own kinsmen had held back from attacking, the mercenaries would not. There was no sign of them anywhere.

There should have been an alarm sounded by now, for surely someone must have seen them. Or at the very least, Darragh would have received word and joined him in the fight.

Yet an unnatural silence stretched over the fortress, shrouding it in foreboding. Ronan waited for what seemed like an eternity, but there was still no signal from the main gates. Had Rhys and Warrick been harmed in some way? Why had they not created the distraction as promised?

The cold encircled them, and Ronan noticed the underlying tension among his men. Whether it was the icy weather or uneasiness, he could not say. The dozen soldiers remained in formation, hidden in the darkness surrounding his father's dwelling.

When the first reddish tints of dawn creased the sky, Ronan finally heard the roar of an attack coming from behind the gates. He waited for his kinsmen to take up their weapons and fight—or at the very least, he expected to see some sign of Odhran's fighters. But again, there was nothing.

He could wait no longer. Ronan raised his hand and signalled his men to join him. With his shield raised and his sword drawn, he shoved the door open and charged inside his father's dwelling.

Only to find that it was empty. There were no children, no prisoners, and no sign of anyone at all.

Had the woman lied to him? Damn her for this. Time was of the utmost importance, and he could not waste it by lingering here.

Ronan motioned for his men to retreat, but the moment they did, mercenary soldiers blocked the doorway. They were trapped inside, unable to spread out their forces. There was no choice but to bring the battle inside so they had the space to fight properly.

Ronan raised his shield, and his sword struck hard

against his assailant's blade. He used his shield to defend the blows while slashing with his weapon. The blade cut through his opponent's flesh, and he let himself fall into the familiar pattern of fighting.

He could only numb himself to the battle while his thoughts turned inward. He had come here to fight for his father and for the children. And if he did not push back their enemies, the failure would once again rest upon his shoulders.

Ronan poured himself into the fight, lashing out at the mercenaries. He hacked at them over and over, releasing all the rage and frustration from the past few months.

But it wouldn't bring back his loved ones.

Ardan and Declan were dead. His father might be gone, too. The weight of guilt was crushing, but he forced it back.

Near the gates, he heard the sounds of more fighting, but it was muted, as if from a distance. He had no time to think upon it, for two men attacked him simultaneously.

His muscles burned, and metal clanged against metal in the dawn stillness. As Ronan struck down his opponents, he barely felt their blades cutting into his flesh. There was no time to consider his own pain— only how he would win.

Behind him, he heard a shout but kept his attention on the man before him. He ducked to avoid a blow and heard the sickening crunch of bones as another man wielded a mace.

In the distance, he thought he heard a faint cry.

And then he realised what the woman had meant. The children *were* in his father's dwelling, but not in a place where they could be seen. The slight noise seemed to be coming from the floor, and he remembered that his father had a small storage space below ground for wine and ale.

The knowledge renewed his inner strength, and he struck his opponent with the shield, knocking him to the ground. The rest of his men had left the house and were now fighting outside. Ronan had only moments to discover the source of the sound while keeping watch over the doorway.

He pushed back the rushes that covered the trap door entrance, but before he could open it, two more men charged inside. One was a seasoned mercenary, a man far taller than most, with massive strength. The other was shorter, but there was a thin smile on his face as if he welcomed the fight.

The shorter man swung his sword, and Ronan blocked the strike with his shield. He lunged with his own blade and barely sidestepped a blow from the taller mercenary.

'Rhys, Warrick!' he called out. But no one came. He knew all the men were engaged in their own fight, but he was outnumbered here. And so it fell to him to defend those prisoners who could not help themselves. Somehow, he had to get the children out.

If Ardan were here, his brother would have done anything to win this battle. He would have sacrificed himself if needed, to save those who were too weak to defend themselves. Could he do less for these children and his own father?

With a renewed spirit, Ronan ignored the pain and exhaustion. He struck again and again, dodging blows and ignoring the minor wounds. A pang of regret caught him when he wondered if he would ever see Joan again.

God above, he wished he had not been so callous when she'd told him of their child. It was something she had dreamed of, and he should have buried his own fears and celebrated her happiness. And now, he might not live to see her grow heavy with child or to see her smile when she held their newborn.

Joan had brought her spirit and her joy into his life, and he didn't want to think of losing her. She had pushed back the darkness, and her courage had brought him from the edge of failure.

She was intelligent, kind, and her heart held enough love for every man, woman, and child of his tribe. If he somehow lived through this, he wanted her to be queen of the people.

His blade moved swiftly, and he defended himself against the sea of blows. He was the only one who stood between these men and the prisoners below the floor. The children needed him to win their freedom. He fought hard, though the odds were not in his favour.

And when a blow caught him on the back of the head, he staggered forward, raising his shield in defence. Pain blasted through his skull, and he sank to his knees before all went dark.

* * *

Although Aileen had stopped the bleeding, Joan still feared the worst. Her child was in terrible danger, and she did not dare move. Worst of all, she could not ask the healer questions about what to do. Instead, she could only try to rest within the tent and pray for the sake of the baby.

A noise outside caught her attention with the sound of horses approaching. At first, she thought it was only the MacEgan men returning, for she could hear them speaking Irish. But when she heard Aileen cry out, fear seized her. What was happening?

One of the men entered the tent and stared at her. His face faltered a moment when he saw her lying down. He hesitated but then gestured for her to stand.

Joan shook her head. 'I cannot.' She rested her hands against her womb, hoping he would understand.

Instead, he reached down and lifted her into his arms, making it clear that he intended to take her with him. For what reason? She wanted to struggle, but if he dropped her, it might harm the unborn child. No, it was better to see what he planned.

He carried her outside to where the others were waiting. The four guards left behind were on the ground, and Joan could not tell if they were dead or only wounded. She met Aileen's terrified stare, praying that somehow they would be all right.

Her attacker lifted her atop his horse and swung up behind her. Before he could ride away, she spoke her husband's name. 'Ronan Ó Callaghan.'

He turned back to study her, and she spoke two other words he might understand. '*Flaith*. Clonagh.'

There were few words she knew, but *prince* was one of them. And he would undoubtedly recognise *Clonagh*. Was that where he was planning to bring her? It was possible that Ronan's stepbrother Odhran had sent these men.

A stillness descended over Joan along with a sense of calm. Though she did not dare risk running away for the sake of her baby, neither would she go meekly into captivity. Instead, she would watch these men and wait for the right moment to free herself.

They rode in the direction of Clonagh, and every mile brought her excruciating pain. Joan bit her lip, trying to keep herself calm. When they reached the halfway point, one of the men lifted Aileen down and abandoned her in the meadow while they rode away. Joan prayed for her safety, though she knew not if the healer would go back towards the camp or await the MacEgans where she'd been left.

Undoubtedly, the men were bringing her to Ronan as a hostage. The MacEgans were already at Clonagh, along with her brothers' men. The moment they saw her, they would know something was wrong and would try to help. Joan squared her shoulders, gathering her courage.

To distract herself from the pain, she centred her thoughts on Ronan. Though it still hurt that he had not wanted the baby, she believed he would come to accept it and perhaps even love the child in time. He was strong and kind-hearted, a man who deserved a second chance. Above all, she hoped he was safe.

But when they drew closer to the fortress, she saw men and women staring at her. She knew not what had happened here, but the MacEgan soldiers were no longer fighting. The Normans also stood at attention, holding their weapons and shields.

Her heart pounded when she saw a richly dressed man and an older woman in embroidered silk standing at the far end of the fortress. It must be Odhran and Queen Eilis. But when there was no sign of Ronan, her heart began pounding. Was he alive?

The horseman slowed when he reached the centre of Clonagh. Joan's entire body ached from the riding, but she kept her mind alert on her surroundings and her enemies. She looked around and was relieved to glimpse Rhys and Warrick on the opposite side.

But from the thin-lipped smile on the queen's face, Joan knew she had been brought here for a reason.

Odhran spoke a calm command in Irish, and the soldier dismounted and lifted Joan down. He held her for a brief moment, allowing her to steady herself. Her knees were weak, and the immense pain in her abdomen was still there. But she had to gather her wits and think of what to do.

Ronan must not be dead—not after all the trouble they had gone to, bringing her here. No, they were using her as a prisoner to manipulate him and her brothers. When she caught Rhys's eye, he shook his head slowly in silent warning.

It felt as if she were caught in a chess game, and she did not know who was the sacrificial pawn.

Ronan awakened, feeling as if his head had been split in half. He winced and sat up in the darkness, only to hear a familiar voice.

'I thought you would not return, my son.'

The sound of his father speaking struck an emotional blow to his heart. Though it had been only a few months since he'd been gone, it felt like an eternity.

'I did come back,' he answered. 'Twice, though you did not know it.'

In the darkness, a hand reached out for his. Brodur's palm was freezing as he gripped Ronan's hand. 'Odhran will never surrender my throne.'

He had suspected that but didn't know how to respond to his father's prediction. 'Did my men free the children?'

'No. Odhran moved them elsewhere.'

Ronan had hoped that someone would get the children out, but it now seemed that he had failed again. Frustration bore down upon him, though he had done everything in his power to save them.

'Where are we?' he asked Brodur.

'Inside the Mound of Hostages,' his father answered. He gripped Ronan's palm harder and murmured, 'I am glad you are here. I wanted to see you again before I die.'

'You won't die,' he said quietly. He put his father's hands between both palms and tried to rub warmth into them. 'I have two armies here to rescue us.'

'Their efforts leave much to be desired.' In the darkness, he could not see his father's expression, but he read the sardonic air.

So did mine, Ronan thought, remembering the lost battle for the children. He leaned back against the frigid wall, trying to gather his thoughts of what to do now.

His father coughed heavily, and Ronan moved closer, steadying him. 'How did you get two armies to help you?' Brodur asked. 'We haven't that many allies.'

'I married the daughter of a Norman lord.'

His father coughed again, but this time, it was mingled with laughter. 'Why am I not surprised, Ronan? You've always had a way with women.' But there was a faint note of censure there, almost chiding.

'Joan agreed to the match,' he said. 'She is a good woman, Father. Beautiful, with dark hair and blue eyes. She always wears white.' A heaviness settled within his gut, for he knew not whether he would see his wife again. He wanted to believe that the armies would fight for him, that he would overpower Odhran. And at least Joan was safe at Killalough where no one could harm her.

'Would that Ardan could have lived to see her.' His father's voice was rough with emotion.

Although he knew the words were not meant to bring him pain, Ronan could not stop himself from saying, 'I accept the blame for my brother's death. And not a day goes by that I don't wish I could have changed what I did.'

'You were not to blame for it.'

He couldn't believe his father's words, though they were spoken with kindness. 'His son died because of me. Ardan lacked the will to live after Declan was gone. So I *am* to blame, and I will never forget this.' He pulled his hand away from his father's. 'I will restore your throne as best I can. But I realise it will never atone for my mistakes.'

'I grieve for their deaths, just as you do,' Brodur said. 'And I know you regret what happened.' His father reached out to touch his shoulder. 'But I forgive you, Ronan.'

The words should have been a balm, but instead, they sliced open his inner wounds. Forgiveness was something he didn't deserve.

'I will try to make amends,' was all he could say.

'I know you will.' Brodur squeezed his shoulder. 'But if something happens to me, you must take the throne from Odhran. Do whatever you must to claim it.'

He didn't know what his father was implying, but he would not stop until he had reclaimed Clonagh for Brodur. Yet there was another question he had to voice—the fate of the queen. 'And what of Eilis?'

His father sighed. 'Her ambitions were greater than I'd guessed. I thought she would be satisfied as queen, but I was wrong. Exile her if you wish, but she cannot be trusted.'

For a time, Ronan was silent. 'I am sorry for all of this,' he said at last.

'So am I. But at least I had the chance to say fare-well to you, my son.'

The emotion in his father's voice seized his heart, for he didn't want to imagine Brodur's death. Ronan reached out for the older man's hand and swore, 'I will make it right somehow.'

'I know you will.'

Joan was permitted to sit near Odhran and his mother, but two soldiers stood at her back with their daggers drawn. Though she tried to remain calm, her nerves were taut with fear. If she dared to run, they would cut her down.

Dear God, what should she do? They would use her to influence Ronan and try to force him to surren-der. She couldn't allow that to happen. And yet, she was too weak to fight back—not without the threat of harming her child.

When she looked back at her brothers, they were standing side by side, their faces locked upon hers. Although their tension was evident, Warrick gave her a slight nod of reassurance.

It looked as if they had planned something, though she knew not what it was. They had the numbers on their side and soldiers who could easily cut down Odhran's men. Yet, why were they waiting? Were they attempting to negotiate? Or had Ronan ordered them to stand down?

She had to trust that they would guard and protect her. In turn, she would do what was necessary to pro-tect her unborn child.

'Bring the prisoners,' Odhran commanded. One of the taller mercenaries went to obey, and he returned a few moments later, accompanied by an older man with a long grey beard. His clothing was tattered, but she could see that it had once been a silk tunic. No doubt it was Ronan's father, King Brodur.

Though she did not know him, his eyes softened when he caught sight of her. It was as if he knew who she was, and she ventured a slight smile. His expression held regret, as if he doubted he would survive this day. Joan rested her hands upon her womb, letting him guess what he would.

And he returned a genuine smile.

In that moment, something shifted within her. She did not want Ronan's father to die, or any of his people. With another glance to her brothers, she stared hard at them and then back to King Brodur, letting them know her wishes. Too many had died, and she knew what Ronan's father meant to him.

Then the mercenary returned with her husband. A spear was pointed at his back, and his hands were bound in front of him. Ronan walked slowly, and she saw dried blood on his neck. She drank in the sight of him, so glad that he was alive. There was shock in his expression when he saw her, and she flushed with her own guilt. Had she remained behind at Killalough, she would not be a hostage now.

Are you all right? he seemed to be asking.

She tried to nod, though she was still afraid for the baby.

The men brought Ronan before Odhran, whose expression turned smug. The new king spoke in Irish, and Joan turned to the men behind her. 'What is he saying?'

One of the Ó Callaghan men stepped forward and translated the words for her sake, and she listened closely to their conversation.

Odhran directed his next words to Ronan. 'You thought to attack us, did you?'

'You already attacked our forces at Killalough,' he countered, remembering his wedding day. 'And you imprisoned the Ó Callaghan children. I thought only to save them.'

His stepbrother shrugged, not bothering to deny it. 'But you did not succeed. And now the people see you for what you are…a failure.'

The man's arrogance irritated Joan. He was behaving as if he was above everyone else, when truthfully, he was a tyrant. To the translator behind her, she directed, 'Tell him my words.'

Then she took a step forward and addressed Odhran. 'A true king would never need to hold hostages to keep his throne. Your reign is a false one built upon fear, not a birthright.'

After the man translated for Odhran, his face reddened with anger. 'If you married Ronan in hopes of gaining a throne, it will never happen. He killed his nephew and his brother.'

If he thought his words would shock her, he was mistaken. 'Their deaths were an accident, and he grieves for them. The people know the truth, and so do you.'

'Ronan is a coward, nothing more.'

She didn't believe that for a moment. Ronan had sacrificed everything to bring help to Clonagh, and he was doing all he could to prevent needless deaths. She could see the tension in the people's faces and how they looked to him for leadership.

One of the men jabbed his spear lightly at Ronan, forcing him to step forward. Odhran regarded him. 'As punishment for your rebellion, you will die. But before you are executed, you will watch the death of either your father or your wife. Only one will live.'

It felt as if the blood had drained away from her face. Panic clawed within her as Joan tried to decide what to do.

Ronan's face remained stoic. 'I would never make such a choice.'

'If you do not choose one, then both will die. It matters not to me.' Odhran motioned towards his soldiers, and two of them seized Joan by her shoulders. They jerked her to stand up, and one pressed a blade to her throat.

Her mind was screaming at her to struggle, to fight for her life against these men. But then, a strange calm descended over her. She squared her shoulders and faced Odhran. To Ronan, she said quietly, 'I trust in you.'

She heard Ronan's father speak in Irish, and the translator relayed his words for her sake. Brodur was urging Ronan to sacrifice him, so that she might live.

A sudden anger roared through her, that this was

happening at all. She would not simply stand here and let Odhran kill her husband or anyone else.

There was no curse and never had been. There was only misfortune and sorrow—and she would not remain passive while her loved ones were threatened. She had come to love Ronan and the unborn baby within her. She could not let anything happen to either of them.

She had full faith in Ronan and in her brothers. But it didn't mean she could not also fight herself. Upon the ground, she saw a stone the size of her fist.

She had the element of surprise. And she intended to use it.

Ronan didn't like the look in his wife's eyes. Joan intended to fight for her life, and he could not risk her being hurt.

'Ronan,' his father said. 'Save your wife and let her go with her brothers. I am old and have lived my life. You know he will kill me anyway.'

But Ronan couldn't turn his back on his father. He had already caused the deaths of his brother and his nephew. The thought of losing Brodur was unfathomable. Then, too, he knew that his stepbrother was lying. Odhran would spare none of them.

'I will not choose,' he repeated, and his stepbrother's face tightened with frustration. Ronan didn't know what the man wanted. Was Odhran trying to demean him in front of his people? All around, he saw kinsmen who were only afraid for their children. They wanted no part of this fight.

And then he realised what he *could* do to under-mine Odhran. The man thought he could prevent an attack because Ronan's armies did not want to harm the Ó Callaghan people. But he was wrong.

Ronan knew exactly how to cause the chaos needed to win this fight. He raised his voice so that all could hear. He focused his attention on his kins-men and said, 'This is not your fight. My men have orders not to harm you. Instead, go and find your chil-dren while my men fight for you. Search everywhere until you have brought them back safely.'

His words had the intended effect. The men and women scattered, while the soldiers remained, clos-ing in on Odhran and the hostages.

Then Ronan twisted away from the men holding him, holding out his bound hands so Warrick could slice the ropes. There was a roar as the men charged forward, closing in on Odhran's mercenaries. Ronan seized his own blade and watched in horror as Joan fell to the ground. One of the mercenaries tried to grab her, but she struck him in the face with a large stone. His heart nearly stopped when he saw another man raise his weapon, and Ronan shoved his way towards her, blocking the blow with his own sword.

'Are you all right?' he asked. She nodded, but her face was the colour of milk. He cut her bindings and called out to her brother, 'Rhys, take Joan out of here!'

The warrior cut a path towards his sister and led her away. Relief poured through Ronan to know that she would be safe. But he lost sight of his father as the two armies converged, slaughtering the mercenaries.

In the distance, he heard the cries of children, and the sound brought back the memory of Declan. He fought hard, his blade biting into flesh as he cut a path towards Odhran. And when he reached the man's side, he faced the man who had harmed so many.

'Your reign is over,' he said quietly.

There was a thin smile on Odhran's face. 'It might be,' he agreed. 'But then, so is your father's.'

Ronan glanced in the direction Odhran was looking and saw the fallen body of Brodur. Anguish ripped through him at the knowledge that his father was dead. He had failed again, and grief overtook him. He had gained Brodur's forgiveness, only to lose him now.

A sound of rage tore from his throat as he attacked his stepbrother. He fought against the man who had stolen the throne and murdered his father. Damn Odhran for this.

He let the fury consume him as he struck hard, caught up in a storm of vengeance. Odhran was a skilled fighter, and he evaded Ronan's blows, striking back with his own blade.

'You're going to die today, Ronan,' his stepbrother said. 'And when you are dead, I will take your wife's body and claim her.' A mocking smile came over his face.

Never in a thousand years would Ronan let this man live. He was aware that the fighting all around them had stilled. The children were in the arms of their parents, and both the de Laurent and MacEgan armies had surrounded them. He could no longer see his father's body, and he guessed that it had been taken away to protect it for burial.

Grief and regret tangled up inside him as he swung his sword, over and over. The clashing metal reverberated through his arm, but he felt none of the force—only sorrow that he had lost his father, and there was no one left.

No one, save Joan and their unborn child.

A rush of emotion slid through him, for at least they were safe. Even if he failed now, it would not matter. Joan had the child she desired, and her brothers would take care of her. It was enough.

And yet, he wanted to live to see this baby born. He wanted to see his wife's joy and the softness in her eyes when she looked upon the child with love. Joan would make a good mother; he was sure of it.

Weariness ached within him, but he continued to fight, dodging blows until at last he saw Odhran beginning to slow. He renewed his assault, and when the man lunged, he twisted and sliced his blade into Odhran's side. His stepbrother gasped, and Ronan ended the fight, stabbing him in the heart. Odhran sank to his knees, clutching at the weapon as he died.

A woman's piercing scream tore through the silence, and Ronan caught a blur of motion as Eilis ran towards her son.

But instead of dropping beside Odhran, she unsheathed her own dagger and drove it into Ronan's ribs.

It happened so fast, he was hardly aware of anything, save the fierce pain and the blood flowing down his tunic. His hand closed around the hilt, and the world tipped sideways, making him fall to his knees. He searched through the crowds of people for one last glimpse of Joan. He desperately needed to see her before he died.

But her brother had already taken her away, as promised.

His last thought before he succumbed to the darkness was that he'd never told her that he loved her. And now he never would.

Chapter Eleven

A hot ball of pain gathered within Joan's stomach as she saw Ronan fall. She wanted to scream, but not a sound escaped her. Her heart was shattering into pieces, and she could hardly breathe.

Warrick was already running forward while other men seized the queen. Joan tried to go to Ronan, but Rhys held her back. 'Wait. Aileen needs to see him, to try to heal his wounds.'

'It's too late,' she whispered bitterly. No man could survive being stabbed in the ribs.

'You don't know that.' Her brother pulled her into an embrace, and she clung to him while Warrick carried her husband's fallen body back. The blade was still embedded, and though he breathed, she knew not for how long.

Her fear and grief consumed her, but she could not let the woman who had done this go unpunished.

Joan stood and beckoned for one of the men who had translated earlier to come forward. 'Tell the

Ó Callaghans to put Eilis in chains to await her trial and sentencing.'

The men who held the queen in custody started to obey, but the older woman protested, struggling to escape while she shouted her own orders.

The translator said, 'Queen Eilis says that you have no authority over the Ó Callaghans. She demands to be set free.'

Joan said quietly, 'Tell the people I am Ronan's wife. As such, I will speak for him until he is able to do so.'

He inclined his head. 'As you command, my lady.'

Were it her choice, she would have the woman slain this very moment for attempting to murder Ronan. But all had witnessed Eilis's treachery, and she had to trust that the people would hold the woman captive.

Warrick and Rhys had helped Ronan into a cart hitched to two horses. Joan climbed inside with her husband, and asked her brothers, 'What about the dagger? Should we remove it?'

Rhys shook his head. 'It's keeping him from bleeding too badly. Aileen should be the one to take it out. We will bring him back to the camp so she can treat him.'

She understood the reasons, though she hated the thought of the blade still buried in his flesh. 'The men abandoned Aileen between here and the camp.'

Her brother found Aileen's husband and told him what had happened. Within moments, Connor seized a horse and rode swiftly to find his wife.

They began travelling towards the camp. Another

cart contained other wounded men who also needed care, but Joan paid little attention to them. Instead, she lay beside her husband, holding his hand. His skin was like ice, and she stroked back his hair, murmuring, 'I am here, Ronan.'

It felt as if *she* had been the one stabbed by the blade. Her heart was bleeding for him, and she could not stop the tears. 'You have to live,' she told him. 'You must fight to stay with me.'

Her husband did not speak, but she would not let go of his hand. She could not release the terrible fear inside her, and she rested her head against his shoulder. This man had wanted nothing more than to help his people, and he had faced obstacles at every turn.

The cart jostled along the grass as her brothers hurried to bring them to the camp. With every mile, Joan's own pain intensified. She had managed to push it back earlier, but now, she pressed her hand to her abdomen, praying that her child and her husband would survive.

When they finally reached the camp, Connor was standing with his wife Aileen. Joan learned that he had found her running back towards the camp, and he had brought her there on horseback.

The healer came to the cart and began issuing orders in Irish. The men helped lift Ronan, and they brought him inside the tent to rest upon a pallet on the floor.

Joan started to ask what she could do, but one of the men shook his head. 'Aileen wants you to rest for the sake of your child. She does not want you here while she treats Ronan.'

The healer was already cutting away Ronan's tunic, and she was calling out orders to the men. Her demeanour was like a warrior, fighting against the hand of Death. And though Joan wanted to be there, the men gently escorted her outside.

She walked towards the other wounded men, hoping to find someone she could help, even if it was only to wrap a bandage or wash away blood. She closed her fingers around the wooden cross Ronan had carved, praying that Aileen could heal him. There was nothing worse than being powerless to help a loved one fight to live.

'My lady,' one man called out in a heavily accented voice. She turned towards the other cart of men, most of whom were bleeding or bruised. The man was holding a broken arm, but he directed Joan's attention to another wounded man. The sight of him made her heart quicken. She had no idea how he had managed to drag himself among the wounded, but somehow, he had survived.

'Help him,' the first man pleaded. 'I beg of you.'

His face was burning hot. Ronan tossed amid the sheets, feeling as if his body were on fire. When he touched his ribs, he felt an agonising pain.

'Shh,' came a woman's voice. 'You'll be all right.'

He opened his eyes and saw Joan sitting beside him. She reached out and placed a cool damp cloth against his forehead. He detected the subtle aroma of mint and basil.

'Where are we?' he asked.

'We brought you back to Killalough, along with the other wounded men. You needed time to recover.' Her voice broke, and she added, 'I thought you were going to die. So many nights, I stayed by your side, praying that you would live.'

Ronan hadn't realised so much time had passed. He knew he ought to be grateful that he'd survived Eilis's blade, but in truth, it only brought back the memory of his failure. He grieved for the loss of Brodur, wishing he could have saved the man. He was deeply thankful they had spent a few last moments in captivity together, but he wished for more time. There was an empty hole within him, for now he had no family left.

Weariness and sorrow weighed upon him, but he could not find any words to say to Joan. In the dim firelight, her dark hair was haloed by the flames, and her clear blue eyes held love.

At last, he asked, 'Are you and the child well?'

She hesitated a moment, but admitted, 'I...started to bleed, but Aileen kept me from losing the baby. She bade me to lie down and drink teas.'

He reached for her hand and squeezed it. 'I am glad.'

When she drew his palm to her abdomen, he felt humbled by the presence of their unborn child. And though he would always regret what had happened to

Ardan, he was beginning to understand what lengths a father would go to, if it meant saving his son.

'There is something else,' she murmured. 'Your father—'

He didn't want to speak of Brodur's death. The man had not deserved to die in such a way. Not after all he had done for Clonagh. Grief swelled within him, but he managed to ask, 'Did they bury him already?'

'No.'

Ronan closed his eyes, wondering what Eilis had done with the body. He didn't trust his father's wife to hold a proper Mass.

'Ronan, there is something I must tell you. There is a reason we did not bury Brodur.'

As Joan was speaking, the door to the bedchamber swung open. A man stood at the threshold and remarked, 'There was no need to bury me. Not if I am still living.'

Ronan's attention jerked towards the voice, and he saw Brodur standing there. A wave of thankfulness filled him with a rush of emotion. His throat closed up, and he fought to maintain control. 'Thank God.'

'Your father was among the wounded in one of the carts,' Joan explained. 'My brothers helped him escape.'

'I wasn't about to lie on the ground and let Eilis kill me,' Brodur said. 'Better to feign death and behave as if she succeeded. And when you distracted them, Lady Joan, I managed to slip away among the other wounded men.'

'Were you badly hurt?' Ronan asked.

'Not so badly as you.' Brodur drew closer to the bed. 'But when you are healed, we will return to Clonagh.'

'You should go back without me,' he urged his father. 'You are the rightful king.' It hardly mattered whether he returned at all, but their people needed a leader. Eilis had been imprisoned for her involvement in the rebellion, and justice had to be served.

His father sat down, and his face appeared tired. 'I can no longer be king, and you know this.'

'Why? The people respect you.'

'Not any more. Not after the uprising.' His father's expression was careworn. 'It is time for you to take my place.'

'I could never be king. Not after all that I've done.' Ronan refused to even consider the idea. All his life, he had looked up to his father, knowing he was the rightful ruler. Leadership was never something he'd wanted, and after everything Brodur had endured, Ronan wanted to give the throne back to the man who deserved it. He looked over to Joan, but her expression was serene and calm.

'They do not blame you for Ardan's death or for Declan's. It was an accident of fate.' His father's voice was calm and reasoned. But the unconditional forgiveness was difficult to accept. Declan's death was preventable, and Ronan knew he should have been more alert that day.

'I cannot lead the people,' he insisted. 'They would never accept me.'

'You brought together two armies to overthrow

Odhran. You saved their children from captivity. The *brehons* have already met, and it was decided by the council,' his father continued. With a rueful smile, he said, 'Whether you want to be their king or not, the people have chosen you.' His father rose and departed the room, leaving him alone with his wife.

A hard lump caught in Ronan's throat, and he knew not what to say. He studied Joan, wondering what she thought of this. When she said nothing, he told her, 'I have no desire to be king.'

She reached for a linen cloth and dipped it in water once more, before she wrung it out and laid it upon his forehead. He was grateful for the cooling effect on his skin. 'What do you think we should do, Joan?'

She sponged his burning cheeks and regarded him. 'It was never my wish to be a queen,' she answered honestly. 'But it seems that governing a tribe is rather like being a mother. There are many responsibilities, and no one will ever be fully pleased with your actions. And yet, I suppose there are moments when you look upon your people and see goodness.'

She drew her hand over his face. 'I will go wherever you go, Ronan. Whether you become a king or not, I believe in you. And I have every faith that you would make a great ruler over the Ó Callaghan people.'

He caught her fingertips and drew them to his mouth. Her blue eyes met his, and in them, he saw the emotions she was holding back.

'I was so afraid for you,' she whispered. 'I didn't know if you were going to live.'

'Neither did I,' he admitted. 'But I would have given my life for yours without hesitation.'

'I am glad you did not have to.' A tear slid down her cheek, and he felt the need to hold her.

'Lie beside me, Joan,' he bade her, moving over. She did, and he drew his hand over her face and down to her womb. 'I am going to live. Whether there is a curse or not.'

'You have to live,' she agreed. 'Because our child needs a father.' She leaned in and kissed him lightly. 'And because I need you.'

Although he was still burning with fever, he knew she needed consolation. He was careful to avoid his wound but tried to draw her closer. 'I love you, Joan.'

'I love you, too.' She was crying softly now. 'And whatever you decide, I will be with you.'

He kissed her lips gently and felt the need to console her. But as he stroked the outline of her face, he realised that Joan was right. Leading the people was not about raising his own rank—it was about bringing them together and ensuring their welfare.

If anyone deserved to be a queen, it was Joan. And if his people needed him to become their king, he would not turn his back on them in their time of need. He would take on the mantle of leadership if necessary.

He regarded his wife and drew back. 'Thank you for saving my father's life.'

She smiled at him. 'To be fair, he saved himself.'

'My father is a stubborn man.' And not one who would surrender without a fight.

'Like his son,' Joan answered. For a moment, she lay beside him, and he took comfort from her presence. He drew his hand along the lines of her body, back down to the rise of her abdomen. He imagined a daughter with Joan's face, and was startled at the wave of protectiveness that struck hard. He could easily imagine holding a little girl in his arms, her small hand clinging to his. And he would guard her with his life.

'We must return to Clonagh as soon as we can,' he said at last. 'My place is with them.'

Joan nodded. 'Then so is mine.' She laced her fingers with his in a silent promise. He did not know what he would find when he returned with Joan and Brodur. But he had to face Eilis and decide upon justice.

They could not return to Clonagh until Ronan regained his strength. Instead, Joan sent Norman soldiers to keep the peace until her husband was well enough to return.

She tended to Ronan and tried learning the Irish language as best she could. Though she had feigned confidence about becoming a queen, the truth was, it terrified her. His father, King Brodur, had spent time with her, for he understood some of the Norman language. The older man was kindly, and he shared his knowledge of Clonagh with her.

Joan veiled her fear of becoming queen and spent her days absorbing as much as she could. It did seem that the earlier danger of losing the child had passed, and she had not bled any more. Rosamund kept her company and offered her advice on motherhood. Rhys's daughter Sorcha sometimes climbed into her lap, seeking comfort.

But this morning, the young girl came running into the gathering space, overjoyed. 'Mama is here! Mama has come!'

Joan could not help but smile at the girl's exuberance. She was surprised to discover that Rhys's wife Lianna had travelled so far from home with an infant, but it was possible that he had sent for her.

Joan rose from her place near the hearth and went outside to welcome her. Lianna had vivid red hair, and her new baby son was swaddled and bound to her torso.

Rhys helped her down from the horse and embraced his wife, kissing her hard. He murmured something in Lianna's ear, and the woman sent him a knowing smile. Then Sorcha broke free and threw herself into her mother's arms. 'I've missed you, Mama.'

'As I've missed you, my sweet,' Lianna answered. 'And look, your brother is crying, for he missed you, too.'

A suspicious look crossed Sorcha's face, but she didn't argue. Rhys took the infant from his wife's arms to keep him from being squeezed by his sister. 'Come here, lad.'

Lianna lifted her daughter to her hip before she approached Joan and embraced her. 'I heard that my Sorcha was right, and you married an Irish prince.'

'I did, yes.' She ventured a smile. 'When we arrived in Ireland, unfortunately Murdoch Ó Connor was already dead. Rhys and Warrick set up a new betrothal on my behalf.'

'I look forward to meeting your new husband,' Lianna said. With a look back towards Rhys, she added, 'You've been gone a long time. I've missed my family.' She dropped a kiss on Sorcha's head and set her daughter down.

Her husband only smiled, and a silent look was exchanged between them before he gave the baby back to her. Lianna cradled the infant and said, 'All of us are hungry, if you could see to a meal for us.' Sorcha held on to her mother's leg, as if unwilling to let go of her.

Rhys nodded and went inside. Lianna put her arm in Joan's and said, 'I'm wanting to hear about your new husband. Tell me everything.'

Joan admitted, 'He is recovering from wounds he received in battle. But we are returning to Clonagh in the morning.'

Lianna paused a moment and nudged a stool with her foot so that it was even with the other stool. 'You seem uneasy.'

Joan tried to hide her feelings and behave as if it did not matter. 'There was a rebellion and a good deal of fighting among the people. I don't know what we'll find when we return.'

Lianna bade Sorcha to go and play while she sat upon the stool, gently patting her son's back. 'How does your husband feel about it?'

Joan joined Lianna and sat across from her. 'Ronan intended to bring his father home to restore the kingship. But King Brodur has said that the people have chosen Ronan to be their new ruler.' Though she tried not to reveal any emotions, Lianna knew her too well and read her fears.

'Which means you would have to be their queen.'

Joan let out a sigh and shrugged. 'It is my place to follow where he goes.' There truly was no choice but to accept the role.

Lianna lifted her son to her shoulder, patting the infant as he shoved his fist into his mouth. 'I know what it means to feel alone among strangers. My advice is to befriend the women. Let them help you, and all will be well.'

'I have to learn their language,' Joan said. 'It won't be easy, but I will try.'

Lianna nodded in agreement. 'Learn all that you can.' A mischievous glint formed in her gaze. 'And you need not tell them that you understand every word.'

Joan bit back a laugh at that, for Lianna had once done the same. She had pretended to only speak Gaelic, when in truth, she knew the Norman tongue well.

Footsteps approached, and when Joan turned, she saw her husband standing with Rhys. Though Ronan still wore the bandages beneath his tunic, his strength had returned.

'This is my wife, Lianna.' Rhys introduced her to Ronan. 'And our son, Edward.'

Lianna rose from the stool to greet Ronan. She smiled warmly, sinking into a slight curtsy. 'I am pleased to meet you, Prince Ronan.'

He took her hand. 'We do not use the title in that way here. You need only call me Ronan.' He raised his knee in a mutual show of respect. Then his eyes descended upon Joan, making her feel self-conscious. It was as if he were trying to ascertain whether she was feeling well, and she tried to venture a smile.

'Come and share food and wine with us,' Rhys invited.

Joan took her husband's hand and squeezed it in silent reassurance. They took a place at the far end of the table while Lianna sat with her husband.

Rhys's face softened at the sight of his newborn son, and he took the baby once again. When the food arrived, he arranged Lianna's knife and bread so that they were even with the edge of the plate. A softness caught Joan in the heart, for Rhys knew his wife's desire to have everything in its place. Seeing them together was a glimpse of the future she wanted to have with Ronan.

And it caught her heart, filling it with love once again.

'Do you want Warrick and I to accompany you and your father to Clonagh?' Rhys asked Ronan.

'No. The worst of the danger is over, and we must meet with our *brehons* to decide what will happen to Eilis.'

'Should I stay behind as well?' Joan asked.

This time, Ronan drew his hand to her back. 'No,

a stór. You are needed at Clonagh. The people must have a queen to replace Eilis.'

Though she tried to nod acceptance, Joan still remembered Lianna's earlier remarks, that she knew what it was to feel like a stranger among her husband's people.

Would the Ó Callaghans want an outsider to rule at Ronan's side? It was difficult enough for him to bring a wife home, but she was Norman. If she brought men of her own to guard the people, they might resent her presence.

Uneasiness unfurled within her, making her dread the journey on the morrow. But Ronan took her hand in his and squeezed it. She took comfort from his touch and reminded herself that he would be at her side to offer guidance. His father could help her, too. And she resolved to do her best to help the people. 'I will try.'

'We will leave in the morning,' he said. 'I have been gone for far too long. My father sent word to Darragh, leaving him in command for now, but I must go back.'

She had known this, but Ronan did not appear eager to return. He knew, as his father had predicted, that his role would change once he arrived. The people would demand that he take the throne. And why not? He had saved their children and deposed Odhran with not a single Ó Callaghan harmed during the battle, save himself and Brodur. His bravery marked a man who put his people above his own safety, and

she had no doubt that he would be chosen to rule.
She could only pray that they would accept her, too.

They travelled most of the day and made camp for
the night. Joan could feel the tension rising as they
drew close to Clonagh. Her brothers had packed several wagons with her dowry and belongings, but it did
feel strange to imagine Ireland becoming her home.

When they were alone in their tent, Ronan brought
several heated stones inside to warm the space. There
was a small stone oil lamp to light the tent, and he set
up a fur pallet for them.

Joan knelt upon the ground, for it was too uncomfortable to sit. Her back was aching, and she rubbed
it with one hand.

'I have something for you,' Ronan said quietly.
From his belongings, he withdrew a cloth-wrapped
bundle and held it out.

Joan opened it and saw a silk bliaud in a rich sapphire blue. She touched the silk, not knowing what
to say. It had been years since she had worn a gown
of any colour at all.

'Do you like it?' he asked.

'It's beautiful. And…it's been so long since I've
worn anything so fine,' she admitted.

'I would like to see you wear it when we go to
Clonagh,' he said.

She understood that this was about more than
wearing a fine gown. It was about setting aside her
fears and embracing a new life. No longer would she
only wear white or let herself worry about a curse that

did not exist. Wearing the blue gown was a means of showing that she had put the past behind her.

'Will it bother your people to see me dressed like a Norman?' She wondered if it would only draw attention to their differences.

'They know who you are. You need not change anything about yourself.' She folded up the gown and then rubbed at her aching back again. Ronan noticed it and said, 'Why don't you lie down and get some rest?'

She knew he was right, but she did not want to sleep just now. It had been weeks since he had touched her, ever since he had learned about the baby. She yearned to have his hands upon her, and she asked, 'Will you help me remove my gown?'

He hesitated. 'You might be more comfortable wearing it. It's a cold night.'

'Then perhaps you will warm me,' she said, leaving no doubt of her intentions. At that, his eyes flared with heat.

He reached for her laces and slipped them free, one by one. Her breasts were fuller, and he brushed against them with his knuckles as he helped her lift the gown away. Beneath it, she wore a linen shift.

Her breasts were sensitive, rising against the fabric in the cool air. His gaze locked with hers, and she removed the shift, letting him look his fill. 'You steal the breath from me, *a ghrá*.'

And with that, he kissed her, drawing her down to the fur pallet. She shivered from the cold, but he undressed, warming her with his bare skin. His hands moved over her swollen breasts, down to the slight rise of her womb.

Then he moved behind her, and she felt the hard ridge of his erection against her spine. Her body went liquid against him, and a gasp shuddered from her when he caressed her breasts.

'Your back is hurting, isn't it?' he guessed, moving his hands lower.

'It is.' But he was distracting her from the familiar ache as a craving filled her deep within. She wanted his body joined with hers, to lose herself in fulfilment.

'I think I know how to ease you,' he murmured, pulling back for a moment. She waited for him, her body feeling poised on the brink of anticipation. Though she didn't know what he intended to do, she closed her eyes, letting her fingers graze against her swollen nipples. Instantly, she felt the pleasure gather between her thighs.

And then Ronan was behind her, his slick hands moving against her lower back. He had coated them in oil, and he began massaging her spine.

'Does that feel good?'

'Yes…' she breathed. Just now, she wanted to curl in a ball and moan with relief. The gentle pressure of his palm against the ache felt so good. But as his hands moved up her back, his touch aroused her even deeper. She wanted her husband so badly, and she reached behind her to curl her palm against his shaft.

He froze at her touch, and she drew her hand up, sliding against his erection until her thumb stroked the blunt tip. He inhaled sharply.

'Joan.' He spoke her name as if he could hardly bear the caress of her fingers. She needed him badly, and God help her, she was so wet for him. This time, she parted her legs, guiding him inside until he was fully seated within her. For a moment, he held her in position, his chest pressed to her spine. She could feel his length stretching her, and she moved against him, loving the sensation of him buried deep within.

'Do you want me to keep rubbing your back?' he asked, his voice rough as he struggled for control.

'You may touch me anywhere you want. As long as you are inside me.'

At that, he drew both arms around her, sliding his slick hands over her flesh. She thrust against him as he circled her nipples with his thumbs, and cried out with the delicious friction. Ronan moved lower until his hand found the hooded flesh above where they were joined. He encircled it, penetrating her again as he did.

From their position, he could not take her deeply, and she was overwhelmed by the shallow thrusts that stroked her. Every sensation was heightened, her flesh so sensitive, she arched against him as she convulsed. He kept the pressure gentle, but rubbed her swiftly, until she shattered, gripping his flesh inside her.

Only then did he claim her fully, thrusting hard from behind. She met his penetrations, backing against him as he filled her and withdrew. Though she tried to stifle her moans, she could not stop the high-pitched gasp as he took her deeply, plunging until he gripped her hips and emptied himself within her.

For a while, Ronan lay with his arms around her, and she nestled against him. He kissed her hair and murmured, 'I didn't hurt you, did I?'

'No.' In the stillness of the night, she took comfort from her husband. It would not be easy to take her place among strangers, but at least she had Ronan at her side.

Chapter Twelve

They entered the ringfort with Brodur leading the way, while Ronan followed with Joan at his side. Two dozen men accompanied them, but there were only smiles of welcome from the Ó Callaghan guards. Even so, Ronan could see the weight of frustration upon his father's shoulders as they entered Clonagh. Brodur appeared both resolute and melancholy.

Earlier, he had asked his father what he wanted to do about Eilis. There came no answer, but he sensed what the answer must be. Yet he couldn't begin to imagine how a man could sentence his own wife to death. If it were Joan, he simply could not do it.

They were welcomed by Darragh when they reached his father's house. His friend seemed on edge, but at least his son Ailan appeared to be well and in good spirits. Joan smiled at the sight of the young boy holding on to his father's leg.

'I am very glad to see you are both healed from your wounds,' Darragh said to Ronan and his father.

'We were fortunate,' Ronan replied. He addressed

his father and Joan, asking, 'Do you want anything to eat or drink, now that we are home?'

Brodur shook his head. 'Later, perhaps. I want to see Eilis first.'

Joan deferred to his wishes, and Ronan understood that his father needed to confront his wife over what had happened.

Darragh's discomfort heightened. 'I will bring you to her. But there is something you should know first.'

Brodur shook his head in dismissal. 'It can wait.'

But Ronan saw his friend's tension rising and intervened. 'What is it, Darragh?'

'You should know that our people obeyed your orders precisely. They did not lay a hand upon Eilis.'

A sudden knot of unease tightened within Ronan. 'What do you mean?'

'She was the one who ordered Odhran to take the children as hostages. The rebellion was hers from the start, and the *brehons* met to decide what should be done.'

'It is my decision and only mine,' Brodur said darkly. 'Take me to her now.'

Darragh pried his son away and sent him back to his mother. 'Follow me.'

He led them away from the house and towards the far end of the ringfort. Ronan took Joan's hand. 'You may want to wait here.' He didn't know what had become of Eilis, but he wanted his wife nowhere near the queen.

But she shook her head. 'No. I think I will come with you.' She walked alongside him and took his hand.

He didn't understand her reasons, but he said, 'Eilis is unpredictable, and I don't want her to frighten you.'

Joan only smiled. 'She can do nothing to me, Ronan.'

Darragh brought them to the other side of the small stone chapel. Ronan expected his friend to lead them towards the souterrain passage where Brodur had been kept prisoner. Instead, he was startled when Darragh stopped before a freshly dug grave. 'She is here.'

Brodur went completely still. 'What happened? How did she die?'

Darragh was about to speak when one of the older *brehons* approached. The man leaned heavily upon a walking stick. 'You gave orders that we were to hold Eilis prisoner, and no one should lay a hand upon her. That is exactly what happened. Not one person from Clonagh went anywhere near the queen.'

Understanding finally took root and Ronan regarded the *brehon*. 'She starved to death.'

The old man met Brodur's gaze. 'Thirst, I believe. After she was imprisoned, we left her there for a sennight. No one saw her. No one spoke to her.' He paused and added, 'No one laid a hand upon her.'

Brodur appeared to have aged several years in that moment. His complexion was grey, and Joan went to his side. She took his hand and murmured, 'I am so sorry.'

The king shook his head. 'No. It had to be done. I would have sentenced her to death. She could not be allowed to live after what she did to the children.'

The old *brehon* lowered his head. 'We wanted to spare you that, my king. After we met, we spoke with the people, and all were in agreement.'

'Give me a moment alone,' Brodur said at last.

Ronan took Joan away, and she moved into his arms. He translated the *brehon's* words for her and his wife nodded. In a quiet voice, she murmured, 'They wanted to spare him that decision. If he had exiled her, Eilis might have tried to rebel again.'

Ronan knew she was right. 'They were married for five years. He was lonely in his later years. She brought Odhran from his foster family only within the last year. But I suspect she never loved Brodur. Not if she was capable of such malice.'

Joan walked with him back to the centre of the ringfort. The ground was wet from frost, and her breath formed clouds in the air. 'Will your father be all right?'

Ronan nodded. 'I believe so. In time.' He stood with her a moment. 'I don't know what will happen now that the rebellion is over. Or what will become of us.' He rested his hand upon the small of her back as if to draw comfort from his wife.

She turned and embraced him. 'We will stay together, Ronan. And we will raise our children in a home where they know they are loved.'

'They will be loved,' he agreed. 'And I will guard them with my life.' Though he had never imagined he would be a father, he found that the idea no longer bothered him. Instead, he was content to give his wife her greatest desire. Ronan drew his hand down to their unborn baby. 'Would that my brother could have lived to see our child.'

Joan kissed him lightly and smiled. 'Somehow, I think he knows.'

Summer

It was one of the hottest days Joan could remember. Her hair was damp with perspiration, and all day, her back had been aching. She had wanted to wade in the shallow end of the stream for relief, but her ankles were so swollen, she could hardly leave their home. She had teased her husband that if she walked out to the pasture, others might mistake her for one of the cattle.

Throughout the winter and spring, Joan had practised learning the Irish language. Being immersed among the people of Clonagh had helped, and she could now understand most of what they were saying, though she was aware that her accent was terrible.

Ronan had summoned Aileen MacEgan to stay with her during the past fortnight, but there were no cures for Joan's discomfort now, save giving birth.

She walked outside, resting her hand against her spine. The baby had dropped low, and it felt as if she were carrying a heavy stone within her womb. Aileen was watching over her, while she made a cup of tea with herbs. 'It won't be long now,' she predicted.

'How can you know?' It felt as if she had been with child for over a year.

'Because you are already having labour pains,' Aileen said. 'Your back is aching with them.'

It was nothing new. For the past fortnight, her womb had contracted with daily pains, though naught had come of them. And yet, she saw the look of worry on Aileen's face.

'Am I too old to have a baby?' she teased.

The young woman shook her head. 'No more than I.' Though she tried to smile, she brought the tea to Joan and said, 'May I see if the child has turned yet?'

Joan nodded, and sat down, letting Aileen feel her hardened womb. The child's elbows and knees seemed to poke out, making it seem more angular.

The woman sighed. 'I did not want to make you worry, but you should know that the baby is breech. I was hoping it would turn on its own, but we may have to prepare for a different birth than you imagined.'

Joan rested her hands upon the unborn child, trying to push back the rise of fear. 'It's dangerous, isn't it?'

Aileen nodded. 'For both of you.'

She tried not to let the worry overtake her, but she had heard stories of difficult births from other women. And given her age, it might be even worse.

'Can you turn the baby?'

'We will keep trying,' the healer promised. 'Drink this tea to help relax you. If you are not so anxious, your body may allow the child to turn on his own.'

Joan obeyed, sending up a silent prayer that the baby would indeed move into the right position. While she knew that many women survived a breech birth with a healthy child, there were also others who died in childbirth.

'Do not tell Ronan,' she warned as she rose from the stool. But no sooner had she taken a few steps when she felt a slight burst and her birthing waters broke. The fluid soaked through her gown down her legs.

'Aileen?' Her fear grew stronger, and she motioned towards the damp wool.

The young woman seemed to transform before her eyes into a healing warrior of strength. 'It will be all right, Joan.' She reached out and took her hands. 'Trust in me.'

'I am afraid,' Joan confessed.

'Every woman is afraid.' Aileen squeezed her hands. 'But I will help you.' She loosened Joan's laces, lifting the bliaud away until she was clad only in the thin, linen shift. 'You may keep your shift on, but you do not need all these layers.' Then she summoned a maid, sending for both the midwife and Ronan.

'I don't think my husband will want to be here,' Joan protested. She didn't want him to know about the possible problems—especially when neither of them could do anything about it.

'He deserves to know that you are in labour,' Aileen said gently. 'He need not stay here with you.'

But the worried look in the healer's eyes did not reassure her. She gripped her hands together to keep them from shaking. Her womb continued to contract, growing rock hard as she started to lie down.

'Let me help you,' Aileen said, bringing several

pillows to help her sit upright. 'When the midwife arrives, we will both try to turn the child.'

'Have you done this before?' she asked.

'Only once,' Aileen admitted. 'But Darerca and I will do what we can.' She reached out and took her hand. 'You must try to rest as much as you can. We don't know how long this will last, and first babies often take many hours.' Though the healer tried to sound calm, Joan hadn't missed the tension in her face.

When Darerca arrived, Aileen spoke with the midwife in a low voice, whispering in Irish. Joan couldn't quite tell what they were saying, but the midwife's expression turned grave, and she nodded.

'It is dangerous to try to turn the baby since your waters have broken,' Aileen said, 'but we will try it once.'

Darerca guided Joan to get on her hands and knees. Then she and Aileen began to push against her swollen womb, trying to turn the baby. Pain radiated through Joan so violently, she clenched her hands against the pallet. Although the women attempted to manipulate the child and force the baby into the correct position, Joan already knew the truth. It was no use.

At last, they bade her to lie on her back once again. 'Rest a moment,' Aileen said. 'I must talk with Darerca a moment to see what else we may try.'

The women stepped outside for a little while, and Joan could only fear the worst. Neither of the healers appeared hopeful, and she rested her hands upon her unborn babe, praying silently.

The door opened again, but this time, Ronan came

inside. His expression remained shielded, but he came to sit beside her. 'How are you, *a stór*?'

'I've been better,' she said, letting out a slow breath as another contraction took her. 'Our child has decided he wants to be born this day.'

He reached out and offered his hand. 'It will be all right, Joan. Aileen and Darerca are the finest healers. I have confidence in their skills.'

She wanted to believe that, but her fear was stronger. Yet, she thought it might be best to pretend as if there was nothing wrong. At least, for now.

Ronan did not leave, as she had expected him to, but instead, he remained at her side throughout hours of labour. Her face was damp with perspiration, and the pain never ceased. Aileen and Darerca helped her to walk around, but as the contractions strengthened, she had to stop and hold on to Ronan.

When night fell, Aileen and Darerca made another blend of herbs and asked her to drink it. 'Your body is not widening for the birth of the child,' the healer explained. 'This may help you.'

Joan drank the foul-tasting tea, though she doubted it would do any good. She was beginning to understand the danger facing both her child and herself. Emotions rose high within her, and she didn't bother to stop the tears.

'I'm going to die, aren't I?' she predicted. 'And the baby, too.'

'No,' Ronan said. 'I won't let that happen.' His tone was haggard as he helped her to sit once more.

His hand gripped hers, and he looked into her eyes. 'I swear it.'

But he could not fight this battle for her. She drew his hand to her face, ignoring the tears. 'The baby is breech, Ronan. If the worst comes to pass, promise me you will cut the baby from my body and save him.'

'Don't even speak of such a thing,' he warned. 'It will not happen.'

She squeezed his hand tightly as another contraction took her. Despite his attempt to reassure her, she knew the truth—that she might not survive the birth.

'Promise me you will save our child.' She needed to know that their baby had a chance to live.

He shook his head. 'If you ask me to choose between your life and our baby's, the choice will always be you, Joan.'

She embraced him, resting her cheek against his. 'This may be the only baby I ever have, Ronan. And if I had the choice between my life or my child's, the choice would always be to sacrifice my own.'

Ronan didn't sleep at all that night but kept vigil at his wife's side all through the next day and night. Joan fought hard as the contractions overtook her body, and he hated seeing her in such agony. He brought hot water to Aileen and Darerca, but he knew his efforts were for naught. With every hour, Joan's strength diminished. She was racked with pain, suffering as no woman should.

At last, Ronan could stand it no longer. To Aileen

and the midwife, he demanded, '*Do* something. She cannot endure this another day.'

The older woman sighed. 'Come with me, King Ronan. There is aught I must tell you.'

He didn't want to hear it, but Aileen nodded for him to go. He followed the woman outside, and Darerca said, 'She is suffering badly, and there is almost no progress. The child is twisted up within her and may already be dead. She cannot push, for her body has not changed in preparation for the birth.'

Every part of him froze up with her words, though he had suspected this for hours. The thought of Joan dying was the worst nightmare he could have imagined.

'What can be done to save them?'

The midwife paused. 'I do not know. Joan asked me to cut the child from her, if she dies. Sometimes the child can survive, if it is taken quickly.'

'But Joan would die,' he finished. 'No. I won't let that happen to her.'

'If nothing changes, both will die,' the midwife insisted. 'I have given her every remedy I can, but nothing is working. I tell you this not to frighten you, but to prepare you for what may happen.'

Her warning resonated deeply within him. He knew what Joan's wish was, but he could not bring himself to agree. He loved her deeply. How could he ever give the order for her to be cut open and die?

But he also understood that Joan *would* die if he stood by and did nothing. 'I need to think,' he said. The midwife inclined her head and stepped back.

Ronan trudged through the grounds at Clonagh

in silence. The stars were out and most of the Ó Callaghans were sleeping within their homes. One of the dogs rose from his sleeping place at the threshold and came over to greet him, his tail wagging.

Ronan bent to rub the dog's ears, but inwardly, he felt shaken. His wife and child were dying, and he had no means to save them.

Was this how his brother had felt? The devastation of being powerless to fight death, his heart wrenching at the impending loss. Somehow, after his wife's death, Ardan had managed to go on living for the sake of their son...but when Declan had died, he'd lost his own will to live.

Ronan stopped at the far end of the fortress, resting his head against the fence. He didn't want to imagine living without Joan. The thought of going through each day alone was devastating.

It felt as if Fate had asked the impossible of him. If he allowed the women to cut into Joan, she would likely bleed to death. But if he refused to allow it, both would die.

His gut twisted with fear and self-loathing. If he could give up his own life for theirs, he would do so without hesitation. Yet this was a battle he was helpless to fight. And he knew not if there was any hope at all.

He raised his eyes up to the stars, wishing his brother were here to advise him. As he thought of Ardan, he knew his brother would have done everything to save his family—even at the greatest risk.

Slowly, he walked back to his wife, feeling numb to

the decision he must make. Already she had laboured for two days with no progress. He could not stand by and let her die with the child trapped inside her.

The night air was warm, but it did nothing to allay the frozen chill of his heart. Never in his life had he felt such fear, but he saw no alternative.

Slowly, he pushed the door open and crossed the threshold. Joan was fighting to breathe, her face red with exertion as the labour pains rolled over her. The midwife turned to him in silent question.

'Do everything you can to save Joan,' he said. 'Even if you must cut the child from her body.'

Joan was lost in delirium, feeling as if her body were being ripped apart from the inside. Ronan came to sit beside her, but when he took her hand, his skin was like ice.

'I cannot bear to see you suffer,' he murmured. 'I wish I could take this pain from you.'

'So do I,' she remarked, braving a smile she didn't feel. She could see his own torment as she fought the violent waves of pain. But he could do nothing to help her, and her strength was waning.

'I am afraid,' he admitted. 'The midwife believes we should try to cut the child out.'

'But if we save the child, I will die,' Joan said. Weariness poured through her, and she squeezed his hand. 'Ronan, I am going to die anyway. I cannot bear this pain much longer, and neither can our baby. We have no choice but to try. At least if our child lives, a part of me will go on.'

'I want both of you to live,' he gritted out. He drew her hand to his lips and kissed her knuckles. 'I love you, Joan.'

Her own love swelled through her, and she closed her eyes. 'Even if the worst comes to pass, I could not have asked for a husband I loved more.' She let her tears fall freely. 'Whatever happens, you must not blame our child. It is not the baby's fault. Nor is it yours.'

He leaned in to kiss her lips, and she kissed him back, winding her arms around his neck. Even when the pain caught her again, she only stopped to catch her breath.

'You must know how much I love you,' she whispered. 'How much I will always love you, even if I am gone.'

His face grew stricken, overcome with shielded grief. 'Fight to live, Joan. Our baby needs a mother. And I will not wed another.'

She drew him down to her once more, pressing her forehead to his. 'I will fight until my dying breath.'

He held her for a little while longer until at last Darerca said, 'It is time. We cannot delay any longer, Ronan.'

Aileen gave her a leather strap to bite down upon. Behind her, she saw the midwife cleaning a sharp blade. She had tried to be brave in front of Ronan, but her courage was slipping away. The blade would cut through her, and she would die. It might even be too late for her child.

'You must leave now,' the midwife ordered Ronan.

But he shook his head and came to sit behind Joan's head. He reached down to take her hands in his.

'I will be here with you,' he swore. 'You can break my fingers if the pain is too great. But I will not leave you.'

His promise meant more to her than he understood. If she was to die now, she wanted her last sight to be of her husband's face. From Ronan, she would draw her strength.

Joan reached back to take his hands while Aileen drew near. The healer had a needle and thread prepared, along with a poultice. It seemed that both women had known what would come to pass. And the knowledge only deepened her terror.

To Aileen, he said, 'Connor told me you are the greatest healer in Éire. I hope it is true.'

Aileen met his gaze. 'I will not lie—this is dangerous to both of them. But Darerca has cut in and saved a child before. This is not her first time.'

'Did the mother live?' Ronan asked quietly, meeting the midwife's gaze.

Darerca slowly shook her head. 'Only the baby.'

It was as she had feared. But Joan knew that there was no other choice—not after this long.

'Save them both,' Ronan commanded. 'Do all that you can.'

Joan steeled herself and put the leather strap into her mouth. She gripped Ronan's hands and looked back at him, not wanting to see the gleam of the knife.

'I am ready.'

Chapter Thirteen

The cry of a newborn broke through the silence, and Ronan stared in disbelief at his son. The boy wailed as the healer pulled him free, swaddling him while Aileen cut the birthing cord. The moment he saw the baby, he knew Joan needed to see their boy.

'We have a son,' he said, his voice breaking. He took the infant from Darerca and brought him to rest upon Joan's chest. Aileen and the midwife worked quickly, removing the afterbirth and trying to stop the bleeding.

His wife wept as she smiled at him. 'We will call him Ardan, after your brother.' She kissed the infant's head, but he was aware of how her body had begun to tremble after the birth. He knew not what Aileen and Darerca were doing, but both worked swiftly, stitching the wound.

'He is beautiful,' Joan said. 'Everything I imagined he would b-be.' Her mouth was tense from the pain, but he had never known a woman braver than his wife. She had barely flinched when Darerca had drawn the blade across her womb though he knew how badly it had hurt her.

'Take care of him for me,' she whispered. 'Tell him how much I loved him.'

He didn't like the ominous tone of her voice or the way she was speaking as if she would not be here. 'You will tell him yourself,' he insisted. 'Joan, you must fight to stay with us. Ardan needs you, and so do I.'

Her eyes began to close, and he touched her cheek. 'Look at our son, Joan. See how perfect he is.'

She fought back and kissed their son's downy head. 'He is beautiful.' Her voice was hardly above a whisper. 'And strong-willed, like his father.' She tried to smile, but he could not return it.

He didn't tell her that the child had been folded in half, his head nestled against his knees. There was no question that if they had not cut in, the baby and Joan would now be dead. Yet he could see her trembling and the effort it took to keep her eyes open.

Aileen and Darerca packed a poultice against Joan's wounds, and then the midwife brought over a fur that had been warmed near the fire. 'Put this around your wife,' she ordered.

At the sudden warmth, Joan closed her eyes in relief. 'Oh, that feels good. Thank you.'

The midwife helped guide the baby to Joan's breast to help him nurse. His wife was exhausted, but she did take interest when Ardan latched on. He met Darerca's gaze and understood what she was doing.

Every moment Joan spent with their baby gave her a new reason to fight for her own survival.

In time, the baby lay against her heartbeat, drawing comfort from Joan's skin. She held him, but exhaustion reigned over her.

'Drink, Joan,' Aileen said softly. She lifted a cup of warm tea to his wife's lips, and though he didn't recognise the herbs, he knew they were still trying to save her. 'It will ease the pain.'

'I will stay with them.' Ronan couldn't imagine leaving either his wife or child at this moment.

'Do not let her get up or move,' Aileen warned. 'She must remain as she is for at least a sennight, if not a fortnight. Later, she can try to eat, but for now, let her rest.'

He nodded and turned back to Joan. Her face was pale, but she stared at their baby as if he were everything in the world.

'Is there anything you need?' he asked his wife.

'Just you,' she murmured. 'Hold us while I sleep.' She cradled the baby in her arms, and he lay beside her, protecting them both in his arms. While she fell asleep, he studied their baby, marvelling at his tiny size. Ardan was a miracle, a child who never should have lived.

Yet, he had—and so had Joan.

Ronan knew that the danger was not yet past. A fever could take her, or her wounds might not heal. There were a thousand things that could go wrong. But he watched his loved ones sleeping, so thankful that they were alive. The fist of emotion caught his gut, until he realised his cheeks were wet.

He would watch over them every moment of every day. For he loved this woman with all his being and their son, too.

Summer had waned into autumn, and Joan sat outside by the fire. She smiled as she watched over the people within Clonagh. Ronan had barely allowed her to move during the past few months, but they both knew that her survival was a precious gift they had never expected. Already their son was babbling in a language only he could understand and was beginning to smile.

There were scars upon her flesh, markings that would be with her always. But she would readily bear a thousand scars in exchange for the life of their son. The feeling of his warm body nestled against hers was everything she had imagined it would be.

Her husband came walking towards her with a young animal. Instantly, she recognised it as the gift Sorcha had chosen from the MacEgan stables. The dun-coloured filly was restless, nudging at Ronan's arm.

Joan went to meet him and smiled at the sight of the horse. 'I'd nearly forgotten about her.'

'Connor kept his promise.' Ronan held the yearling steady as she rubbed the animal's ears. Ardan's eyes widened at the sight of the horse, and he instinctively reached towards the filly's nose. Joan pulled him back, but Ronan's hand was already between them.

'When you're older, lad,' he said, nudging his son's chin. He gave the reins to a stable lad and walked alongside them through the ringfort. Although Joan had lived among the Ó Callaghans for nearly a year, many still regarded her with awe. She should not have lived through the birth, and most believed she was otherworldly. Although she didn't believe there was anything special about herself, she did believe in miracles. Her son was living proof.

Though she spoke with several women as she passed, Ronan guided her towards their home. Ardan's eyes were closing, and she knew he was ready to lie down and sleep, as he did every afternoon.

When they were inside their bedchamber, she placed their son in the cradle Ronan had carved for him. The wood held the design of a cross knotted with circles and an elaborate pattern. It had taken her husband months to finish, and he had sanded it smooth. She had never seen anything so fine, and the cradle could be rocked by resting her foot upon one of the runners.

When the baby was curled up in sleep, Ronan drew her away and asked, 'How are you feeling, Joan?'

'Like a piece of glass you're afraid might shatter,' she answered honestly. 'You haven't touched me since Ardan was born.' Although she understood why, she was not about to let his fear come between them.

'You nearly died, Joan,' he said. 'And it would have been my fault.'

She took his hands in hers. 'You fathered Ardan,

true enough. But we cannot live out the rest of our days without loving one another.'

His face grew sober. 'I don't want to hurt you, Joan. And we cannot risk another baby.'

'Aileen said it is unlikely that I'll ever conceive another child,' she said. 'I believe her. But even so, I need my husband.' She reached up to wind her arms around his neck. 'For so many years of my life, I lived in fear. I believed in a curse, feeling as if I could never be happy. But since I married you, I've come to understand that I do have command over my own life.'

She stood on tiptoe to kiss him, and the moment she did, some of his tension dissipated. He took her mouth deeply, and his kiss awakened her desire, making her crave more.

'I love you, Ronan. And I will not let fear take that from us. We have a perfect son, and if he is the only child we ever have, I will be content with that.'

He drew her against his body, and she felt the hard ridge of his need. But the expression on his face held pain, as if he were trying to hold himself back. 'I cannot lose you, Joan.'

'You will never lose me. My heart is yours, now and always.' Joan unlaced her gown, lifting it away. The shift followed, until she was bared before him. His hungry eyes drank in the sight of her, and he reached out to touch her. She drew his hands to her full breasts, thankful that she had nursed Ardan only an hour earlier. He was gentle with her, caressing her nipples before he lowered his hands to the scar at her womb. It was still reddened, but to her, it was a mark of survival.

'I thank God every day that you lived through Ardan's birth,' he said, dropping down to his knees. He kissed the scar, and she rested her hands upon his head.

'I was meant to live,' she said.

'You were,' he agreed. 'And I will love you every day until I draw my last breath.'

'Love me now, Ronan,' she pleaded. 'I need you.'

He stared up at her, and the heat in his eyes was searing. 'Then lie back upon the bed,' he commanded, 'for I have not finished worshipping you.'

She obeyed, but was surprised when he moved her legs to hang off the end of the bed. When he knelt between her thighs, she suddenly felt embarrassed at knowing what he was about to do.

Her fingers dug into the fur coverlet when he opened her legs and moved his tongue to her cleft. She could not stop the cry of delight, and moaned as he began to kiss her intimately. Her body was so sensitive that she could already feel herself rising towards release. And when he used his tongue to stroke her hooded flesh, her breath came in ragged gasps.

His mouth was hot, feasting upon her, while she arched her back in surrender. 'Ronan, I want you inside me.'

He ignored her plea and pressed her higher, relentless as he caressed her with his mouth. She was so driven with need, she could not stop herself as a wave of pleasure crashed within, causing her to tremble.

Only then did he draw back, looking pleased with himself.

'Take off your clothes,' she demanded.

'I think you should rest now,' he said.

But she would not be deterred. Instead, she sat up on the bed. 'It was not a request,' she said. 'Let me see you.'

He seemed slightly taken aback, but when he saw that she would not relent, he stripped away his garments until he stood before her. There were familiar scars, and the one he had received only last year during the battle at Clonagh. But every part of his body was strong and fierce, and Joan knew that he was holding back his needs. His erection was heavy, and she reached out to touch him.

The moment she did, he inhaled, resting his hand upon hers. 'Careful, Joan.'

She smiled wickedly and stood from the bed. 'Lie down and let me pleasure you.'

For a moment, he didn't move, but when she closed her fist around his length, he obeyed. Just as she had, he lay back on the bed. She moved between his thighs and lowered her mouth to his thick shaft.

The moment she kissed the rounded tip, he let out a shudder of air. Joan loved being in command of him, and she slid her tongue down his length, cupping him in her palm as she stroked him.

Ronan was trying not to move, but as she suckled, he couldn't stop the husky growl. 'If you don't stop, I'm going to spill myself within your lovely mouth.'

She replaced her mouth with her hand, and he shut

his eyes while she fisted him up and down. Seeing his intense arousal only made her crave him more. She was so wet, needing him deep inside.

Joan knelt upon the bed and took his shaft, guiding it inside her. Ronan's eyes flew open, and he sat up, taking her waist. 'What are you doing, Joan?'

She rose up on her knees and sank against him. 'I'm riding you.' A smile played at her lips, and she said, 'Lie back, and let me enjoy myself.'

She rose up and lowered herself again, but this time, he clasped her hips, meeting her thrust. 'We shouldn't do this,' he admitted, even as he caressed her breast. The sensitive tip was like a bolt of lightning between her legs, and she quickened her pace.

'I don't care. Nothing in life worth having comes without a risk. And I would risk everything for you.'

She continued to ride, watching his green eyes as he grasped her hips and penetrated her. 'I lived my life in fear for too many years. I won't let myself fall into that trap again. Each day is a precious gift, one that I treasure.'

Abruptly, Ronan stood and lifted her with him, forcing her to wrap her legs around his waist. His strength was shocking, and he raised her up and down, the position causing such delicious friction, she held him tight as he claimed her.

Another climax seized her body, and she cried out with the force of it. Ronan continued to thrust within her, until at last he groaned and spilled his seed deep within. He carried her back to the bed, still deeply sheathed within her body.

Her heart was pounding, but she loved the way they fit together. 'I've missed being with you, Ronan.'

He cradled her body to his. 'As have I, *a stór*.' He held her close, but his hand came to rest upon her scar. 'You are everything to me.'

'I love you. And we will live each day to its fullest, without fear.' She kissed him softly. 'There is no curse. Unless I am cursed to love you…and that is one I will heartily embrace for the rest of my days.'

'Being loved by you is never a curse,' he answered. 'Only a blessing.'

She rested her hand upon his heart. 'A blessing indeed.'

* * * * *

If you enjoyed this story, you won't want to miss the other stories in Michelle Willingham's Warriors of the Night series

Forbidden Night with the Warrior
Forbidden Night with the Highlander

To find out more about some of the characters who appear in this story, check out Michelle Willingham's The MacEgan Brothers series, including

The Warrior's Touch